REDUCE HEAT

CONTINUE TO BOIL

REDUCE HEAT

CONTINUE TO BOIL

J.J. Colagrande

Jitney Books

#MADEINDADE

#MIAMIFULLTIME

REDUCE HEAT

CONTINUE TO BOIL

Chapter 1—

"What?"

"Don't move, baby."

"Am I wet enough?"

"Yes."

"That tickles."

"Don't move."

"Is it in?"

"Yeah. Don't spill it."

"What now?"

"Clench, like you're doing kegels."

"I don't know no kegels, bro."

"The exercises to tighten the pussy—"

"—yeah, I don't need those—"

"—clench your butt, so the powder doesn't fall out."

"It burns."

"You're doing fine. It's in there."

"What now?"

"Just wait."

"I've never done molly," said Jimena. "How exciting."

She fell onto the bed, releasing her ass from its upright position and rolled over to lock her lover in the eye. Her lover. HA!! She didn't even know this guy's last name.

"How long does it take?"

"To plug molly? Not too long."

"Let me see that dick again."

Jimena pounced on her knees and threw him on the bed. She fell onto her stomach and quickly moved towards his groin. Like a frog jumping on lily pads, with three kisses she reached his dick and took one long lick from the bottom of the shaft, all the way up. She mouthed the top of his half-hard shaft, licking the underside, and then slowly head bobbed up-and-down the shaft with slow, wet motions. She liked the curves and slight indentions of the veins on this cock. He moaned, grabbing the back of her head, holding the dark auburn locks away, while she sucked, slow, and then fast, and then slow, sometimes using her hands to rub the wet saliva along the top of the shaft. Rock hard and wanting to give something back, he maneuvered to swing her around without saying a word. Jimena repositioned, expertly dropping her rear-end near his face so that an obedient tongue might soon discover the hovercraft of ass. Little earthling, take me to your leader, said a clitoris, greeted by a tongue that traversed towards a labia. With the mothership properly attended to, Jimena went back to hiking the mountain, a fifteen minute trek, taking in peaks, cliff sides and views. They both tasted clean, a little salty, but clean and warm and wet. Jimena began to feel twirly, like the sugary strings of a cotton candy machine spinning in circles, coming into shape, taking on a sweet clustery form. Whatever he put inside her was kicking in, but not overwhelming, more like a gentle wave riding a swell along salty wet ocean shores.

"I'm starting to feel it."

"You're very wet."

"Shut up and grab a condom."

As he stumbled around the nearly dark room looking for his pants and a condom, Jimena lay on her back. She took a deep breath and reached for a glass of water from the nightstand. She smacked her lips and fell back onto the pillows, which felt softer than usual.

She looked up at the ceiling. The popcorn crevices appeared slightly more distinguished and the shadows from the twilight more pronounced and alive, things she never noticed before.

He returned, mounted her like a bicycle and began to peddle ever so slowly, opening Jimena's valves which were already greased and ready to go. There was little resistance, no brakes needed, as he began the uphill climb. She immediately exploded, not with orgasm, but with dew. Never a huge fan of a prophylactic her wetness enveloped the rubber with honey and they both felt equally engulfed. They both moaned. They both gyrated. Jimena closed her eyes and could see a white light near her forehead. The express train of her lover picked up steam and began to move faster. She needed to control this ride. He had too much dick and was turning her inside out, upside down. She didn't want it like that. "Let me get on top. I want on top."

Jimena climbed on board and with the guidance of her navigation system the schooner departed the port-of-entry again. Slowly, a piston grinded a shaft, pumping in-and-out, in-and-out, and the engine began to pick up steam. This journey admittedly felt strange, new and a little awkward. She felt like a bird flying over a sea, swept around by unpredictable gusts, she could see the vessel clearly sailing below and used it as a beacon, but honestly Jimena didn't feel all aboard. Part of the distance was the condom—between two organic pulsating ripe genitalia lay this rubber sheathe—who in the world actually enjoyed the use of a condom. Still, she knew how much she could take and where it felt good and how to move her hips to rub and ride that shaft to Candyland. Jimena gyrated, climbing the ladder, slowly at first, looking for a bell to ring until she found it. Right there. The bell began to ring louder and louder. She closed her eyes and again a vivid white light covered her forehead and also her face. "It's building." She moved her ass up and down his totem pole and felt the ancient spirit of orgasm open her up like a canyon. She vividly felt like an open canyon ready to push the deluge of a crashing waterfall over the edges.

"I'm going to cum." It was only a matter of a few more rungs up the ladder until an explosion. "I'm cummin. I'm cummin. I'm cummin."

As she fell down into the deepest depths of her own private canyon, he flipped her onto her backside, found a way into the water park and quickly discovered a fun slip n slide. But he didn't come to the park not to ride the biggest roller coaster—he needed to finish the adventure and that meant picking up the pace, burning through the rubber—and he discovered the monstrous roller coaster, sat in the front row and rode the rails into a private oblivion, smiling for the camera, until he came, and with wobbly legs and a disoriented constitution dismounted, falling onto the bed alongside Jimena. They both lay there motionless, puffing and sweating. Jimena let out a deep breath.

"I think I like this molly."

Chapter 2—

       Wynwood (33127) was crazy, sexy cool. A segment of the Downtown area, the arts district existed between the Design District and Overtown, starting on Miami Avenue south of 29th Street, running west until NW 5th Avenue. The same visionaries who revitalized South Beach and developed SoHo in New York created Wynwood from a rough warehouse district for wholesale fashion into an area bursting with creativity and color. A living, breathing museum, the walls of Wynwood were painted with original works from the world's best living street artists. In particular, every year, in December, during Art Basel, the largest exposition of art galleries on the planet, muralists parachuted into Miami like soldiers dropped over a Vietnamese clearing and they looked for a place to "get up" on a wall. Wynwood was a tribute to the street arts movement, the dominating aesthetic discipline of the early twenty-first century. The streets were a political statement in Wynwood. The sidewalks stamped with graphics, street signs covered in stickers. On telephone wires dangled painted cardboard cutouts of sneakers and shoes. Crosswalks were also painted by renowned artists. And yet like a Buddhist monk swiping away a beautiful mandala, the nature of things constantly changed in Wynwood. Murals were covered by other murals, vandals disrespected others, and with coat after coat after coat after coat, the tiny neighborhood constantly smelled like fresh paint. The area had "it" and everyone wanted "it" they had to have "it" understand "it" realize "it" be seen in "it" so the Itness of the area attracted photographers, amateur and professional, and it was common to see models standing around aloof or Hollywood types wandering the area like nobodies. Oscar and Grammy winners made news popping into local coffee shops while production scouts sniffed around like K-9 dogs. The neighborhood was also a figment of a speculator's wildest imagination. Property that once rented for $5 to $10 a square foot now leased for quadruple that. There was irony in Wynwood. There also existed a lot of hipsters and when there were a lot of hipsters irony lingered not too far behind. Artists, gallerists and production companies moved in first, co-existing with the poor and the broken and the damned. These pioneers poured blood, sweat and tears into a start-up neighborhood, in full cooperation and awareness with the real estate developers. And then as the area bloomed and property owners could reap the rewards of their investments and patience, all those who built the neighborhood had to move out. No longer could those who built the neighborhood afford the neighborhood. So many moved away, into Little Haiti, or Park West, or Allapattah, and only the successful stayed. The verdict was not out on Wynwood—on the surface the area appeared booming—but if one lifted only the top layer of the neighborhood's thin veil, they would find a town void of organization, loyalty and camaraderie. Business owners didn't work together. The politics of the neighborhood's development authority and boards were in conflict. And the area was far from bustling. There were as many homeless in the area as people on foot. Wynwood may never reach the pinnacle of Miami success, but they tried. More restaurants and bars entered the tiny neighborhood, some high-end, some hipster.

***

The Timber was a hipster bar but Jimena felt too high to care. Normally places overrun with moustaches and skinny jeans made her hands sweaty, but not that evening. Jimena's constant smile was counterbalanced by a slight edginess in her jaw, but a stick of chewing gum Vilano offered seemed to calm the jitters. She wore big round sunglasses, a graphic Betty Boop t-shirt, tight shorts that accentuated her firm, plump derrière, and flat shoes. Behind her glasses, her eyes beamed with ecstasy as she took in the scene. It was bike night at the Timber. A social. The end destination of a 12-mile pub crawl with bicycles and drunken cyclists sprawled everywhere. They quickly found Dolly among the mass. She usually was located in the center of where the most people stood. The lime green tank top worn when riding helped her stick out.

The Timber had a huge outdoor courtyard, squared off like an abandoned lot, with a dirt floor and picnic tables. Sometimes they played movies outside on the projector screen, or displayed a sporting event that might interest the community, e.g. a Miami Heat playoff game. Jimena told Vilano that she would catch up to him by Dolly and that she wanted to get some water. Smacking her bottom lip, she needed to walk around, see people, listen to music, and not necessarily stand idly amongst a group of sweaty drunk bikers. There was a railroad bar inside with a separate sound system and a big room that hosted dance parties and live music. The deejay played an eclectic mix of danceable songs from the Fifties to today. The air conditioner felt amazing. Everything felt amazing. Jimena ran her fingers along the red vinyl of a booth she slowly walked past. The glass of water the mustached bartender presented her had condensation that she touched to her upper lip. The lighting, although darker than outside, felt cozy and nuanced. In one word, to Jimena, rolling on molly for the first time, all appeared vivid, and she had her dancing shoes on. She scurried towards the dance floor smiling. She closed her eyes, took a deep breath, smacked her lips and swayed to the rhythms, which sounded enchanting.

Jimena wondered why she never tried molly before. Why didn't anyone tell her it made you feel like JELL-O? And that it made your pussy wet. And that it made you want to dance. And maybe even talk, or confess. Wow. How could the world hide such a wonderful thing? And water. Did water always feel so good? She wanted more water. Shit. How long did the feeling last? Hopefully it didn't go away too soon. Because there was a brief moment, a small crack in a window, one song back, for a few seconds the feeling lost its intensity and the vividness turned itself down a teeny weenie notch. Maybe Vilano had more.

Jimena had to sit down. She chose a corner of the room on a bench that ran along the wall, near an air conditioner vent. Sitting down never felt so good. Until she took a shoe off and slowly massaged the sole of her foot. Okay. Sitting down quickly lost its world championship title of Things That Never Felt So Good. Until the pleasure of rubbing her foot quickly relinquished the belt to the air conditioner vent once Jimena focused on the Freon laced breeze. After cooling off for a few minutes, she started to feel cold. She smacked her lips, bought a water bottle from the bartender and ventured back outside into the courtyard.

For a brief moment the transition from a dark indoor room into a well-lit outdoor patio disoriented Jimena but she quickly absorbed the change and welcomed the natural humid air that challenged and then quickly defeated the air conditioner for the title of Best Things Ever.

Her friends were in the same spot and she walked up to Vilano. A member of the bike scene, skinny, with a bunch of tattoos, maybe fifteen tats in all—a year or two older than Jimena, fit and firm, the kid didn't have a car and probably rode his bicycle twenty miles a day. Jimena didn't know that much about him. He worked at an upscale restaurant in the Design District, played bike polo, rode in weekly community bike rides, and liked to drink whisky and PBR. Vilano's real name was Brian. He'd probably be bald by the time he reached thirty but he had a big dick. This was their third intimate encounter and if it wasn't for the size of his dick, they probably would've ended at two. Vilano was too cool for his own good and she saw that.

"You got more?" The words came from her mouth but was that how she sounded? Not like an addict or a crack head, that didn't bother her, Vilano turned her onto this. She didn't have a problem asking him for more candy, especially after the experience they shared back at the apartment. What amazed Jimena was the actual process of speaking. Her words laced and covered with extra air. She could actually feel her breath coming together with her lips and tongue to produce sounds and cadence. It felt different outside, maybe the humidity played a role, or maybe inside she had to talk loud to the bartender so she didn't notice.

"What?" asked Vilano.

"More? I want more."

"There you are," said Dolly, noticing her roommate for the first time. She placed her hand on Jimena's shoulder which felt like someone was blowing in her ear and then she hugged Jimena into a personal Jacuzzi. "You guys missed the pub crawl. I'm so drunk already."

"We were busy," said Vilano.

"Busy getting busy," Dolly laughed.

Jimena's shoulders hunched over with embarrassment but Dolly wouldn't let her sink into the trap. She knew what Vilano gave her and also that it was her first time. "Come, sit down near me," said Dolly.

They found a seat on a picnic table and Dolly lightly rubbed Jimena's shoulders, without causing a scene. It wasn't like a music festival where some girl sat down in an open area wearing a gas mask loaded with Vicks vaporizer as some dude rubbed her shoulders and some other girl waved glow sticks frantically in front of her face, like the Ultra Music Festival, although that didn't sound too bad to Jimena.

Instead, Dolly subtly allowed Jimena to absorb some of the extra benefits of her predicament, without making it blatantly obvious that she was blowing-up on ecstasy—not that anyone at The Timber would really care—maybe a few hipsters would've twirled their moustaches, one side of the moustache in misguided jealousy and the other side in contempt. However, at this particular moment, the light caresses from Dolly had the effect of placing Jimena in a place between obedience and surrender, like a cat picked up by the fur of its neck. "So, first time, huh?" she said.

"More."

"You want more?"

"*Si*, more."

"It's a good batch. I rolled on it last week."

Jimena looked at Dolly who appeared different somehow. They shared an apartment for six weeks but for the first time Jimena noticed just how beautiful Dolly looked. Her physical Colombian features seemed raw and teeming with an indigenous energy and appearance. She looked Amazonian, *thee* female Incan princess of the Miami Bike Scene, her lime green-shirt nothing more than a loincloth seeped in sweaty jungle secrets. She looked amazing. Jimena wanted to talk to this queen. Tell her how she felt. Like a liter of truth serum suddenly shot into her blood stream and all her inhibitions disintegrated into the ether.

"Dolly, you look so beautiful tonight," Jimena began. "Did I ever tell you how beautiful you are? I never really noticed before, I mean I always thought you looked cute, but you're like amazing. I'm so glad I choose you for a roommate. I interviewed a lot of people and from the moment I met you I knew you were cool. I mean, you weren't my first choice but I don't regret choosing you at all. There was this one applicant who just seemed perfect but when she said no, it wasn't a tough decision to choose you. I'm so happy with the vibe we have, me, and you, and Chito too. He's playing a gig in Wynwood tonight, I might go see him, but, you know, I just want to thank you, for introducing me to new stuff, like the bike scene, everyone's so cool and young and beautiful, and I just feel good about everything, you know, like, really great. It's like I'm really moving on, crossing this threshold, and now there's this giant, wild, open frontier for me to explore, and normally, I'm very shy and kind of depressed and anti-social, but I feel really good about things."

If someone actually recorded that mess and spewed it back like a week later Jimena would have probably just killed herself, but, at the time, that's how she felt, and Dolly took it in stride.

"Everything's good, baby," said Dolly.

"It's all good." Behind her glasses Jimena's eyes slowly rolled. She smacked her lips. "But I think I need to walk now," said Jimena.

"You sure?" asked Dolly.

"Yes."

Jimena headed straight over to Vilano and grabbed him aside.

"I want more. Is that okay?"

"Want me to plug you in the bathroom?"

"No thank you, I don't want anything else in my ass, Dumbo, especially not in public. But I like it. It's good. And I want more. Just throw some of your powder in my water bottle."

Vilano looked around the scene at The Timber.

"Okay," he said. "Give me the bottle and wait here."

He received Jimena's water bottle, her true comrade for the night, about three-quarters full, and he dashed towards the bathroom. Vilano returned before Jimena finished the cigarette she'd bummed from Dolly. The best cigarette she ever smoked, a new world record.

"Enjoy."

"How much is in here?"

"Enough."

"Yuck," said Jimena. "It tastes sour."

"More sour the better."

"If you say so."

"Where are you going?" asked Vilano.

"Inside. I'll be dancing."

"Okay, see you in a few."

Jimena walked through the crowded courtyard of The Timber, a labyrinth of chattering bicyclists. To be honest, a change of scene seemed *apropos*. When entering the air conditioned inner bar of The Timber the same vividness in the transition between lighting and temperature greeted her, but with a slightly less novel effect. She could either head towards the dance floor or cut right through the railroad bar and exit out the front door, to a new scene, without saying goodbye to anyone, including Vilano, especially Vilano; for some reason the urge to move, to vanish, to explore a different scene struck her with a tinge of paranoia and haste. The decision came effortlessly as she sauntered out the front door, with her water bottle, into the balmy and inviting Miami night.

***

Look at your life now, Jimena. New friends and experiences, a new neighborhood, a new lifestyle, even further distanced from the brainwashing of that religion, far enough from your parents so they don't freak out over every little thing, and best of all, out of that horrible marriage. This was just the start of the start, the first period in the University of your New Life, the initial dot in the grammatical ellipses of existence … so much to see, not just in Miami, but who knew where? New York? San Francisco? Paris? France? London? Moscow? Shit, there was so much to see just in Wynwood—the whole world existed in Wynwood, in its murals, painted by the interconnected spirits of so many. She texted Chito hoping to catch him before his gig started and she did, just in time, because the power of serendipity was at her very fingers, the synapses of her personal kinetics commanding the keyboard of her smartphone. Jimena felt too damn good as she rode the bicycle she borrowed from Dolly (who had three in the apartment). Chito and the boys were playing at a club like eight blocks away, just on the outside of Wynwood, near the Design District. He said they were coming on soon

so she had the next stop on her itinerary, a small but swanky room called
Ursula, but time did not command her, the streets of Wynwood were
rather empty, as was so often the case most nights, and she wanted to
ride bike. A small but subtle breeze hit her face as she peddled around.
Young Jimena in Wynwood-land, the rabbit-hole, a water bottle in her
purse, bouncing off her thighs as she rode. What a beautiful night! The
moon appeared a day or two away from being full and had not yet
completely risen so it looked like a balloon and cast an extra glow on the
neighborhood. The street lights beamed with a soft orange and the
painted murals on the sides of the buildings burst forth with color and
accentuated patterns. Jimena placed her eyeglasses atop her head so she
could absorb the colors. Her eyes looked bugged, but the art looked
more bugged without glass to interfere. She rode slowly up NW 2nd
Avenue, the heart of the neighborhood, smiling. A few cars passed, and
some kids on bikes, a security patrol car sat stationary two blocks away.
        One mural caught her attention so much that she stopped to
examine it. Jimena was not an art aficionado—she had neither the
training, upbringing or experience to even understand the nuance or
symbolism of art—but she wanted to learn—art appreciation another of
many callings that whispered to her during cubicle daydreams. She
could barely tell Warhol from Dali, mostly she just liked the nudes,
anything with the naked human form, but the mural she stopped to
admire called in her some latent feeling which beckoned contemplation.
        On the side of a white building on the corner of 27th street,
there was a black silhouette of a girl holding a batch of balloons. The girl
in the mural had a pigtail and wore a skirt and was not yet a young lady
and definitely in her childhood. The balloons lifted her, slightly off the
ground. If she let go of the balloons the girl in the mural would surely
land safely on the floor, maybe twisting her ankles slightly, but if she
held onto the balloons, which certainly appeared the most improbable,
risky, and dangerous of all possible outcomes, it also definitely seemed
without question like her desire. What little girl wanted to let go of a
batch of red balloons when there was no telling how high you could soar
or where you would land. Jimena stood for a while spellbound.
        "You know who that is right?"

"Excuse me?"

Jimena turned to see a young man standing behind her. He stood alone, smiling, pointing at the mural. Wearing khaki pants and a cotton button down shirt with a graphic tee underneath, he seemed a little hyper, like he couldn't stand still. He sort of rocked back and forth on his heels, but his eyes looked alive with passion. They were hazel. Jimena held them for too long. They looked beautiful. She caught herself, smacked her lips, and threw down her sunglasses.

"Do you know what you're looking at?"

"A girl with balloons."

"Yeah, but who is the artist?"

"Does it matter?"

"Yes," he said. "And it should matter even more in Miami."

"Okay then," said Jimena. "Who painted it?"

"When the student is ready, the teacher will appear."

"Huh?"

"I need a beer," he said, walking away with that same smile, playful and mysterious, yet also a little disdainful. Not condescending, but really more of a hopeless smile. "Peace out."

Jimena watched him walk away. He had a nice ass. It rounded out his khakis like a bubble, or even a balloon, but not flabby. He wasn't fat or necessarily skinny, more just like a man who grew into his body and bones. Jimena placed him at thirty-five, maybe younger. She liked older men, found them more distinguished, mature and attractive physically. She wondered if he was going to turn around OR really just leave her hanging there. She gazed at him like a confused peacock and would've ruffled feathers if she had some—instead she rubbed her scalp, smacked her lips, and stuck her tongue in and out of her mouth quickly like a thirsty iguana in the sun. Wow, he really wasn't going to turn around, not even for one last smile. He kept walking, without looking back, until he popped into a bar about a block down the road.

Jimena licked her lips. She needed a fresh stick of gum. She also needed some water, not magic water, but some regular drinking water, but instead she took a huge gulp from the magic sour fountain. After making the crankiest face in history, she turned back to the girl with the balloons. The image lost a little of its hypnotizing effect but firmly chiseled itself in her memory. Time to leave Wynwood-land. Jimena hopped on her bike and wobbly headed to Chito's concert at Ursula. After almost falling, she regained balance and rode into the night.

***

Another wave of the molly hit her. Was that how this drug would work? Like the ocean, arriving in waves, like a hyped-up crowd at a sporting event, all standing up at once, throwing hands in the air, and then sitting down until the wave came back. The ebb-and-flow of her serotonin levels moved like the soundboard at Chito's concert. Keen sounded sweet, real crisp, better than any live music she heard in a long time. This was the third occasion Jimena saw Chito's band and she liked their sound, a synth quartet, poppy, electric, fresh, danceable, totally catchy. And they were nice guys too, not just Chito but the three other band members, she met them all, their girlfriends, friends, manager— quickly Jimena was welcomed into the small inner world of Keen, which consequently spread out into the wider world of Miami, for Keen played in every mid-sized venue in town, and they were even beginning to get constant gigs up in Broward, down in the Keys. There was a tour planned for Florida: West Palm Beach, Orlando, Tampa, Gainesville, St. Augustine—they had a growing vibe. They didn't win Best New Band in the *Miami New Times* but the band received the People's Pick, which was better; besides, it wasn't Keen's fault the editorial board wanted to choose a rock band since an indie synth band won the year before. Ursula was a swanky bar in Midtown Miami, between Wynwood and the Design District, across the street from the huge mall that wasn't there five years previously. The neighborhood was also known as Edgewater (33132) and its biggest social issue was not gentrification, crime, drugs, poor schools, poverty or the homeless, but whether or not to allow Wal-Mart to infiltrate the area with a megastore. Opponents argued a super Wal-Mart would hurt small businesses, clog traffic, and that the mighty Wal-Mart wasn't abiding by strict zoning laws, but under the surface it appeared quite evident that real estate speculators didn't want a store that attracted low-income customers. City Commissioners, real-estate speculators, mortgage brokers, for a decade have had an obsession that they were sitting on the lost neighborhood of gold, of course it didn't matter that most residents of Edgewater skirted the edges of poverty. Sans a few sky rises near the water, the median income of 90% of the area's residents hovered around $20,000. A Wal-Mart wasn't the worst idea in the world for Midtown. But Jimena, rolling on ecstasy for the first time in her life cared nothing of the politics of the burgeoning area. All she knew was that her new roommate was in an awesome band and the bar she sat in seemed cool.

Ursula's posh interior design felt balanced and extra comfortable. Cushy couches with soft pillows lined the walls of the bar and surrounded the stage located in the middle of the room. The art on the walls appeared chic, mosaics of dead musicians, blown-up photographs of models from the Sixties. Jimena sat a little to the side, with a decent view of the band, but removed enough to melt into the cushions of the couch and avoid conversations. Her leg was restless like a student struggling with a marathon test. She smiled behind her glasses and nodded to the catchy rhythms, but needed a few minutes to herself, without talking, without being noticed, if possible. She stroked the velvet couch with her fingers and chewed the fresh stick of gum she procured from the bathroom attendant in the ladies room. With one deep breath another wave hit her and soon she felt like dancing. Licking her bottom lip quickly, she arose from the couch and bopped and shook and gyrated, moving to the music and the lights of the trendy hole.

Keen only played a six-song set and it ended quickly. There's always that awkward moment when the music ended, especially when you knew the members of the band. What happened next? The crowd usually filled with genuine satisfaction from the aural pleasure it just received, they feel satisfied, but also want more. In a small venue like Ursula, approaching the band to offer pats on the back, or phrases of admiration appeared eminent. But what if an encore was on its way? You didn't truly know until the deejay started up and then what? Jimena stood there like a statue. The deejay indeed pumped out a song and the show was over. Friends and well-wishers slowly moved toward the band, which also had to work tearing down equipment.

Jimena felt anxious and nervous and her palms turned sweaty. She scurried outside and bummed a cigarette from some hipster. Not wanting to stand around, she gracefully thanked the guy and walked away from Ursula. What the hell was that about? What? What's wrong with a little fresh air, a walk around the block, she was sweaty from dancing and Ursula was packed.

By the time she made her way back inside Ursula, everyone was milling around, overpriced drinks in hand, enjoying the deejay's tunes, now unplugged from the band. Much more relaxed, Jimena walked up to Chito, who was just about done breaking down his drum kit.

"Look who it is?"

"Hey roomie," she said, licking her lip. "Nice set."

"Thanks for coming. You okay?"

"Me? Yeah, definitely."

"Are you alone?"

"I left Dolly and Vilano in Wynwood."

"Too much bike scene?"

"Too much bike scene."

'I feel you, bro." Chito finished packing his drum kit. "Hey, want to go to a party?"

"I don't know, maybe. Where is it? "

"Little Haiti, like a few blocks from the crib."

"It's not that place with the swingers and gay doctors."

"No, this is a Gemini party at The Mukti Family Warehouse."

Jimena licked her lips like a lizard and took a sip of the sour water. "Gemini party? Warehouse? Sounds like serial killer shit."

"Gemini's get in free, that's all. Can I have a sip of your water?"

"Um, I don't know."

"It's okay, bro. I like molly."

"How do you know?"

"It's written all over you."

She felt nervous. "Maybe I should go home."

"Nonsense," said Chito. "You're safe. You're good. It's all good. You look fine, Jimena. You look beautiful actually and styling. You ain't got nothing to worry about. No one's judging. Well, maybe at Ursula these bitches be judging, but not at Mokti. You'll like it there. Trust me."

"Okay, Chito," said Jimena. She felt nervous but it began to morph into safe. She looked at her roommate who was smiling, kindly. His eyes glowed. He looked beautiful. She felt trust and the truth serum returned, as she handed over the bottle of sour water. "You know, Chito, I feel so blessed you are my roommate. Like really lucky. You are such a nice guy, so authentic and it's like really helping me, you know, since I left my marriage and everything is so fresh and new. It's like I'm living for the first time in my life and even though we've only lived together for a few weeks, I just want to thank you for the role you are playing."

Chito laughed, sipped the sour water and returned it.

"It's all good, Jimena. Tell me more at Mokti. I want to hear. But I have to pack up now. Want to throw your bike in the van and just come with us? Or I should text you the address."

"I'll go with you guys, if that's okay."

"Cool, let's roll. You're going to like Mokti, you'll see."

"Mokti, huh? Okay, bro. If you say so. I trust you." She gulped her sour water, not yet aware that by the time the ride ended, she would've stayed out until ten-thirty in the morning.

Chapter 3—

Jimena woke up in her own bed with the devil by her side. It was night, dark, and the apartment felt too quiet. The clock read 11:34pm which seemed like a weird awkward number. How did that old song go? Should've been dead on a Sunday or something? The feeling she felt was possibly worse than death. Poor Jimena didn't know where to start. Should she get some water? The walk to the kitchen was without gravity. Her head pounded like it was the dangling clapper inside of a Church bell after a funeral procession. She was the Liberty Bell, a symbol of freedom from the city of brotherly love, but cracked and broken. Dilapidated and distorted. For every ounce of pleasure she felt last night, a pound of empty pressure now held her down. Every stimulation from the day before now transformed into a miserable burden. She wore it like a sweater in the summer, sticky, unwanted, out-of-place. Who could help her? She almost turned to God to fill the emptiness with substance, to dash a sprinkle of light upon her darkness for it really felt like the devil raped her. Jehovah, sweet, dear, forgiving Jehovah, please if you can help me right now . . . but to turn to God was futile for she had abandoned that alter years ago. Science surely had an explanation for the way she felt? Was this sudden mood a chemical imbalance? Did she remember someone saying something about serotonin levels and the after effects of molly? When on it, serotonin levels were enhanced and everything felt extra good because serotonin was a natural chemical in the brain that controlled moods, but when off-of-the-molly your serotonin levels dropped real low so you felt extra shitty. But this. This horrible depression. Was too nice. Of a word to describe. What. Befell. Poor Jimena. It hurt. She felt shattered and fragmented into a million little Jimenas and she did not recall signing up for it.

This was a Tropical Depression, the second named-storm-of-the-season, forming right in her bedroom in The Place and it quickly forecast to morph into a Category 2 Hurricane Jimena.

"Chito," she yelled. "Chito—are you home? Dolly?"

No one. Just Jimena with a noose tied around her neck and a swirling depression that intensified with every aching breath. Classic cause and effect. Too good to be true. She felt way too awesome the night before to think there wouldn't be consequences. For every happy and *vivid* thought and breathe she experienced from her adventures in Wynwood-land, now she was doomed to three times as much misery, darkness and suffocation. It seriously felt like her insides were gutted from her belly and wrapped around her neck. Jimena was empty inside and suffocating outside. She felt cold and hot. The juice didn't do anything. A shower didn't help. The toast she made only wound up in the bathroom toilet. The slow unwinding of time didn't make anything easier. The fact that she had to work in the morning definitely didn't help. Bookmakers in Las Vegas put the odds at 100-1 of Jimena making it to work. Every thirty minutes, the odds were rising. Just how dedicated and strong was that Cuban work ethic instilled in her? If someone believed in Jimena, they could make a killing. She'd call them a sucker.

How on earth could Jimena work? Seriously? You want her to scan medical charts, talk to and educate doctors, and enter complicated codes into a computer? You think Mrs. Perez or Claudinette will ever, ever, ever see Jimena like this? Don't count on it. Missing a day of work definitely didn't make her feel proud, but sick days existed for a reason.

She stayed in her bedroom, even when Dolly came stumbling home drunk at around two. She didn't feel good, there was nothing anyone could do—this was a ride-it-out-keep-it-to-yourself kind-of pain.

Chito never made it home, but he may have helped because he was also on molly, maybe he knew or had something to make it feel better. Actually, maybe Dolly did too. Jimena crept from her bedroom, in pain, like she just had an abortion. She gently knocked on Dolly's door.

"Enter."

"Hey, do you have anything to make me go to sleep?"

"What's wrong, darling?"

"I just want to sleep."

"Do you need a Xanax?"

"Oh my god, yes."

Dolly, down to her night ware, a baggy t-shirt and panties, removed the portable computer from her lap and found an orange bottle. She shook it like a *maraca*—Jimena couldn't tell if she was gauging how many pills she had left, or being a little playful, or maybe both.

"Can I have two?"

"Yeah, sure. They're pretty weak. Only-half-a-milligram."

"You're a lifesaver."

She escaped Dolly's room with a remedy and managed to avoid conversation, explanation, recapitulation, engagement. She did not have it in her. Jimena had nothing inside her. Jimena was a shell of Jimena washed up on the shores of Jimena at low tide. In the kitchen, she washed both pills down at once with a healthy shot of white wine.

Respite, relief, reward, redeem, re-evaluate the situation back in bed. Was it worth it? Was the adventure worth it? Was the molly worth the next-day feeling? She didn't know if anything was worth the dick of the devil in your mouth, ass, and pussy all at-the-same-time. It astounded Jimena to think that all of her adventures happened within one long Saturday night. Did she really have sex with two different people, two different genders, at two different places? Did she? Jimena did. She certainly did. Her vaginal area felt a little sore actually but thinking back, oh, boy, maybe that was worth this ride on the dick of Satan? No, impossible. No way. She felt horrible. She couldn't even feel enough to feel horrible. She felt empty, invisible, not there.

She currently felt worse than the worse she ever felt. Great. A new record for the worst feeling ever. The only difference at least this emptiness was a by-product of a really good time.

***

Jimena Quintero lay in bed, curled inwardly, all sixty-two inches of her body covered in a moist sweat. The night felt brisk and the air conditioner hummed—it was the quirk she hated the most about herself—when nervous, she perspired. She hated the idea of exposing her anxieties with clamminess. What a weak, revealing tell.

Just thinking about it made her sweat more.

The clock read three. At eight am she'd wake-up and call Perez Medical to tell them the truth, she felt sick and couldn't work. She might make her voice sound hoarse. Although physically ill she was mainly sick in the head and needed to trump-up the charges. She'd then fall back asleep and hopefully all would heal. It couldn't get worse. Could it? Demons bounced off walls, literally, little shadowy monsters, whenever she opened her eyes. Luckily the Xanax worked a little. Jimena a light weight with pharmaceuticals. A good night's sleep should do the trick. Time healed all wounds. But what if there was no such thing as time.

***

You woke up at one-in-the-afternoon inside of a sinkhole. Your soul's erosion must've summoned the devil to bubble the bedrock and limestone underneath the surface of The Place. You can't see—the collapse, the roof, the remnants of any particles—nothing's visible. The apartment, furniture, brick and stucco all vanished. No roommates or friends. The dark cavernous space you occupy is cold and dank with yesterday's memories. Humans create sinkholes as a disposal site for various types of waste. This isn't the devil's doing. Your sinkhole is a private enterprise created for your own stink. It smells. You smell.

Is it therapeutic to smell your own stink? Jarring enough to wake you up and look for a cleansing? Or, does it hold you back, bring you down, and remind you of just how hopeless your situation seems? This rotten, stinky pit-of-despair. What if you don't even smell it, Jimena? How could you not. You stink. You mean to tell the world that you honestly can't smell your own stink. It seeps from your arm pits, your feet, your pussy and breath. You're decayed and a corpse, Jimena. Your skin merely formaldehyde to preserve the death you carry around. You're posing like an alive, vigorous lady. Who are you kidding? You're miserable. You think you've earned your freedom, leaving that freeloading man, filing your mother's preaching and Watchtower leaflets

into an invisible and antique cabinet, but you're just as trapped as ever,
Jimena. You hate your job. And you know it. It makes you sick to have to
sit in that cubicle, reading medical charts and lecturing doctors. You hate
that you're embedded in the health care industry, that you're making
money, a lot of money, for other people, humans you don't even respect
or like. You hate that fucking job and everyone at it. And it's eating at
you slowly, like maggots, termites. You can feel them inside of you right
now, crawling and gnawing. You're dying to quit Perez. You've been
secretly looking for an exit strategy for months. But you can't quit. You
fucking can't. Not now. Not as long as you continue paying the
mortgage at your old apartment. What's the exit strategy there? Kick
that motherfucker out? Apply some pressure on him to move out?
There's a statute of limitation on how many months you will pay for an
apartment you don't reside in. Leverage in leaving a marriage is only
worth so much because you're not happy. You want to leave Miami. You
want to see the world. You need to fucking see the world. You're not old
enough at twenty-three to realize you can't run away from your
depression. You're naivety thinks that if you leave Miami, escape to New
York City or San Francisco or Portland or Anywhere Not Here, you will
feel better, like this cloud hovering over you will dissipate with
California sun. You can't run away from yourself, Jimena. But these are
hard-earned truths you must learn on your own. So, figure-it-out. find
an exit strategy, devise a contingency plan, even though you know you
can't leave for good, that much you recognize, not as long as your
mother lives. As much as you want to, there's still the noose of her health
wrapped around your skinny little neck. But traveling certainly is on the
table, and you deserve a holiday, a few of them, but not right now. You
couldn't even leave if you want to. Not while stuck in this sinkhole,
engulfed in your self-made darkness. You are useless until your
serotonin levels balance out. Useless. You don't possess the ability to
succeed. Luck will never tap your shoulder. Opportunity has padlocked
the windows. Success has leapt over you like a hurdle in its way, kicking
you in the process, knocking you down. You are a doormat for others to
walk on. Nobody cares if you take another sip of water, chew another
grain of rice—you're a waste of life, Jimena. How does it feel? Is this

what you wanted? Was it worth it? Was the hippie model you went home with at Mokti worth it? The headache you feel—the soreness in every limb. Was the oily massage and cunnilingus worth it now? You know you have to work tomorrow. You can only lay in your stink for so long. So take a whiff, Jimena—savor your funk like it's a vintage Napa Valley wine, for this is the odor of your depression, your failure and fears—this is the smell of your wasted youth.

***

Jimena had to leave the house, her room. She felt decent enough to move, gravity began to return to her in full around sunset. A long-hot-shower proved highly effective, like a video game character collecting power-up life-force points. She allowed the water to coat her face and the back of her neck as she leaned forward. The water-pressure at The Place was surprisingly strong, but unfortunately, the water only remained hot for fifteen minutes before gradually losing its heat. Also, there was the teeniest tiniest hint of sulfur in the water which tweaked the showering experience. She'd mentioned it to management who had sent over maintenance. A nice Ecuadorian man swung by the apartment to gauge the issue by running the water. He quickly said it was an issue beyond his control and an engineer would come through. But that never happened. And when Jimena followed up with The Place management they said they'd send the engineer sometime this week. She reminded herself to call management again to confirm. Miami, like no other city in the United States, operated on a platform where little to nothing got done without follow-ups, reminders, and constant pressure. Jimena learned that from the corporate world of Perez, the labyrinth of scheduling around her mom's health care, and owning an apartment in a high-rise; valuable lessons for anyone, let alone a lady of twenty-three.

Jimena still felt shittier than any shit water. But at least the sinkhole closed a tad. Jimena felt empty but could see again. After her shower, she meandered around like a zombie, her small frame slowly finding clothes. No one was home. She chose wisely when picking roommates. They were never home. One of them was probably at Winston's, the punk-rock dive-bar walking distance from the apartment.

The apartment she needed to get out of.

Jimena texted Jackie—since moving to Little Haiti, she hadn't seen Jackie, or Sucio for that matter—which was expected. Grove-rats didn't leave The Grove and now they jokingly called Jimena a hipster because she lived so close to Wynwood. But time could not come between true friends. Some say you could count on one-hand the true number of friends you will have in your lifetime. Acquaintances will enter and leave constantly, but true friends endure.

Jackie was definitely on the hand. Even more during times of crisis. So towards The Grove Jimena began to move down the wide Biscayne Blvd also known as U.S.1. But she didn't travel far. A neon sign caught her attention somewhere in the Upper Forties: TATTOO. Instinctively she pulled into the parking lot, but leaving the car required more reason than instinct. Should she get another one? Yes. The answer a resounding yes. It wouldn't take long and she could go to The Grove afterwards and chill with Jackie. Do you know why Jimena exited the car? Do you know why she walked inside of a strange tattoo parlor not far from home? Because she wanted to feel the tattoo needle. She needed to feel something and the pinching and spotting of fresh ink on her body gave Jimena exactly what she needed: pain. She longed for the stinging of that needle so much Jimena wound up getting two tattoos, one on her upper right arm, and the same design on the wrist of her same arm. Choosing an image she wanted on her body came effortlessly. She didn't need to look at a catalogue, when asked she replied: I want a noose.

Two months earlier

Chapter 4—

Medical coding should come with a prescription of anti-depressants. The monotony of trudging through patient files, dozens per day, hundreds in a month, thousands every year, *ugh*—Jimena Quintero must've perused ten thousand files during the three years she worked at Perez Medical—a far cry from her childhood dream of shooting photos for *National Geographic*. Perez was the fastest growing medical center in the Southeast. With over fifty practices (thirty-two in South Florida) the Perez family quickly trotted down a pathway toward billionaire status. Each office was a self-sustaining infirmary with doctors, nurses, receptionists and medical coders.

Jimena learned such fun facts as a coder. Did you know almost one-out-of-two women in Miami have had abortions? That's an ICD-9 635.92, a legally induced complete abortion without complications. Want to guess how many have had more than three abortions? Ask Jimena.

She'd say abortion will always be legal if for no other reason than it is logistically impossible to curb the quantity of women who have them, even if illegal. That's an ICD-9 code 636.92, an illegally induced *complete* abortion without complications, viewed in charts weekly.

How about victims of rape and sexual abuse? Want to know how many carry herpes or other STDs? You have a 097.9? That's a burning case of syphilis. You better take care of yourself, girl, there's no cure for a 042, but you could live with it, just look at Magic Johnson.

Was there a single scorecard with more secrets than your medical record? And there was a young and bored Jimena Quintero, sitting in a cubicle, listening to indie music on Pandora, depressed, sifting through your broken, damned and diseased secrets. There was a code for every one of them. She looked for patterns, misdiagnoses, wasteful spending. How could this person need two Pap smears in one year when they're only nineteen and on birth control? Misdiagnosed.

Working full-time, a normal nine-to-five gig, not some late night zombie shift, not some hustle and flow machinery of stereotypical Miami, but a full-time job, with honest benefits and a honest check, was the least Jimena could do, for herself, sanity and the honor of her family.

Medical coding wasn't ideal, she didn't dream in ICD codes, it didn't make her wet, but she knew the business, plus there existed room to grow and the gig would not require a degree.

A medical coder was the intermediary between billing and practice. They possessed familiarity with insurance plans, rules of regulation and compliance which changed and evolved constantly. In addition, coders needed to possess a fluency in anatomical and medical terminology. They were an important cog in the machine. Insurers relied on them to prevent fraud and eliminate waste and doctors needed them to get paid. Annabelle Perez, the matriarch of the operation, she who could get a Senator on the phone in minutes, who hosted at her home world-class entertainers, owners of sports teams, foreign dignitaries, presidential candidates, who turned down reality television fame. Mrs. Perez, with her stiff collagen lip, augmented chest and Botoxed forehead, knew Jimena well, and of her record at spotting wasteful spending, and of her pace at coding and billing, far ahead of any others. Mrs. Perez would greet her, always in Spanish, *más vale malo conocido que bueno por conocer, Jimena*—better the devil you know than the devil you don't. Jimena would smile and nod. The devil always lived in the details.

For such an important spoke in the wheel, she still hated the job. The monotony of combing through records in a cubicle felt tedious, even if she could listen to her music, or sneak time on Instagram, or buy and sell things on Craigslist, which she loved. The best part of her job was definitely telling doctors what to do. Physicians with their God complexes, educating them made her feel alive and on edge, as if claws just sprung from her fingernails—what, you think you're better than me, *hiss-s-s*. Excuse me, Dr. Baum. This patient should be considered major depressive disorder manic type with recurrent episodes, not simple depression, circumstantial or occasional, as you reported in the Pt's chart. It's quite clear, doctor, this patient's been on Lexapro and Zoloft for over a year and has been hospitalized several times for panic attacks (ICD-9 code 300.01) and erratic behavior. Sorry, but this is misdiagnosed.

Part of Jimena wanted to become a doctor since she saw their existence as relatively simple minded, not altogether different than a car mechanic. She could definitely handle the task. Education was the issue. As a home schooled student, test-taking wasn't her stronghold and just thinking about seven years of college made her palms sweaty. Miami-Dade's Medical Campus offered entrance into a Physician's Assistant program after two years. She'd looked into it during down time at work. Jimena could easily stretch five hours of work into an eight-hour day.

PA's were the future and just as important as a doctor. What else could she do with her career? To evolve as a coder meant more certifications, maybe entrance into management, consulting, operations? The sexy allure and excitement of mid-level management was too much to contain for a twenty-three year old. She wanted to wander the earth, even if only for a year, the desire to explore gnawed at her constantly. She could always come back to coding, if PA school didn't work out. Ugh, where was she going? Seriously. She lived in *that* fucking cubicle.

The cubicle was attached to another cubicle. For years, on the horizon of her peripheral vision, Jimena could view the top of her neighbor's head, a cropped Claudinette: half of a chalky black forehead, her latest hair style, certain months of the year natural and kinky, other times conditioned and coiffed, combed over, slicked back. The styles of Claudinette's hair, over and beyond the rocky landscape of her computer screen, were to her like the mountainous coasts of the Pacific. Jimena knew more about Claudinette than she needed to just by proximity. How she passed gas after eating pizza and it smelled like a wet and flooded car in the summer; when she sucked her lips and sighed she felt frustrated, maybe with a code, maybe just with life; from overhearing phone calls Jimena knew that Claudinette's baby-daddy was useless and philandering; she knew Claudinette's mother was never the same after the earthquake; she knew Claudinette was pregnant again and would birth her third baby soon without wavering (for she absolutely did not believe in an ICD-9 code 635.92). Every time Jimena learned of someone's pending pregnancy or even spent time around children, at some point within the hour she clicked open the Aztec-like-calendar of birth control just to confirm, again, that she didn't miss a pill.

Claudinette and Jimena were cordial but far from close friends. It was more of an age and lifestyle difference, than cultural. Sometimes they lunched together, mostly off-property from Perez Medical, sometimes at Chef Creole up the road from the North Miami office. Claudinette turned Jimena onto some of her favorite Creole dishes like stewed chicken or steamed conch.

"Guurrl," said Claudinette, her head rising above the gray cubicle partition. *"Plee-tay-dem-hayfones-ooff?"* She pointed to her own ears so Jimena understood the body language.

"Huh?"

"Lunch time."

"Oh."

"Oh-you-wanna-stayy-here, or, oh-you-wanna-get-out-of-diss-damn-playcce-wit-me, hmmm? Maybe-we-go-to-one-of-yo-places-too-day, hmm?"

"Not today, but thank you."

Claudinette smacked her lips and sighed, turning around with raised eyebrows, a slightly sassy facial expression indicating both disapproval and apathy with her cubicle neighbor. Claudinette couldn't relate to Jimena's quiet tendencies. The young Cuban-American who listened to music day-after-day, seemingly unplugged from the affairs of the office. Jimena didn't have one single close friend at work. She politely minded her business and went about work with a quiet diligence. Not completely anti-social, she'd small-talk. The consensus on Jimena was that she was nice, hard-working, and excellent at her job, just different. Different how? Jimena put her headphones back on and proceeded to finish up some charts. She'd leave the office, but not to eat. Instead, a half-day, she had to take her mother to the doctor again.

***

Inez Quintero stared out the window as her daughter drove east away from Little Havana towards Jackson Memorial Hospital downtown. They passed the Woodlawn Park Cemetery on Eighth Street and 32nd Avenue. Jimena noticed her mother peek inside the manicured sanctuary since the black steel gate remained open for afternoon visitors. The place looked empty and let it remain that way for today did not look like a day for a funeral. Nor even a time to mourn. The sun shined too bright and the blue of the sky looked too young and crisp. It always rained when someone died, that's what her mother always said. Jimena often wondered what her mother remembered from her youth, as far back as six, when the revolution began, because for one thing, Inez did not fear death. What was it *mami*? What did you hear that numbed you? Did one of your neighbors wail so deep it seemed to strike a simultaneous chord with the summer thunder resonating off of the distant foothills, or was it the time your *tia* came through the front door of your modest house soaking wet shrieking the name of her husband? The rain fell so hard on the roof that foreign afternoon there was no arguing with the verdict dealt from the Almighty Judge. Death of course was nothing new, yet over the years, Inez specifically noticed when He called for his servants, without exception He sent the sun away. Jimena heard it all the time. Her mother didn't fear death for Jehovah would provide the eternal peace and rest afforded in His kingdom. Yet that did not mean she would surrender to His beckoning. He had called previously, but just because He called did not mean it was time, for Jehovah's voice and call were constant. Besides, when time, the call would not be heard. You'll know. You'll be welcomed into His kingdom.

"*Donde hay patron,*" Inez said, "*no manda marinero.*"

"*No, mami. Hacer de tripas corazon. Esta no tiempo.*"

Jimena knew her mother well enough to catch the melancholy and cryptic tone of such phrases. And she would not feed it. What the boss says does not always go. No mom, don't think like that. It's not time. What can't be cured must be endured. The last thing Jimena wanted was to toss the slightest kindling onto her mother's passions for it would only lead to a Bibling down. "*Dios que da la llaga, da la medicina.*"

"*No, mami. La salud es la mayor riqueza.*"

Jimena turned the radio up a few decibels to let her mother know that she was not going to engage her. Think positive, think healthy, and if you have to meditate on religion, keep it to yourself, mom. This trip to the doctor will not morph into a dogmatic soliloquy about Jehovah. And His welcoming ways. And His all-knowing timing. This was a trip to the urologist, a throat and mouth specialist. Nothing more, nothing less. It took Jimena four hours in-the-middle-of-the-night to isolate this particular specialist and maneuver through the labyrinth of proper Medicare paperwork so that the referral could be covered. Plus, she dropped by the office of the specialist a month ago to make the case for why she should be seen. The specialist, a Turkish immigrant who worked for the University of Miami's research facilities at Jackson Memorial, Dr. Hamash Ozid was the best in the region and did not see just anyone. His career was a hexagon pulled in six directions, and like everything in Miami, a phone call would not suffice. Jimena had to go in person to secure the appointment, which only guaranteed a consultation, not any treatment—under the pretense that maybe, just maybe, Dr. Ozid could use her mother as a case study.

Inside the doctor's office, along with the paperwork and triage, Jimena joined her mother in the examination room, since she would have to translate and explain. Indeed, a medical chart spoke for itself. And so does Stage IV cancer, which Inez had already endured for two years.

The poison long ago made its way down to the bones and into her blood stream. Like a gypsy free to wander, of all places, the cancer chose her jaw. Stick your chin out and take it on the jaw for a piece of your bone will literally drop because it needed removal as soon as possible. This much they knew. The procedure was actually pretty simple but it required a specialist. And after cordial introductions with Dr. Ozid, the question still remained: would the cartilage of a sixty-eight year old woman's jaw grow back—cartilage metastasized by Stage IV cancerous cells and if it didn't, could she survive without it? It was a good question and one Dr. Ozid did not know the exact answer to. Based on the X-Ray films that Jimena brought from the Radiologist at her mother's primary care facility, there would still be enough bone in the area to barely keep her jaw intact and maybe, just maybe, more bone could regenerate. Dr. Ozid was a tall and hairy man with bushy eyebrows. In between lecturing, performing surgeries, publishing, traveling for symposiums, and dabbling in medical business, he liked to visit Boston and spend time with his daughter, an undergraduate at Emerson. Indeed, he would help Inez and perform the surgery. He diagnosed the risks as minimal and admitted the regeneration of the cartilage interested him enough to maybe even warrant a study. Most of all he agreed to help because it touched his heart that this woman's daughter would take care of her mother. It wasn't quite like that in his native country and he thought how sweet it would be if his daughter did the same, although he doubted he would ever need her to, the idea still warmed his heart. So the surgery would be done, he declared, within a week, a simple snip-snip incision and a chop-chop saw, and follow-ups.

"As you know, this is not a cure. It's not going away," he said.

"We're aware, Doctor Ozid," said Jimena.

"Okay then, schedule an appointment with the ladies up front and we'll see you soon. Make sure she doesn't eat anything solid for twenty-four hours before the operation."

"Will she have to spend the night?" Jimena was already thinking about her dad and how they could hide this from him. If she did have to spend the night, what lie could they concoct?

"No, we'll have her in-and-out in two hours."

"Thank you. We're very grateful." Jimena stood to shake the doctor's hand. Her hands never felt sweaty around anything clinical. These things never made her nervous. Still her eyes inevitably teared up.

"*Gracias, senor*," Inez also stood to shake his hand.

***

It was dusk and beautiful, the sun a plump red cherry sinking over the western suburbs and Everglades. Downtown the streets and buildings glistened in a pink hue and everything seemed more vivid and alive than usual. Across town on the beach and in Wynwood, photographers cracked their knuckles at the natural lighting and counted down the minutes. The drive home was quiet. Inez stared out the window as Jimena worried how she could maneuver time off to take her mother to the surgery. What could she say? Another family emergency?

Jimena sighed and her sweaty palms gripped the steering wheel harder. Why did she have to take care of this all by herself? She sucked her teeth.

There was just her, no one else.

"*Jimena, no le diga al padre.*"

They sat idle at a traffic light. Jimena looked at her mother's light brown eyes, hazel at times, yellow and green in a certain light. They held strong embers, her mother's eyes. One thing about her mother that Jimena admired was her strength. The small framed Cuban lady was a fighter. She lived with cancer for years, never complained. Inez hid it from her husband, neighbors, sisters in Jehovah, no one knew. Her mother was hard and sharp like a nail, even with the preaching she didn't care what others thought, *lo haré a mi manera*, I'll do it my way. Inez Quintero was a strong woman and Jimena without a doubt would carry her mother's strength and fortitude into the future, but not in the name of Jehovah, or anywhere near a Watchtower.

"*Mami, no se preocupe.* Of course I won't tell dad." Are the secrets of the dead guarded more than the secrets of the living? Inez's husband of forty-seven years had no idea about her cancer, in any of its stages. She decided long ago to keep it a secret. It'd upset him five times more than her. It'd trigger an episode, probably more than one. It'd trigger a series of episodes, a novella of episodes, who knew how many seasons, how many episodes. Eduardo would blame himself. He'd wish to die. Hide in rooms. Stay up all night anguishing about Cuba. He'd relive the years in jail. Hear the gunshots. Fifteen episodes per season. You lie to save the ones you love. They could say they were going to the dentist.

This time the lie would be relatively easy.

Chapter 5—

"I left him."

"No way-y-y," said Jackie. "*Dale*, come inside."

Jimena entered Jackie's condo and sat down on the couch.

"So, is it for good this time?"

"Yeah."

"Finally," said Jackie.

Jackie Trujillo was one of those old-school Cuban-American girls from Miami. Not like the new Lady J's who spelled their name with a "y" like Yulanquis or Yanaira or Yaneisy. Jackie had a few years on Jimena and already owned her own business in Coconut Grove, a little spa on the good-side of Grand Avenue that specialized in pedicures, manicures and massages. They met years ago and were immediately drawn to each other. They were both ex-Witnesses. They learned this at a house party in the Gables, a U of M college vibe, beer pong, flip-cup, BMWs lining the street. Jackie made a comment about how it still felt weird to toast people when drinking. When some guy asked why, she shrugged and awkwardly said she was raised that way. Jimena picked it up at once and later pulled Jackie aside. *You were one of them too, huh?* Jackie looked at Jimena and immediately understood. Jimena had been out of it longer, a little after the ex-communication at eighteen. Jackie left on her own accord but not until her early twenties.

"Exactly how many bong hits do I have to inhale if I want to croak?" asked Jimena, sitting on her friend's black leather couch. She still wore her baby blue scrubs from work.

"You can't die from marijuana, stupid."

"I can die trying," said Jimena, picking up the glass bong.

"Bro, stop eating shit," said Jackie. Everyone born and raised in Miami (who didn't attend private school) called each other *bro*, regardless of their gender. "Take a freaking shot."

Jimena let out a sigh. She was spaced-out on the television.

"Jamison or Johnny?" asked Jackie.

"Surprise me."

Jackie stood in the kitchen of her Coconut Grove apartment and poured two healthy shots of Johnny Walker Black. She joined Jimena on the couch. Regardless of gender in Coconut Grove, a majority of people drank scotch or whisky rather than vodka or anything too fruity.

"When did you leave?" asked Jackie.

"Am I supposed to feel anything?"

"Thirsty," Jackie poured her friend another Johnny Walker Black on the rocks. Jackie wasn't overweight but neither was she skinny. For a scotch drinking gal from The Grove, she had sex appeal. "You know, I didn't want to say shit because it's not my business, but that relationship ended a long time ago. Sometimes you stay because you feel you have to." She sat down next to Jimena and offered her a drink. "Sometimes you stay because you have nowhere to go. It's like a container of milk in the fridge. The expiration date passed but you're not ready to throw it away until one day you realize how bad it smells and you toss it."

"Shut up, stupid."

"No, but seriously, are you okay?"

"I feel fine. No tears, no regrets. I feel relieved."

"Where are you going to stay?"

"I guess with my parents. My mom needs me."

"You can stay here, but all I have is a couch."

"I'm working. I need stability. There's a room at my parents."

"Well, you know, stay until you can get your own place."

"You want to go out for a little, Jacks?"

"*Dale*, you don't have to ask me twice, *pero*," Jackie pointed at her scrubs with raised sassy eyebrows. It's not like she could borrow clothes from Jackie, who didn't wear a size zero.

"Let me run to my car, I have some clothes."

***

A woman walking alone in Miami at night had to keep her eyes open and her mouth shut. Jimena was not some ugly, dilapidated, forlorn figure at a bus stop. She had shape, maybe not in her Perez scrubs, but underneath her loose fitting clothes lay a firm and fit body. Yeah, she stood a measly five-foot two and weighed a buck-oh-four. She probably could've been a jockey if she had the skills or desire, but it wasn't like she had the face of a horse; on the contrary, she locked pretty, beautiful even, a mix of an adorable mutt, not unlike the Terrier / Yorkies who wandered the streets of Miami. She rolled along with her Cuban *mestizo*, not so dark—her bloodline mainly Spanish of course, but there was Irish (the few freckles) and a hint of Japanese (those lazy eyes) somewhere in her stew. Maybe even Haitian if you stirred the pot and considered her ass. Not many Spanish women had *that* much cushion and *that's* saying a lot. Ass and hair was how Jackie used to refer to Jimena, before Jimena cut off her auburn black hair and settled on the bangs a few months previous. The bangs accentuated her face. brought out her tiny impish ears and highlighted her light blue eyes (definitely Irish in the stew) and cured brows. "So-o-o-o, like," Jackie shifted her body on the couch. "Frankie's gone. Like literally? Good for you, girl."

Those not embedded in an unhealthy house can clearly see just how inevitable it was for the foundation to crumble. Over time, the building will no longer pass inspection, and the inspector will issue its condemnation. But no one was truly entitled to inspect anyone else's property except those who lived in it. The inspection must come from within. Of course anyone could see that Jimena and Frankie lived in a decaying institution. Their relationship was Detroit.

An eighteen-year-old disgraced Jehovah's Witness who lived at home with a practicing Witness mother and a bipolar Cuban father will take the next ticket on the fastest train to Get-Me-The-Fuck-Outta-Here – at least Jackie saw it like that. "Let's celebrate at The Sandbar."

"Ugh. Sandbarf. I don't know, Jacks."

"*Oye*, you got a better idea?"

***

Coconut Grove (33133) was like an athlete on the wrong side of thirty; there's some game left, but the glory days existed mostly in the past. The Grove was indeed the oldest neighborhood in Miami, although it has been modernized over the years. Its side streets were covered in rich, tropical foliage, typical of the southern hammocks. Peacocks were also known to wander the residential areas of The Grove causing havoc with their loud mating calls and dances. Many a roof has needed replacement, many a car hood dented, by the stomping of a peacock in search for a peahen. They were horny birds and mated often, like most in Miami. At the same time to witness the colorful fowl wandering the narrow streets of Coconut Grove added to the area's charm. Then there's the storied Peacock Park, not named after the fowl, but the Peacock family, London grocers who emigrated to the United States and opened the first hotel in South Florida in 1883 called the Bay View House, right on the water. The hotel was eventually turned into a school and then demolished and transformed into a park. Jackie's condo lay across the street from the park, behind the Coconut Grove library. Peacock Park was also the countercultural hub for Coconut Grove during its heyday in the Sixties. A gathering spot for hippies, keen to the West Village of New York, the park hosted concerts and love-ins. The park created the bohemian reputation The Grove carried to this day. It was also where Jim Morrison was arrested for public indecency as he may or may not have whipped out his Peacock during a controversial concert in 1969, an event that inarguably led to the demise of The Doors and arguably ended the Sixties. The Grove has maintained its charm but lost its trendiness to neighborhoods like Wynwood, Coral Gables and South Beach. The neighborhood carried that Florida weirdness that certain writers and media outlets loved to highlight, but in reality it was as stale as the bread the line cooks fed the pelicans off the marina's restaurants. Still, the east side of Coconut Grove will always end on the bay and house those who loved the sea and its turquoise Caribbean luster. There will also always be a night life in The Grove with a plethora of bars named after a sea pun like The Porthole or Barnacle or The Jelly Fish.

Jackie lived close enough to Grand Ave so they could safely walk and stumble home from any of the bars, a mission they would indeed accomplish. As long as colleges like the University of Miami and Florida International existed for a Thursday night college night, ladies like Jimena and Jackie could bounce around and drink, for free.

Bouncing with Jackie in The Grove was more like a strange routine than a special night out. She recognized the bouncers and security people at the door. Bartenders knew her drink before she opened her mouth. Regulars scurried up to them whenever possible. They weren't birds to prey on, vulnerable, easy to trap or cage. They were indeed more like peafowl, roosting in bar stools, taking flight only to flash their plumage on the way to the next place. Although celebrating her newfound independence, a somber melancholy followed Jimena, reminding her to drink, to forget the complicated knots she still needed to untangle—simple inquiries like, Jimena, what comes next exactly? After three drinks her questions and fears sunk into an abyss.

Running into Tony Sucio helped. Sucio was a generous man, light-hearted but a little dark and gothic, jovial, opinionated yet funny, a wild boar of The Grove. He could handle his weight in liquor and the longer the night, the more unpredictable the roar of Sucio.

The girls were inside a bar called The Vessel, just one of many watering holes in The Grove decorated with paraphernalia from the sea, fishing nets, anchors, taxidermied swordfish or marlin, tons of snarky tin signs with a nautical theme: *NOTICE: Street Girls Bringing Sailors In From The Street Must Pay For Their Room In Advance*, or, tin signs with a sarcastic pirate undertone: *If I Had Known I Would Live This Long I Would Have Taken Better Care of Myself*. They saw Sucio outside with his long greasy black hair, talking to some college girl on the street. He put his finger on her chest and when she looked down, he poked her in the face.

Jimena ran outside.

"Soose."

"Hey," he said, giving her a hug. "Where the party at?"

"Come inside," said Jimena.

"Are you with Frankie?" he asked, following her into the pub.

"We broke up," said Jimena.

"About time," said Sucio, giving Jackie a hug. "Hey you."

"What's good, Sucio?" said Jackie.

"Dude, it's crazy. I just saw some guy getting head in an alley."

"No-o-o-o-o," said Jimena.

"Literally?"

"Yeah, bro. Like a block away."

"Dirty," said Jimena.

"Let me buy you a drink."

"It's Ladies Night, we're drinking for free," said Jimena.

"Yeah, but that's swill. Let me get you something good."

Sucio ordered three Johnny Walker Blacks, splash of Coke.

"So you left, huh?"

"Yes, yesterday night."

"That's awesome," said Sucio. "To your future."

They bashed together their glassware and drank.

"Everyone saw this coming except me," said Jimena.

"Well, you know, you're a loyal person," said Jackie.

"Bro, royalty over loyalty. You need to treat and see yourself like royalty, like you're a fucking queen," said Sucio. "The only good thing about loyalty is that it breeds devotion, which leads to sacrifice. And when you learn how to sacrifice you've earned an ingredient in love."

"Loyalty matters," said Jackie.

"It does, but so does self-preservation," said Sucio.

"I feel fine," said Jimena.

"Bro, you should feel fine," said Sucio. "You're young as fuck. Hot as fuck. You haven't done shit yet with your life and you have the whole world right here." Sucio cupped his hands together. "You can have the whole world and every day it's just more and more possible."

"He's right," said Jackie.

"Of course I'm fucking right, bro," said Sucio, in his fast cadence, usually indicative of a bump or two. "You know what you should do? You should get a tattoo. You have any tattoos?"

"No," said Jimena.

"No," said Sucio. "Like really?"

"I like tats just Frankie never wanted me—"

"Let's get a tattoo. I'll get one with you," said Sucio. He turned to Jackie. "We should all get ink tonight. Let's drink some more and then we'll go by Joey's place. He's good with ink."

"*Come mierda,*" said Jackie. "Stop eating shit."

"I'm down, I like it," said Jimena.

The three of them had a few more rounds and Sucio began to wander around the bar talking to girls. Jimena liked the idea of getting her first tattoo. She always liked tattoos, especially on women. She followed dozens of tattooed girls on Instagram. #tattoogirls #suicidegirls #hotgirlswithtattoos #Jimenadugchicks #chicksoverdicks #fantasy #tattoo Jimena just never had a chance to get ink. Her mother's religion forbid it as pagan and Frankie thought they were a little raunchy. *Ha, to fucking irony.* She drank. Jimena always thought tattoos were exciting and symbolic. The occasion totally called for something and a tattoo seemed perfect. She didn't allow Sucio to forget his promise and soon they all walked to Joey's, a tattoo parlor on Grand Ave. Jackie hung with them but didn't want a tattoo, however, she knew Joey for years. Jimena always wanted Japanese lettering on her body. #dontjudge #letJimenachoose #shenevergetswhatshewants #sowhatifJapaneseletteringispasse. Jimena found the gesture simple yet also resounding, plus, she possessed Japanese in her blood, from her mother's side. The image received over thirty likes on Instagram when posted the next morning. Combing through a book of symbols, she found it. Although transparent and a tad commonplace it was apropos: the lettering for freedom. It ran down the left side of her ribcage.

Chapter 6—

    Little Havana (33125) rested directly west of Downtown Miami; in fact, as soon as one crossed the Miami River they technically entered Little Havana, although locals would argue the area transformed into Little Nicaragua then Little Honduras and then Little Havana. Either way, as soon as one crossed the Miami River to the west, the median household income dropped by about fifty thousand dollars. It was easy to see. The dilapidated Spanish architecture and wide, sparse streets littered with nomadic refugees illustrated the poverty, but the more west one ventured the more the neighborhood came alive with color, cleanliness and pride. The heart of Little Havana was undoubtedly Calle Ocho (8th Street) and on this strip beat the rhythm of the city. Once the ubiquitous hub of the Cuban exile community, many have moved even further west into the suburbs of Kendall, maybe Westchester, but the fingerprints of Cuba without measure defined the neighborhood.

    The Quinteros lived in the neighborhood since Eduardo and Inez both left Cuba together by airplane in 1978; together they pooled their life savings and money given to them by their relatives to purchase a 4,000 square foot lot with a two-bedroom house and a little guest *casita* out back. Over the course of the years, Eduardo put his sharp carpentry skills to use by adding on a whole other back room to the house, as well as a swimming pool and deck. They rented out the back portion of the house as well as the *casita*. Eduardo converted his home into a revenue generator. Jimena usually played property manager and handled all things related to the tenants (placing the ad on Craigslist, interviewing them, delegating the rental agreements and communicating any issues or complaints) since neither Eduardo nor Inez spoke English.

    She'd been staying with her parents for two weeks and it was two weeks too long. She hated having to live by their rules. It didn't matter that she was a grown woman. When she lived with Frankie they didn't care what she was up to, but now they wanted to know where she was going, when she'd arrive home, who she was with. Plus her mom was always a sentence away from Bibling her down, not to mention the Jehovah flyers that popped up on her nightstand or kitchen table. Plus, her dad held her in slight contempt for leaving the marriage, for in his antiquated and somewhat misogynistic ways, a lady, a Cuban lady, did not act in such a manner. Jimena could hear the echoes of their fighting.

"*El casado quiere casa, y costal para la plaza.*"

"*No, Eduarado—en tiempos de guerra, cualquier hoyo es trinchera.*"

Her father argued with fury how married people needed a home of their own, but Inez, more modern in many fashions would defend Jimena: any port will do during a storm.

There were some obvious advantages to living at home, the biggest of course a rent free existence. Minor conveniences also brightened her day, like how her father prepared a *tostada* and *café con leche* for her before she ventured off to work, or how her mother washed her clothes and folded them so well. It was also convenient in case Inez needed anything health related; for example, her jaw, which was already successfully operated on. But for the most part Jimena tried to spend as much time away from the house as possible. Work kept her busy as she recently finished a major Power Point presentation and now went back to coding. At night she bounced to The Grove to hang out with Jackie. The first hurdle seemed cleared. She definitely left Frankie and had no plan to return. Frankie was in a mild state of denial and texted her at least once a day with stupid and pointless queries asking if they could meet, to which Jimena always replied no. She already changed her mailing address to Little Havana, closed their joint checking account and spoke to a lawyer about divorce. Since she paid the mortgage on the condo, basically his rent, he was in no position to act any kind of snide.

However, she needed to save money. Before she could afford any divorce proceedings, she wanted to move into her own place. It looked like she would have to find some roommates, not the best situation in the world, but hardly the worst. Jimena figured after two or three paychecks she could afford a place and the deposit and security fees. If she rented a three-bedroom apartment and placed all the bills in her name, she could rent out two of the rooms for a flat fee and basically live at a reduced price herself, basic property management skills, check.

Although Jimena swallowed resentment against her parents for her unhappy childhood, she owned a bigger grudge against the house. The house in Little Havana to her was like a prison, an encampment of old haunted memories filled with the years she felt trapped, longing to escape. She spent too much time in that house, in that room. Those middle school years were torture. On the weekends her mother would take her along on missions and she would stand in the background while Inez canvassed the strip mall across the street the dog track on Flagler Street preaching the word of Jehoviah, handing out pamphlets that wound up in the garbage or on the floor. Sometimes students from her class would see her standing behind the crazy women on the streets screaming about religion. Or, even worse, they would knock on the door of one of her classmates, only to have it slammed in their faces. Sometimes Eduardo would show up in the parking lot of the mall and yell at Inez for forcing Jimena to tag along on her mission. He would scream in Spanish: Are you crazy, woman? Can you not see what you are doing? If you want to act like a loon with your crazy religion, feel free, but do not take my daughter with you. He'd grab Jimena and take her home, back to her room. It was always such a scene.

Kids at Citrus Grove Middle School were not kind to Jimena, who was already a pipsqueak due to her size. Those who saw her on the streets remembered and they whispered. Jimena was an easy target and they bullied her, pouring milk on her head during lunch, hitting her in the neck with spitballs in class, ganging up on her in the gymnasium during dodge ball. She was always the last one picked. Many avoided her in any in-class group assignment. Those who did befriend her—outcastes themselves—often could not understand why Jimena wasn't allowed to attend their birthday parties at the Super Wheels roller rink or the Venetian Pool or Chuck E. Cheese. What do you mean you didn't get anything for Christmas? Are you Jewish? Jimena, who are you going to dress up as for Halloween? Why can't you go trick-or-treating? Why can't you come to the dance? Join the gymnastics team? Drama club?

She didn't really have an adequate answer. And she felt like an idiot because she couldn't watch television and had no idea about the pop culture of her generation. Sometimes she would fight back on the playground, on occasion with her fists, or a stick or a rock. Her father never yelled at her when she was suspended. He would yell at Inez for forcing their daughter into what he called The Cult. No matter what the circumstances, Jimena always wound up back in that bedroom, alone, with her tears and anxiety. She had no toys, no games, no computer, just an internal clock that could not wait for her to grow up, and that room, that gray room, with the gray carpet and wallpaper, which she never liked. The wallpaper was gray with a white floral pattern, Baroque looking, ornate, like white henna painted on the foot of an Indian. She would stare at the wallpaper for hours and see in it some sort of pattern or code, like her DNA, so alive and mysterious but stagnant for the white floral pattern stuck to the gray background going nowhere.

It only morphed into something worse during high school when her mother decided that Miami High would only corrupt her daughter. Instead of finding a charter school that might have corresponded with Jimena's personality, Inez wanted to protect her daughter from the temptations of the world so she had her home-schooled, which only pushed her further away from whatever friends she had in middle school, and kept her more and more in the house.

Eduardo battled with Inez about their only child—he yelled how it was wrong to shelter a kid, how if anyone knew of isolation it was him, and she, his wife, knew that, or did she forget? Yet even when he won a fight, he never won the war. Although he never stopped his argument, over time it just became something to bicker about. And Eduardo himself always gave in for he was a busy man, working sixty hours per week as a carpenter, around the city and sometimes in the Caribbean where he used his hands to build countertops in retail shops.

Even though her father was her greatest champion, she still felt closer to her mother. Her father was not a stable man. It was no secret that Eduardo spent seven years of his life in jail, in Cuba, during the peak years of his existence, from age seventeen to twenty-four. It was no secret that Eduardo's father, uncles and three older brothers were murdered in cold blood after the revolution. His family in Cuba had been involved in politics for generations—his uncle indeed the mayor of a small town outside of the city, closer to the hills, and when the revolution overthrew Battista, the Quinteros were not loyal to Battista, nor were they on board with Castro. And that's all it took to have a gun lodged to the back of your head. People with political affiliations that differed from the revolution were seen as a threat to the revolution and they were killed. These real-world problems haunted the streets of Little Havana to this very day. If Eduardo was six months older he would not have ghosts to wrestle, nor would Jimena even exist. As a seventeen-year-old, Eduardo was seen as a boy by Castro's regime and instead of being shot in the back of the head, like his father, uncle and brothers, he was put in prison for seven years. He spoke about it to his daughter but she would try to shut him up, change the subject, steer the conversation elsewhere, for her own good, and more importantly his. She didn't want to see her father's gray-blue eyes search his mind in a distant and cloudy manner. The pain hurt. She had no longing to hear about the prison they kept him in, an old 17th century Spanish fort converted and surrounded by a dried out mote. That was where they killed the prisoners, with an inhumane brutality, in a dried out mote. His room, a rock, a slab of rock with only a peephole the size of a small envelope, faced in the direction of the mote, that was all they allowed him to see, his brothers, cousins, father, best friends, all killed right before his eyes. And then after seven years they let him go, just like that, you, you're free to go, he never knew why they let him go, but they did, but not without constant harassment in the village he lived in, at the university he attended. They probably freed the young man as a means of promoting fear amongst those who thought otherwise. They called him a traitor, dissident, revolutionary, rebel, don't trust Eduardo, they whispered, as if the mass slaughter of his whole family weren't enough, they wielded a branding iron on his soul, and they attacked and destroyed his pride, the one Cuban value, pride, why? For twelve years they lived under Fidel until finally they left only two years before the boat lift. Sometimes it's better to cross-over into the mystery of the ether at a young age, in the name of some cause that won't be forgotten, rather than carry un-healable scars into old age.

To Jimena, the house in Little Havana must've been what jail was like to her father, a place of solitude, loneliness, of no do-over's and immeasurable regret, of tears and fears. But Jimena, unlike her father, ran away, escaped, albeit her route led straight into a marriage arguably comparable to imprisonment; clearly there existed a foggy and gray area.

***

One day after work, as Jimena slowly trudged through the rush hour insanity of I-95 leaving North Miami, she received a phone call from her mother. Her father needed a ride. He was playing dominos in the park. Maximo Gomez Park, or Domino Park, was a refuge for refugees. Located on the outer edge of Little Havana, the small park hosted a contingent of jovial seniors, who sipped strong coffee, smoked robust cigars, and wore guayaberas with white tank tops that covered up huge guts while playing game after game of dominos and chess. One could hear the shuffling clank of dominos if in the vicinity, and despite the vagrants and marijuana dealers who hovered, the park was rich with tradition. It represented a fine symbol for the elderly to remember what it was like to play dominos back in Cuba. Sometimes one happy memory that could be recreated will cancel out ten that are hard to forget.

Eduardo was already waiting for his daughter near the curb so when she pulled up he hopped right into the car. Since Eduardo retired from carpentry full-time, he also retired from driving. If one could avoid the experience of driving in South Florida, they'd be foolish not to.

He smelled of sweat and stale cigar smoke. Jimena often didn't know what to say when around her father, which only made her palms sweat. She told him, *en Español*, that they had to stop by the pharmacy to pick up some medicine for mom. Eduardo grunted in approval and pointed to the new baseball stadium that was recently built. He started to lament about the misfortunes of the Miami Marlins and how wasteful it was for the taxpayers to build the stadium. Jimena knew nothing about the sport or issue and often wished that she had a brother. "*El mayor aborrecimiento, en el amor tiene su cimiento,*" he said.

The greatest hate springs from the greatest love. What was the old man talking about? Jimena understood her father enough to comprehend that he was shrewd and could speak in metaphors. For example, in this instance, she questioned if he was referring to a city's love for a baseball team, or Jimena and her situation with Frankie. From the day Jimena arrived back home again it was clear her father didn't endorse the concept of divorce. He and Inez were married forty plus years and that was the way it worked. Everyone's trapped, there's no escape plan. When Jimena didn't respond to her father's didactic statement he tried a more direct approach.

"*El que la sigue la consigue,*" he said.

(If at first you don't succeed, try again)

"*Ay, papi. Es como hablar a la pared.*" It really was like talking to a brick wall. Jimena sighed and rolled her eyes. What part of it's over do these people not understand? Especially her dad who foreshadowed this divorce on her wedding day. As if Jimena wasn't nervous and sweaty enough already, Eduardo pulled her aside to specifically reinforce the notion that marrying young might not be the brightest idea.

Jimena pulled into the Walgreens without pursuing her father's subtext. Little offbeat comments from the peanut gallery only pushed her to pursue finding her own place faster. The Walgreens on the corner of 12th Avenue and SW 1st Street was loaded with character, both in the patrons it attracted and the design of the building. The site was deemed a historical landmark in 2001. It used to house the tire and car specialist Firestone. The building, with its circular shape, and covered outdoor parking lot, belonged to a different era. The eighty-four feet long, thirty-six feet high W-A-L-G-R-E-E-N-S sign above added to the time warp.

Jimena asked her father if he wanted to wait in the car. He responded by opening the door and walking towards the entrance to the pharmacy. If only he knew the purpose of the medications Jimena was picking up for his wife, oh, boy. Inside the air conditioned Walgreens, the place teemed with customers. Jimena immediately ventured to the back to wait on line at the pharmacy. Pharmacies in Little Havana were different compared to the rest of the country. For example, if you felt sick and needed antibiotics (amoxicillin or penicillin) one could find them in

Little Havana without a visit to a doctor or even a prescription. Little neighborhood perks like that often went unnoticed. Eduardo wandered, eventually settling on the candy aisle. He picked out a few chocolate bars (his guilty pleasure) and gave them to his daughter along with five dollars. Then, he sat down in the waiting area and stared into space.

A group of three teenagers with greasy hair joined the line to pick up prescriptions. They were noticeably loud and giggly, stoned on at least marijuana. Who knew what they were picking up at the pharmacy? One of the teenage boys was wearing a hat with an image of Che Guevara, which caught the eye of Eduardo, who immediately stood up and grunted. As Jimena was paying for the prescriptions and candy, she heard the voice of her father yelling in Spanish:

Do you know this man you wear on your head? You fool. Like a crown you wear his image—do you know what he did? Are you Cuban? Your own people he killed Thousands of your people. You wear a cold blooded murderer on your head like a crown. What an ignorant and misinformed fool you are. Your parents have raised an idiot child and should be ashamed.

"*Oye,* relax, old man," said the kid wearing the hat.

"Come on, dad," said Jimena. "*Vamos,* let's go."

Her father had tired, defeated eyes, always with a tint of red in the sclera. Her dad's eyes also had a beautiful dark blue in the outer circle of the iris, with a light brown ring around his black pupil. The rings gave him the eyes of Neptune, and even though they appeared broken, they were also gentle. Jimena wished she could've communicated better with her father. She wished he was more active in her life, especially regarding all the religious bullshit she endured. He could've fought a little harder, pulled her in a different direction, but she could forgive her dad, for even when sitting on the old green couch in the living room, he was seldom home. She nudged Eduardo away from the kids as everyone watched them leave. He was breathing hard and mumbling curses under his breath. *Always a fucking scene.* She sighed.

***

It was the last Friday of the month and Jimena managed to convince Jackie and Sucio to leave The Grove (a miraculous feat in its own right) and join her in Little Havana for *Viernes Culturales*, or Cultural Fridays, the monthly block party the neighborhood hosted to support the local art galleries in the heart of Eighth Street. Sucio and Jackie had been hooking up lately. It wasn't the first time they'd crossed the awkward blurry line between friend and sexual partner.

The night looked clear, the moon shined bright, and the air filled with the upbeat rhythms of salsa and meringue bursting from speakers outside restaurants and also a live stage. Domino Park was packed with its regulars and the cigar rollers were out in full force. The three walked around the art galleries with *mojitos* in hand, checking out the assortment of colorful art.

"Bro, I don't understand how any of this art is different," said Sucio, pointing to an acrylic painting of a banana on a plate, surrounded by oranges. "It's obviously a cock-and-balls. And look at that painting of the candle next to the headphones, cock-and-balls — and that one over there — the tall tree with the two little trees beside it — everything here is a picture of cock-and-balls. Fuck, bro — take a few pictures of my cock-and-balls, we'll hang em in a gallery and call it art — I'm telling you."

"No one wants to see your cock," said Jackie. "Or dangly balls."

"My balls dangle strong and low because I'm a *meng*," said Sucio. "Not some skinny *flaco cholo*, like you're used to, Jackie."

"Let's eat something," said Jimena.

"We're talking cocks, and you're hungry. Nice one, Jimena."

"Shut up, Soose."

The three of them settled on street food as a vendor just pulled back the aluminum foil on a huge batch of *paella*, only five dollars a plate. The ladies found a place to sit at a table outside a restaurant that let them stay there as long as they bought drinks, which Sucio covered.

While they ate, a slew of kids rode by in the middle of Eighth Street, making noise, screaming and cheering, riding fancy and colorful bicycles, from fixed gear and beach cruisers to mountain and multi-seaters. After the first wave of riders flashed by, what appeared as an army of cyclists followed — some wore costumes, some kicked skateboards, some pulled rigs with amplified speakers booming loud and obnoxious {{{BASS}}} for twenty city blocks and at fifteen-minutes. More than two-thousand riders zoomed by the scene in Little Havana.

"What is this? Some sort of race?" asked Jimena.

"No, bro, it's Critical Mass," said Sucio. "Today's last Friday."

"What's Critical Mass?" asked Jimena.

"It's awesome, bro," said Sucio. "It's a community bike ride. They meet at the Government Center and ride bikes all around town, like a 12-mile route, they change the route every month, and then it ends at a bar downtown and everyone gets drunk. I love Critical Mass."

"Sounds like fun," said Jimena.

The tiny street in Little Havana was extra packed. Locals lined the sidewalks with Smartphone cameras, cheering loudly chants of *dale! dale!* abound, mojitos raised high in salutation—*salud!*, couples put down forks and knives and plates of *arroz con frioles*, old folks left the tables of Domino Park to check out the commotion, moviegoers outside the Tower Theater waited before entering to see the latest foreign indie film, men raised their cigars in approval. For a good five-block stretch it felt like a community uniting marathon of cheers.

"I want to participate," said Jimena.

As the group of riders teetered out, hearty clusters of bicyclists morphed into light patches, and then lighter patches, until eventually the ride was reduced to a pack of stragglers whom tried to catch up with the lot, as cars and buses resumed full control of the boulevard.

***

The night was still young and the three meandered around the art walk, settling near the live music and courtyard filled with vendors. They spent time browsing merchant's wares and dancing to the all-male band on stage who kept a tight and fast rhythm with a barrage of bongos, drums, maracas, as well as a stand-up bass and keyboard. The seemingly endless *patta-pa-pa-pa-patta* had Little Havana moving hips to dances like the mambo, bachata, salsa and meringue.

Viernes Culturales ended early enough that the event would adequately serve as a springboard into another neighborhood and another adventure. Jimena specifically felt frisky.

***

Coral Gables (33134) was fairly close to Little Havana but the neighborhoods couldn't appear further apart in style, design and class. The median income of an average household jumped five levels and it showed. The streets stretched wider in Coral Gables; the traffic lights beamed brighter; dogs looked more groomed and the restaurants seemed cleaner. Coral Gables, home to private fundraising dinners during political seasons—by day, candidates, usually Republicans, partake in photo ops and meet-and-greets at Versailles, the Cuban restaurant in Little Havana, but at night they ventured to The Gables to appease the big donors with whatever they wanted to hear—promises to reinforce the embargo against Cuba, pledges to increase travel restrictions to the island, and of course, tax cuts, always tax cuts.

Swing, Coral Gables swing, for upper-middle class Miami needed to celebrate. Swing lawyers and businessmen and women, medical professionals and bankers. Swing salespeople. Swing you sons and daughters of old Cuban money. Jimena grew up a few blocks from Miracle Mile, a shopping haven during the day, for high-end fashion, wedding dresses and catering companies. She once had a job on the Mile, at Radio Shack. She must've been seventeen and maybe it lasted a month. She was that young girl who deflected technical questions to a co-worker. The one who rang you up, could maybe find some batteries or a cell phone charger—the extent of her technical capabilities. But at the register, she swiped the Platinum cards and saw the BMW keys attached to chains left on the counter, from men and women only a few years older than her. They swam in money and celebrated it with pride. Not every Cuban-American left the island as a political refuge. Not every Cuban-American spent years in jail, in squalor and wasted youth. Not every Cuban-American was scarred for life. Many left with as much as they could carry, sans their lost land—a giant fist shake at the old island, one big swipe of a card. Today, these people were further away from Cuba than ninety miles—Coral Gables, where Cuban-Americans sang Tupac on karaoke nights. A young Jimena, when choosing her next job after Radio Shack, never felt comfortable in The Gables, and turned toward the weirdos in The Grove.

"And why are we here exactly?" said Jimena.

"I don't know, let's try something different," said Jackie.

"I used to get my coke here," said Sucio. "Where the party at?"

"Used to?" asked Jackie, laughing. "Nice pinky-nail, bro."

She grabbed Sucio's right hand and held it so Jimena could see the elongated pinky nail. "Ooo, do you have any?" asked Jimena.

"I don't know what you're talking about," Sucio said.

The three of them walked along Miracle Mile, looking for a place to invade. Attacking a bar with a pool table and a juke box was too much to ask of the neighborhood so they eventually occupied a fancy Irish Bar with a deejay and a dart board. Settling at the oak bar, Sucio ordered a round of drinks and when they arrived he snuck off to the bathroom.

Jackie looked at Jimena and flared her nostrils.

"Does he think we're stupid?" she laughed.

"Sucio."

"So, how are you getting on at home?"

"Ugh."

"Your mom Bibling you down?"

"Almost every day," said Jimena. She began to imitate her mother, speaking in Spanish. "Now, Jimena, when you go out to these places at night you must not allow your eyes to keep looking at that which is unclean or immoral. When you see sin, it is Jehovah's way to turn away. I swear just listening to her makes me want to stick a nice hard dick in my mouth. I swear, Jacks—and it's crazy too because I've caught that woman sneaking to the dog track to gamble."

"Well, she's sick so."

"I know. And I love her but it's challenging. Sometimes I want to just tell her, mom, I'm sorry, but your religion is bullshit to me. I don't even believe in God, mom, I'm sorry. You can believe in whatever you want, but stop preaching your shit to me. But I can't say it. I just can't."

"What ya talking about," said Sucio, back from the bathroom.

"Nothing," said Jackie.

"You want to play darts?" said Sucio. The girls looked at each other with ambivalence. "Hey, you," he asked some guy sitting alone a little down the bar. "You want to play darts with these hotties and me?"

"You talking to me?" the guy said.

"Come, on. Let's play some darts, bro."

The guy looked at the girls. They smirked and nodded.

"Sure," the guy said. "Why not."

"We'll play Cricket, teams, Jackie and me versus you two. What's your name?"

"Blake," he stood, walking towards them. "Blake Thomas."

"I'm Sucio, this is Jackie."

"Nice to meet you, Blake."

"I'm Jimena, guess we're partners."

"Are you good at darts?"

"Me? Sure," said Jimena, as her palms began to perspire.

Cricket is a game where you have to close out certain numbers on the dart board: 20, 19, 18, 17, 16, 15 and Bull's-eyes. When you hit three of the number, it opened for one team to accumulate points on until the other team hit it three times and closed it out. The game was over when all the numbers and Bull's-eyes have been closed and whoever has the most points wins. Sucio allowed Blake to throw first and his first dart landed on the red Triple 20s line.

"Damn, bro, nice dart," said Sucio.

Blake's next two darts hit the 20 and they were up 40 to 0. "Nice, partner," Jimena gave Blake a pound rather than a sweaty high-five.

"Fuck, bro, I think we're in trouble," said Sucio. "We need to close out twenties. I'm glad we didn't gamble with this hustler."

Blake was a good looking guy, white, about seven inches taller than Jimena. He had black hair, combed back, and a lighter complexion than he should, considering he lived in Florida. Jimena figured he must not tan or get out much. He wore a red Polo plaid shirt tucked into a pair of khakis, accentuated by a black belt and brown loafers. Jimena figured him for a lawyer or accountant, definitely white collar, maybe an IT guy, maybe even sales of some sort.

Sucio hit two 20s, so Jimena could point them if she wanted to. The first dart that Jimena threw missed the board completely and came dangerously close to a waiter that walked by. "Oooops," she said.

"Dam-m-m-n, bro, incoming," said Sucio, "duck, Jackie."

"I thought you said you were good at darts," said Blake.

"Um, yeah," said Jimena. "Just a little rusty I guess." Her next two darts at least hit the board although she didn't score any points.

***

They played a few games of darts, drank a couple along the way, and wound up sitting back at the bar. The deejay was spinning retro music from the Sixties off of his Mac computer.

"Even the Irish bars in Miami have a deejay," said Blake.

"Not like that in Ohio, huh?" said Jimena.

"I want to go back to The Grove," said Jackie.

"Yeah, let's keep moving," said Sucio.

"I like it here," said Jimena.

"I can drive you home," said Blake. "If you want to stay."

Sucio and Jackie looked at each other. What should they do? Jimena was obviously drunk, but she wasn't a child neither, and nor did Blake seem like anything other than a nice guy.

It boiled down to Jackie, who deemed the situation safe.

"Do you want to stay here?" she asked.

"Yeah," said Jimena. "Don't worry about me. Go. I'll be fine."

"Okay," said Jackie. "Holler at your girl tomorrow."

Sucio and Jackie said good-bye and left them at the bar. Jimena had a nice sized cocktail, a Johnny Walker Black and Coke and Blake ordered another beer. "Are you good for now?"

"I'm fine, thanks."

Jimena's eyes looked a little sunk and blood-shot, but inside she felt like Wonder Woman, like she could keep going, right till the break of dawn. She processed the tidbits of information she learned about Blake so far. Age: 31. Last name: Thomas. Sign: Libra. Favorite movie: *Anchorman*. Favorite book: *Cat's Cradle*. Sports team: Cleveland Indians. Favorite actor: Jonah Hill. She learned how he grew up in Ohio, went to The Ohio State as an undergraduate, attended law school at Nova up in Ft. Lauderdale and landed in a firm off Brickell that specialized in corporate litigation. What she liked most about Blake was his ethnicity: White. No offense to her own people, but she thought staying away from Latin men made a lot of sense.

"What's the furthest place you've traveled?" asked Jimena.

"St. Petersburg, Russia," he said, adjusting his glasses.

"That sounds so exotic."

"I'll take Miami any day."

"You're crazy. I want to get out of here."

"Why?"

"Miami sucks. Try growing up here. Everyone's a phony. Or a gangsta idiot. It's sunny every day. The cops suck. Public transportation sucks. Driving is a nightmare. Our politics are corrupt. Everyone moves away and there's nothing to do but get fucked up. Shall I continue?"

"You don't think it's changing?"

"No."

"Why don't you leave?"

Blake caught the eye of the bartender.

"Because my family lives here."

"You're lucky. I miss my family. Want another drink?"

Jimena put her hand on his thigh and rubbed it up to his groin, stopping at his penis. "Why don't we go back to your place?"

***

Blake didn't live far so it only took five minutes to arrive at his condo. On the way she looked at her phone and saw two text messages, one from Jackie checking in, and another from Frankie: a simple and stupid 'Hey" incoming at 2:30 in the morning, a few minutes ago. Seeing that message did not make her regret or second guess what she was about to do; it didn't matter that they were still technically married; it only made her more angry towards him. That good for nothing motherfucker! Does he think I'm actually going to respond? What balls on him to dare and try and contact me so late, as if what I do is any of his business? Maybe he should've thought first before he stalked Jimena's friends, taking pictures of them at the beach, setting up a hidden camera in the bathroom when guests showered, creating a secret folder on their home computer and hiding the illicit images in a folder named "JOBS" – ugh, what a fucking douche. She's gone and not coming back. Plus she's paying his rent—that good for nothing, scumbag—Blake was the first man she went home with and that motherfucker was not going to ruin it.

It only made her want it more. And the alcohol certainly didn't prohibit the mood. How many *mojitos* in Little Havana multiplied by a few scotches in Coral Gables divided by her one-hundred-and five pound frame, in addition to the glass of Cabernet he poured for her as they sat on the couch and settled into the space. She noticed some plaques, apparently homage to his alma mater, framed images of a sold-out football stadium. The décor of the apartment also emphasized the colors of his old school, red and gray, showcased by blankets tossed over the couch and chairs as well as a maroon carpet and gray painted walls.

"You know this is Canes country?"

"I'm aware of that."

"Green and orange, not red and gray."

"Well—"

"You must not get laid a lot."

"Pity sex," said Blake. "Lots of pity sex."

This Midwestern corporate lawyer could have his way with her. He could litigate Jimena in more ways than he could possibly imagine. "Is your bedroom red and gray also?" she said.

"Want to see?"

"Thought you'd never ask."

Jimena followed Blake into the bedroom. Once inside she pushed him on the bed and jumped him. No small talk, no negotiating— certainly no arbitrator—maybe a little pretrial discovery—but they had each other right where they wanted. This was an open-and-shut case.

***

Jimena's phone buzzed again. To Jimena, deep in slumber, the buzzing sounded like a vibrator, for Jimena wandered this strange dreamscape where she shopped at a mall, but in the middle of the forest, the scene like a flea market or Renaissance Fair, and this one merchant, a familiar wench, held in her hand a purple vibrator, and she turned it on for Jimena's amusement.

The semi-continual buzzing of the phone woke Blake up. It was not an alarm. Someone tried to contact Jimena, repeatedly. Blake, still tired and needing rest, grabbed the phone with the intention of placing it in the living room, but when he glanced at the screen and saw sixteen missed calls from Mami, he decided that he better wake up Jimena for it must've been urgent.

It was nine-thirty in the morning. The sunlight in the room, not overwhelming, but still present, could injure a vampire, which was how they felt after the previous night's festivities.

"Jimena, wake up," said Blake, nudging her.

She rolled over and moaned.

"Jimena, wake up," he said louder. "Your mom's calling you."

"Huh?"

"Your phone keeps ringing. There's like a hundred missed calls from your mother."

"Let me see." She reached for the phone, sighed, scratched her frazzled locks and leaned up in bed. "What time is it?" A stupid question considering she had a phone in her hand.

Again, her phone buzzed with an incoming call.

"*Que paso, mami?*" From the other end of the line a bombardment of oratory Spanish filled Jimena's ears so fast it was hard to understand. To Blake it sounded like a warbled and distant echo of: *patta patta patta.* "*Lentamente está hablando demasiado rápido.* Slow down, *mami.*" Jimena jumped up from the bed, fully alert to her mother's words. She listened. "*¿Dónde está? ¿Qué es lo que quiere decir el armario?* The closet? Why the closet? *Mami, parada, parada, por favor, no llores.* Don't cry, stop, stop, okay, okay, *voy a estar allí. Vendré ahora.*" Jimena disconnected from her mother and immediately started looking for her clothes.

"Is everything okay?"

"Yes, no, I don't know," she said dressing. "I have to go."

"Right now?"

"Why does he act like this?"

"Do you need a ride?"

"No, I have to go." She started crying.

"What happened?"

"I fucking hate my father sometimes."

"Jimena, you don't have a car. Let me drive you."

"No, I have to go." She was already dressed and heading for the door. "I'm sorry." Jimena opened the front door and left the apartment.

Blake stood in the hallway wearing only his underwear. Confused would hardly do justice to his state of mind. He would never see Jimena again, they didn't even have each other's contact info, and even if he did, he wouldn't put it to use. He will convey to his lawyer buddies the story over drinks at the Gordon Biersch on Brickell Avenue. And when home for the biannual game against Michigan, he'll laugh about it with his old frat buddies. Every time Blake Thomas tells the story it will always end the same. And you think white girls are crazy?

***

Jimena found her way to a major intersection, Le Jeune and Miracle Mile, where she waited on her Uber driver Ricardo in a blue Toyota Corolla, what else? Wearing the same clothes from last night, aware of the looks she received while standing on the corner with tears in her eyes, knowing she could never face the boy she met last night (who wasn't her type anyway), she called her mom to let her know she was on the way home and also press for more details.

The bottom line: Eduardo locked himself in Jimena's closet at seven-in-the-morning with a .22 caliber pistol and a promise to shoot himself. This was the shit you dealt with in the Quintero family. You didn't call the police, or the psycho ward at Jackson, you dealt with it.

Just like the time he locked himself in his bedroom for three days before Christmas, a holiday the Quinteros stopped celebrating when Inez became a Witness. Or the time Eduardo went on a hunger strike for ten days during the Elian Gonzalez fiasco, a media event that transpired walking distance from their house in Little Havana. What about the time when he pulled Jimena from school? He drove her to Key West, in silence, all the way down to Mile Marker Zero, to the southernmost point of the country, and into the salty blue horizon he stared for hours and cried. Do you think that scared the shit out of Jimena, who was only ten years old and in fourth grade? Did everyone's dad act like this? Instead of experimenting with baking soda and vinegar and paper machete volcanoes, Jimena had to watch her father's breakdowns—a tough, hard-working man (most of the time)—that would just crumble and decay like another structure not up to code.

There were other incidents: the rope-in-the-attic; the fishing trip in Islamorada; the prostitute and the guest house; the two-week disappearing act in 2007; the piano teacher's rabbit; the invisible friend playing soccer; the Telemundo protests; the bathroom and the hurricane.

You never knew when he would lose his grip, but it happened inevitably. You wanted to believe it was a harmless joke—a publicity stunt—but there existed a real sense of danger and it was enough to push the institution of their small family to a brink, time and again.

What if he really shot himself? What if? Oh my god. He wouldn't do it, no way. Jimena knew exactly the root of this scene. It reeked of her father's way of seeking attention. Indeed, a publicity stunt. He did not like it when Jimena stayed out late. Since she moved back he often tried to enforce a curfew. Except there was no way Jimena, a grown woman, a married woman, on her own for years, would abide by a curfew. It didn't matter whether she stayed under their house and she had to play by their rules, a curfew wasn't happening, not on this planet. And last night, a Friday, *her* Friday after a long week at Perez, she stayed out all night, didn't call, never let them knew her whereabouts. She could've called, that wouldn't have been asking too much, but she didn't, it slipped her mind, and there's no do-over, only a promise and a next time. And now her dad felt undermined, like no one ever listened to him, like his existence didn't matter. He had no position or role or authority and it made him shrink and fall backwards into darkness, trapped, isolated, alone, just like when he rotted away in jail all these years ago, so he locked himself in his daughter's closet and took with him a pistol, for dramatic effect, for the possibility. Yeah, Jimena knew the scene, episode, script, but at the same time, she never knew for sure.

When Jimena arrived home she found her mother sitting in the kitchen on the phone. Her mother's tears had dried up for the moment. Inez's sister-in-Jesus calmed her down on the phone, long distance crisis management. Witnesses had a certain knack for calming her down.

Meanwhile, Jimena entered her bedroom. It was too quiet.

"*Papi, está usted aquí?*"

She could imagine him in the closet, sitting on the carpeted floor, surrounded by shoes, dresses and his old clothes that no longer fit, for they used the closet space for their old clothes.

"*Papi, estoy en casa.*"

Nothing but creepy silence.

Jimena sighed and knocked on the closet door.

"*Habla conmigo. Para mi, por favor. Lo siento, papa.*"

She tried to turn the doorknob, but it jammed. The doorknob had a lock that could be turned from both the inside and outside of the closet. Surely he either had or hid the key.

"*¿Quieres llorar?* You want me to cry, *papi?*"

Jimena began to sob. She threw herself on the bed and cried.

"*Déjame en paz,*" said Eduardo. "*Es demasiado tarde.*"

"*No, papi, estoy en casa.* It's not too late."

"*Déjame en paz, Jimena.*"

"Fine. You want to be left alone. I'll leave you alone."

Jimena walked out of her room and entered the kitchen.

She grabbed the phone from her mother and hung it up.

"This is fucking bullshit, mami. I can't take this anymore. I'm going to have dad institutionalized. He's fucking nuts. I mean my *loco* dad is locked in the closet with a gun."

"*Cálmate, Jimena,*" said Inez.

"Don't tell me to calm down." Jimena rubbed her runny nose on her sleeve. "I'm sick of being here. I want to be free. I want to live," she spoke in English and yelled at her mom.

"*Cálmate, Jimena.*"

"Why is he doing this?"

"*Estaba preocupado por usted.*"

"Ugh, why was he worried?"

"*Porque.*"

"*Soy una mujer hecha y derecha*—I'm a grown woman, mami."

"*Pedir disculpas. Dígale a su casa, a salvo.*"

"I already did that. Yes, I'm sorry. Yes, I'm home safe."

"*Que necesita tiempo, Jimena.* He need time."

Heeeaa needa tyyme—her English as broken as her man.

"Fuck my life."

Jimena handed the phone back to her mother and sat at the kitchen table. Another storm they would have to ride out. Another Hurricane Eduardo, another Category Four, heavy rain with wind gusts up to 120 miles per hour. Flash Flood warning in effect. Get them storm shutters up, stack up on supplies, and pay extra attention to another emotional round of squally feeder bands.

Around one in the afternoon, Inez couldn't take it anymore. With frayed nerves she left the house to seek council in Kingdom Hall. She wanted to pray in peace to Jehoviah, for an answer, for Eduardo to find the fortitude to calm down and return, for her own state of mind.

***

Left alone in the house, Jimena returned to her room.

"*Mamá ha dejado. Estamos solos,*" she said.

Again, nothing but silence. To fill the void Jimena thought if she played music it could possibly bring her father back. She thought of one particular song. She knew he loved it. It was a popular folk song, a symbol of Cuban pride and romantic love: "Guantanamera." On her laptop, she found an old version of the song by The Sandpipers, an American folk band from the Sixties. Right before she played the song she repeated to her father that they were alone. And when the song ended, Jimena let silence fill the room just long enough before she broke it, apologizing. And then she played the song again. Jimena and her father had a connection to the song. During their trip to Key West, to Mile Marker Zero, her father had repeatedly played "Guantanamera" on the car's CD player. Over and over he played "Guantanamera." And now she would do the same. And when the song ended again she allowed the silence to re-enter the room before apologizing to her father. "*Lo siento, papi.*" And again she reminded him that they were home alone and again she played the song. Jimena knew the lyrics by heart; the first few lines were so beautiful, from a poem by Jose Marti: *Yo soy un hombre sincere / De donde crece la palma:* "I am a truthful man from the land of palm trees." Every time the song played on the radio or at some public event, it always made Jimena remember the trip to the Keys with her father. *Y antes de morirme quiero / Echar mis versos del alma:* "Before dying I want to share these poems of my soul." If it wasn't for "Guantanamera" Jimena would have probably reported her father's actions, at least to her mother. But she never did. The road trip to the Keys was their secret. "*Lo siento, papi,*" said Jimena, playing the song again. "*Estamos solos.*"

After forty-five minutes, in between the song, Jimena heard a *click.* Fuck. Was that a gun cocking or the rattling of a lock? Eduardo exited, placed the pistol on the dresser and hugged his daughter.

Chapter 7 —

A suicide attempt is coded by the method used in the attempt and often use "E" codes. E codes describe the circumstance causing the injury, never the nature of the injury. Therefore, they aren't used alone and never as the principal diagnoses.

Example:
W955.0-Suicide attempt by firearms (Handgun)
E950.2- Suicide and self-inflicted poisoning by sedatives & hypnotics (sleeping pills)
E953.0- Suicide attempt by hanging (strangulation)

Sometimes the cubicle at Perez Medical wasn't the worse place in the world. Buried in charts, locked into the Vampire Weekend channel on Pandora, alone, it passed the hours well enough. Work had altered its course, like usual. Jimena never wound up training doctors in New Orleans or Kentucky, all the preparation for naught; instead, Perez scooped up a few fledgling medical practices in South Florida and began the integration of hundreds of new patients into their network, which meant a whole new project for Jimena. Each new patient usually came with a novel's worth of paper, and most fledgling practices weren't electronic or anywhere as organized as the well-oiled Perez facilities. Want to talk about organized? Care to see the big hawks make money in health care? Perez Medical had its own in-house IT department. They had technicians on staff developing original software specifically for Perez Medical; considering how often medical coding evolved, staffing in-house technicians and software developers put them light years ahead of smaller practices, many in comparison weren't even digital yet.

Jimena had about one hundred patients she needed to audit and consolidate. This current project would probably take her about two weeks to complete. The process was fairly easy, just time consuming. She had to scan the charts page-by-page into a Perez network computer and at the same time look for any discrepancies or missed diagnoses. When all the patient files were converted from paper to digital, she then needed to produce a spreadsheet with her findings and send it to Mrs. Perez directly. This was how the Perez's received payment from Medicare. It boiled down to the proper collection of data and organized documentation from patient encounters. Medicare's model was based on a HCC (Hierarchical Condition Categories) payment template broken into 79 HCC categories, connected to specific diagnosis codes...z-z-z-z-z-z-z-z...Jimena's spreadsheet included an in-depth HCC Review of every chart for current and new found HCC codes, suspected at risk conditions by HCC group category, and the date the billing must be submitted before a year expired. Medicare mandated patients must be updated every twelve months. Unorganized physicians lost money from the giant cash cow others milked so well. On a project like this, Jimena could probably finish twenty patients in a day, a pace faster than other in-house coders who averaged ten, so, she slowed it down to create spare time on the clock for the creation and organization of her own HCC (Hierarchical Condition Categories)—two new categories beyond the seventy: HCC80: Find A Place to Live and HCC81: Roommates.

The incident with her father occurred a week ago, the day before she began looking for apartments on Craigslist. Ideally, Jimena could afford a one-bedroom or a large studio loft and live alone, but considering she was paying $700 a month carrying Frankie on their mortgage, it would be mathematically impossible to live alone. She needed roommates, just how many? If she rented a three-bedroom apartment or house and put everything in her name, the lease, all the utilities, she could sublet two unfurnished rooms and secure herself a suite for practically free.

First, she had to choose a neighborhood. Any area close to Frankie or her parents was a non-starter, so that automatically excluded Little Havana, Coral Way, Coral Gables, The Roads, Downtown or

Brickell. She also had zero interest in living out west. The last place a newly single young woman in Miami wanted to live was the suburbs, so that eliminated Kendall, Doral, Westchester, Sweetwater, or Coral Terrace. Living in the country or sticks would've been better than the suburbs, but the sparse barrenness of such an area turned her off. Jimena wanted to live, not hide, so Cutler Ridge or Homestead were out of the question. The Keys and Pinecrest and Broward were too far. Overtown, Allapattah, North Miami and Opa Locka were too ghetto. The process of elimination left her a few areas: South Beach, North Beach, Miami Shores, Midtown, Little Haiti, or Coconut Grove. Living on the beach sounded like a perfect launch pad into the next chapter of her life, but parking loomed a nightmare, plus it was expensive, especially for the size of the units, not to mention the annoying tourists. Most people who live in Miami probably go to South Beach a handful of times all year, if that. Coconut Grove was definitely a possibility but the more Jimena thought about it, the more she felt like moving to The Grove would be *too* familiar, convenient and predictable. Sure, it would've been great to live near Sucio and Jackie, but what about venturing into the unknown, taking a risk? Midtown was an up-and-coming neighborhood, on the cusp of the Design District and Wynwood, both burgeoning with culture and change. Change was the keyword. Jimena longed for a big change and she wanted to live in a neighborhood morphing into something unique and dynamic. Unfortunately, change also attracted speculators and a lot of the real estate in the area was expensive for Miami. Three-bedroom, new condos in Midtown were renting for $2,500 or more.

There was one apartment complex that continued to attract Jimena as she perused the Craigslist ads. It featured three-bedroom apartments for an affordable $1,100 and highlighted amenities like a gated community, swimming pool, gym and free parking. It was promoted as located in the "Design District" and they had an excellent marketing team, with ads constantly popping up on Craigslist, where ads were devoured in the free stream. They offered move-in specials, like one month's free rent. The community called itself "The Place."

The Place. The pictures in the ads looked cute. Colorful, quad-complexes (four units to a building) attached to other colorful quad-complexes, surrounded by lush green well-manicured foliage. The colors really stood out. Lime green, Shasta orange, aqua blue, very Florida. Jimena drove by during a lunch break to take a tour. The neighborhood was definitely closer to Little Haiti than the Design District, but not by much, and there was a gate with twenty-four hour security, plus the neighborhood was only ten minutes away from the main offices of Perez Medical. The day of her visit shined bright and the landscapers had recently spruced up the facilities. Before Jimena even entered the property manager's office she already knew she found her home. On the walking tour, the pool looked huge and attractive, with a few young guys out tanning. The real-estate agent tried to place Jimena in a three-bedroom unit in the back corner of the complex, but it appeared dilapidated and a little sketchy, especially compared to the buildings on the interior blocks. Also, Jimena did her homework on "The Place" at Yelp and Google Reviews and already knew not to rent in the back for there were issues with rats and roaches. The Place was a two-block by two-block development. Over five hundred units were scattered across the square shaped compound. Some units lined the interior city blocks while others lay behind those on the outside. The buildings on the inner core of the development definitely appeared more modern and manicured for they gave the place its impression to guests and outsiders. Jimena negotiated with the agent shrewdly. He insisted there were no units in the interior and that if she wanted to move-in right away she'd have to settle for an apartment in the back. Jimena called his bluff, thanked him for his time and started to walk away. She knew how many ads they were running on Craigslist; also, with all the move-in specials they offered, they had plenty of properties. The agent was just trying to do his job by filling the worst units first, maybe some newbie from up north would fall for that routine or some first year college student, but not a native Miamian who knew everything was a hustle #hustler #everyday #305tillIdie. It worked too. Jimena hadn't walked more than five yards before he told her to wait. There might be a unit available, he said, in the front, but he didn't know if maintenance had it ready.

The agent guided her to the unit, located on the first floor of a building near the main office, swimming pool, gym, and mailboxes. It looked ready to Jimena. The unit wasn't brand new nor the appliances upscale, but the place would suffice. It looked quaint. Three decent sized bedrooms, unfortunately only one bathroom, but two entrances, one in the front leading to the street, and a back door that opened into a cute little grass courtyard. She liked it on the spot.

After filling out the application and dropping off a deposit fee, Jimena had to wait a few days to pass a standard security background check. Early one Wednesday she received a phone call. Everything was ready. They had the lease for her to sign, set of keys, and a parking decal.

HCC # 71 — Residential Security

***

"Can't go to lunch today, Claudinette."

"*Waa-chu-meen?*"

Claudinette had the baby, a beautiful boy named Jacques. Jimena missed the shower, which made her feel awful, especially since Claudinette liked to throw it up whenever possible.

She returned from having the baby just in time for the new project from Perez Medical. Claudinette exhausted her two-week vacation pay during the pregnancy because skipping a pay cycle when living check-to-check hurt more than post-partum depression. Maternity leave? No way. The idea of a twelve-week unpaid maternity leave was inconceivable to a single mother of three. Besides, take more than two weeks off at Perez Medical and you might not be welcomed back. In Miami, in Latin American and Caribbean cultures, the concept of maternity leave was as foreign as playing lacrosse or joining crew. Even if the land of their ancestors in Europe received months of paid maternity leave, their mentality did not transfer along with its imperialism. "Signing a lease," said Jimena. "Moving."

"*A new ahpawtmint,*" she was excited. "*Where-you-move?*"

"The Place."

"*Doo-doo Place?*"

"You know it?"

"*Meh-knee Hay-shun live near da Doo-doo Place, it Little Haytee.*"

"It's The Place," said Jimena, laughing. "The."

Jimena always laughed when Claudinette's accent sounded heavy, although she really shouldn't. Sometimes it happened to her too. Certain words brought out her *Spanglish*. Words like Achilles, blurry, air-filter, slurry, error, marrying—anything with a double *rr*—in addition, occasionally the *Spanglish* would pop up in her writing—a "y" inexplicably replaced a "j"—for example, in an email Jimena might write: the patient has mayor problems. And a doctor might joke: I don't see the relevancy of this patient's political sensibilities towards the mayor? Claudinette, who spoke Creole as her native language, also stumbled over grammar's hurdles, mainly verb agreements. She might compose a business email: *Mrs. Perez collect the files from me yesterday*. Sometimes with tenses, in a private message on Facebook, to one of her friends, Claudinette might write: *he want to treat me nice*. In many, if not most professional emails, in Miami-Dade County, subjects and verbs were like Israel and Palestine, they didn't always agree.

***

HCC #72—Roommates

Jimena Quintero could maneuver Craigslist like the best of them. She bought, sold, found, gave away, announced, hired and scored practically everything off of the online classifieds. Securing two house mates should amount to a minor mission, if that. She posted the ad, with attached pictures of the empty apartment and bedrooms available, in three-hour increments. The headline read 'Roommate Wanted for Midtown Apt.' The price box read '$500' and the location parenthetical indicated (Design District/Little Haiti). She kept the copy succinct: 23-year old female seeks two roommates to share a three-bedroom apartment. $500 includes all utilities, internet, electricity, and cable. Month to month lease. One month ($500) deposit, no exceptions. Pet friendly. 420 friendly. Check theplacemia.com for all complex details.

Jimena's email blew up like the world was poisoned and she held the antidote. Within a twenty-four hour period, she received over sixty responses. She swam, with her destiny in tow, in a massive pool of categories, each holding its own genetic codes to unlocking the future: gender, age, ethnicity, job, relationship-status, time spent in Miami, lifestyle, sexual preference, type of transportation, level of education, birthplace—so many niches within each. If she wanted a twenty-something female model from Europe in town for a few months, or a late twenties male recently moved down from Boston with a graduate degree and a desire to teach, or a 19-year-old male undergrad from Broward who was taking classes at the Art Institute, or a twenty-something male recently divorced Brickell accountant who drove a motorcycle.

It was exciting, for sure. Whoever she chose could almost definitely affect her life in one way or another. They could possibly introduce her to new scenes, styles, people, places. Did she even want a friend or just someone to share space with? She never had a roommate before. Jimena thought it would probably be best if she found one guy and one girl, to balance out the energy. Two guys in The Place would probably lead to her cleaning up after them. And there was no way in the world three girls could co-exist in one apartment with one bathroom.

Some of the responses were creepy. Like the few emails she received from fifty-year old men who didn't speak English, or spoke English but didn't work—or the couple of twenty-somethings who felt inclined to include a picture of them without a shirt—or the overweight African-American who offered her body for rent—and of course the obligatory response from some pervert who sent along a picture of his dong. Some of the responses seemed way too revealing: like the nineteen-year-old who admitted to selling cocaine—or the girl that just broke up with her boyfriend and had to go into all the details of his infidelity with her ex-best friend. Some of the responses were just strange—like the girl who mentioned Justin Bieber and Selena Gomez four times in a long, run-on sentence, or the couple who wanted to share a room but weren't in a relationship, or the guy from Colombia who wanted to know if it would be okay to have a pet spider monkey. Miami.

Most of the Craigslist responses came from normal people, a lot of folks that just moved to the city, or were passing through for a semester or a season, a lot of students and plenty of locals as well. Jimena liked the responses from applicants that included links to their Facebook pages. She found the gesture mature and saw it as a clear and open glimpse into that person's life. During downtime at work, she busied herself setting up appointments with those potentials that she pre-screened. Jimena scheduled two consecutive meetings per day, after work, at dusk, when Miami was at its prettiest, when the city crawled inside your senses and tickled them silly. The routine was simple. She walked the prospective roommate around The Place, showing off its amenities, answering questions, business-like, and then they ended back in the unfurnished apartment, where she had a couple of chairs, and they talked personal. Soft amber light of the fading day warmly filtered through the single small living room window. Part of a large palm tree blocked the view, a subtle vignette of Florida beauty, and behind that telephone wires with little birds peacefully perched, attracted to the electricity. Most people try to sell their best selves in situations like these, while others stayed authentic. The most important challenge in choosing a roommate was understanding the difference between the two.

***

Transcript: Final Round: Contestant #1: Dolly Robbins

Jimena: So you don't have a car?
Dolly: Nope. I ride bike everywhere I go.
JQ: What happens if it rains?
DR: I get wet. [both laughing] Or I will Uber sometimes.
JQ: That's so cool you don't have a car. I totally respect that. I hate my car. I always get tickets and driving is so frantic in Miami. I just need a car because sometimes for work I have to drive all over the place.
DR: Do you even have a bike?
JQ: No, I want one though.

DR: I have two. You could borrow one of mine, but you should definitely get one of your own. There are also free or cheap bikes at the Co-op all the time. I'm in the Miami Bike Scene.

JQ: Cool. I don't know what that is, but it sounds cool.

DR: Have you ever heard of Critical Mass?

JQ: Yes. One night in Little Havana I saw the big marathon of bicyclists driving down Calle Ocho. That's the Miami Bike Scene?

DR: It's the city's biggest event. The actual scene is a little smaller. You know, we ride bike a few times a week, long rides, like twenty miles. We play bike polo. Things like that. It's fun.

JQ: So, how often are you home?

DR: I'm like never home, Jimena. I work downtown, like a regular nine-to-five chick in one of those big buildings. I work with lawyers, as a paralegal, like I said—

JQ: Do you hang with lawyers?

DR: No, most of those guys are douchebags, but you know, after work, I usually head out, to a bar, maybe in Wynwood or Downtown, or we go on bike rides. I fucking love Miami. I like to enjoy it by being outside as much as possible, and then I come home and go to sleep.

JQ: You said you were from Colombia?

DR: Yeah, we lived there until I was eleven, but I mainly grew up here, in Broward actually.

JQ: Do you use the kitchen?

DR: Hardly ever.

JQ: How many tattoos do you have?

DR: Shit, let me see. I think I have eleven. Do you have any?

JQ: One, but I want more. Do you have a boyfriend?

DR: We just broke up. That's why I need a new place. I was living with Edgar for like a year-and-a-half, but then he cheated on me, that motherfucker, so, that's that—

JQ: I'm sorry—

DR: Don't be. I fucked his best friend. It's all good. You?

JQ: Getting divorced. Long story short, I married too young.

DR: {laughing} we'll have the Single Ladies Club up in here—

JQ: Tell the truth, sista. {laughing} So, Dolly, do you party?

DR: In moderation.

JQ: Yeah, me too.

DR: I like the apartment. It's cute, but a little kitschy.

JQ: I mean, it's unfurnished, so there's a lot we could do with it.

DR: I don't need much.

JQ: I have furniture at my old apartment, some things, like a couch, living room set.

DR: Well, if you need help with anything, let me know, even if you choose someone else.

JQ: I'm thinking I want one girl, and one boy—

DR: I wouldn't want to live with two boys. It'd be a pigsty.

JQ: Girls can be catty.

DR: I used to work at the Fetish Factory. I've had both, babe.

JQ: Interesting.

DR: It's whatever.

JQ: Well, Dolly, I'll definitely let you know what I plan to do. I have a few more people to chat with, but I'll give you a ring and let you know what I'm thinking, either way, I promise …

DR: Cool, I mean, yeah. Like I said, even if it doesn't work out, give me a ring, we can grab a drink. I have friends that live in The Place and I go to Winston's sometimes to see a show.

Transcript: Final Round: Contestant #2: Jason Corbin

JQ: So, you said you were a bartender?

JC: Yeah, I work in Wynwood at The Sour Pickle. It's cool. I used to work on the beach, at The Pearl, in the Oysterbar, but I wanted to get away from the beach. There's so much more happening on this side of the bridge. I live on the beach now but I want to move closer to my job.

JQ: What are your hours like?

JC: Pretty straightforward. I work Tuesday to Sunday, from six to two, on Friday and Saturday we get out later, like four or five—

JQ: A bartender, huh? Do you party? It's okay, I'm not a cop.

JC: {laughing} Let's keep it real—a bartender on the beach and in Wynwood who works 'til five in the morning is doing cocaine, sometimes. But, you know, everything in moderation.

JQ: I appreciate your honesty. And I like to party, a little. I mean I'm open to new things. But I don't want this to be like a party house?

JC: I feel you. Our house should be like our temple, or a sanctuary, or in the least a place to relax and take care of ourselves.

JQ: You seem pretty fit.

JC: Yeah, I work out. I hit the gym a couple of times a week. I'm not like a muscle head, but I try to keep it balanced. I like to swim and jog, also. And I play basketball like once a week.

JQ: Anybody ever tell you that you look like Jude Law?

JC: I have not heard that. But he's cool in *I Heart Huckabees*.

JQ: On a scale of 1-10, how clean are you?

JC: Oh, gosh. I'm not the cleanest guy in the world, but I definitely pick up after myself, don't leave dishes around, I take out the garbage. I'm probably like a 7 or a 8, for a dude. {laughing}

JQ: Are you from Miami?

JC: No, I'm actually from Mississippi and grew up in the Big Easy in Nawlins. And then I lived in the ATL for like five years, and I've been in Miami for three years.

JQ: That's so cool. I've never been anywhere. Why are you looking for a roommate, Jason? You could afford to live on your own?

JC: I could, you're right, but you know, it's cheaper, I can save money, and I'm not tied down to anything. I don't like being committed.

JQ: {laughing} Commitment issues, huh? I see.

JC: No, it's not like that. {laughing} Well, actually, maybe a little.

Transcript: Final Round: Contestant #3: Rachel Wooten

JQ: So, Rachel, are you from Miami?

RW: No, I'm from Sarasota. Know it?

JQ: Yeah, it's by Tampa. Pretty cool. And you mentioned on Craigslist you're a dancer and currently a junior, at New World, is that right? What is New World? Is that the symphony?

RW: New World School of the Arts? It's an arts school, downtown. The symphony is called New World and they do have a fellow program but we're different. Our campus is actually integrated with Miami-Dade, Wolfson. They have a high school and college program. The college program is actually an extension of the University of Florida, so when I graduate I get a degree from U of F—it's a fairly competitive program—funny you mention the symphony, some of my friends are classical musicians but have nothing to do with the symphonic New World.

JQ: You sound pretty cultured.

RW: My mom was in the New York City Ballet company—

JQ: Wow, is that what you dance? Ballet?

RW: No, I'm more modern, some hip-hop.

JQ: Do you get gigs dancing?

RW: I've been in a few videos, Flo-rida, Rick Ross, Khalid; they like to add a little cream in with the cinnamon flavor we have down here in Miami. You know those big video shoots out at some mansion they rent, or on some yacht, stuff like that. I was a Miami Heat Dancer too.

JQ: What? That's so cool. What are you doing looking for a roommate in The Place? Why aren't you living in a high rise on the Bay?

RW: {laughing} We don't make a lot of money. Heat Dancers make minimum wage for rehearsal, and $100 per home game, and more for the playoffs. There's only like fifty games a year so we really don't make that much, maybe a little more for appearances. Being a Heat Dancer was fun but you do it more for like building a resume to move on to something, like landing a gig on Broadway, or dancing on tour with some pop artist or something. I mean, if I wanted to fuck a player and get set up with something on the side, but that's not my scene.

JQ: So what do you do for money?

RW: {laughing} Right now I'm actually stripping.

JQ: Really? No way.

RW: Yeah, like two days a week. At Scarlett's—it's easy money.

JQ: That's kind of cool.

RW: You're pretty enough.

JQ: You think so? My tits are too small.

RW: People like your body type. Petite is hot. You've got a look.

JQ: Thanks. So, what's your lifestyle like?

RW: I eat organic, do yoga, lots of coconut water.

JQ: Do you party?

RW: Yeah, some Molly, some coke, I'm not a big drinker. I smoke weed. My boyfriend is an EDM deejay so we go out on the Beach, like Liv, Story —by the way—I'm like never home. I sleep at his apartment five days a week. We haven't been dating that long and we're not quite ready to move-in, so that's the reason why I need a room, and why get my own place if I'm like never there, you know what I mean?

JQ: The best roommate is the roommate that's never home.

RW: So that's pretty much my story.

JQ: Well, if you want the room, it's yours.

RW: I'm looking at other places, but you seem really cool.

JQ: Cool beans—just let me know when you know. I'm meeting with a few more people too, but you know, no matter what happens, it was awesome meeting you.

RW: Same here. I'll let you know, Jimena.

Transcript: Final Round: Contestant #4: Dali Rencio

JQ: What do you think of The Place?

DR: {laughing} It's not The Grand, bro—but I've been here before. I have a few friends that live here. I think everyone in Miami has lived in this place at some point or another.

JQ: {laughing} You're the second person to tell me that, Dali—

DR: Please call me, Chito.

JQ: {laughing} Okay, Chito, so you said you were in a band? What instrument do you play?

DR: I play drums in a band called Keen. We're actually nominated for the Best New Band in Miami in the *Miami New Times*. You ever hear of that Latin band Mana, they're from Mexico—we sound like them but more indie and pop. Our sound is sharp, crisp and very keen.

JQ: So you must like play a lot of gigs?

DR: Yeah, we play gigs a lot. We have a residency in Wynwood, and we play at Winston's, like right across the street. Living here, you'll hang there, if you like to party. We play at The Pickle and at Garbo in the Design District and Blackbird in Brickell. We play all over the place, just after awhile you have to space out gigs so you don't play yourself out.

JQ: Will you be playing drums at home?

DR: {laughing} No, you don't have to worry about noise. We have a warehouse where we rehearse. It's up the road, off of 58th street.

JQ: I don't know that area, actually.

DR: {laughing} Bro, it's weird. There's a warehouse, two down from us—it's a secret swinger's club for gay men. Super low key. I've been inside—it's lavish, all decorated to look like the Garden of Eden, but there are sex rooms everywhere, glory holes, swings and shit—

JQ: Are you gay? It's okay if you are.

DR: No way, I have a girlfriend. Just I've been in that place because the owner likes our music so he's shown us around. Their clientele are like these rich Jewish doctors from South Beach. They live like double secret lives, with families and million dollar houses and then they sneak away at night, lie, or not, to their wives, and come to this swinger's club. They throw a party like once every two months. It's super crazy. The Mukti Family Warehouse is also near there.

JQ: What's that?

DR: Mukti? It's the visionary arts scene, cool transcendental stuff. Their parties are awesome, like DMT, mushrooms, all that trippy hippie shit. Thought you said you're from here?

JQ: {laughing} I'm just coming out-of-my-shell, you can say.

DR: Miami's a pretty small scene. I know a lot of heads.

JQ: So why look for a place to stay with strangers?

DR: I just need a room, babe. A place to crash. Not complicated. I'm moving out of a house where everyone was friends. There's like six of us. It turned into too much drama. I'm cool with everyone, but I want a fresh start. I'm not looking for friends. That's not to say we can't be friends, you're welcome to chill with me. Does that make sense?

JQ: Sounds like you just go with the flow. Chito, do you party?

DR: Yeah, we party. Go with the flow . . . I like that.

JQ: Does your girlfriend have her own place?

DR: No. She still lives at home with her family, in Pinecrest.

JQ: Are you home a lot? Do you have a day job?

DR: Not really home. I work as a freelance graphic designer . . .

JQ: Do you go into an office?

DR: I usually work from home. Or, sometimes I'll go to a café.

JQ: Well, I'm out of the house at 8:30am, back around six.

DR: That's usually when we're rehearsing, around six.

JQ: Passing ships. I kind of like it, Chito.

Chapter 8—

Park West (33132) was a tiny little club district of Downtown, sandwiched between historical Overtown and the U.S. 1 Corridor of Biscayne Boulevard. Parts of the area possessed a twenty-four liquor license, while other parts of the area were broken and damned. An estimated 320 homeless people lived on the streets. State laws allowed the displaced to stay on the street, as long as they were offered a bed in a shelter and refused. The city wanted the outcasts gone so the neighborhood could develop. But The Homeless Trust, with a fifty million dollar budget, didn't see the warehousing of the estranged as the answer, so they stayed on the streets. Ironically, the beds cost the City and the Homeless Trust $900 per month, considerably more than a furnished studio with all utilities included, in most area codes of Miami. But some were meant for the street, not a shelter. Jimena heard them say it themselves: I'm like a bastard dog, born from an abandoned mutt bitch, I'd only shit myself and wail if put in a cage or the pound.

When the U-Haul pulled up to the cracked sidewalk in front of The Complex, a few homeless turned with mild interest which waned when they saw three people jump out. One to two people were vulnerable pray but three represented a crowd and harder to engage.

"Bro," said Sucio, first onto the sidewalk from the U-Haul. "They keep saying how this neighborhood's changing but I don't see it, even if they break ground on a convention center."

"Are your new roommates settled yet?" asked Jackie.

"Um, Chito's moving in tomorrow," said Jimena. "And Dolly, I'm not quite sure. She's waiting on some bike friends to help her out or something. Funny. None of them have cars."

"I can't believe you almost lived with an ex-Heat Dancer, bro. That would've been sick, I would've been over the house all-the-time. Sucks she chose somewhere else," said Sucio.

"Let's go inside," said Jimena. She didn't want to stay at The Complex any longer than necessary. Her skin stuck to her pink tank-top and the back of her neck perspired, but not from the heat. She felt nervous, like trespassing on some government facility where you once worked but lost clearance. The fact she trekked this walk into the apartment four thousand times made her more nervous, for she knew every crack on the path, could nod to the rhythm of the rusty squeak when the front metal gate opened, timed the exact arrival of the elevator to a millisecond, and could write five text messages before arriving on the third floor for it was the slowest elevator ever. Jimena knew what accessories lined the doors of her neighbors, the wooden wreath on 3A, the cokehead's door in 3B still needed a paint job, and there's that gnome outside of 3C. How many times did Jimena look at that gnome and wonder if they really traveled the world.

"Let's do this," said Jimena. "Hit and run."

Inside the apartment, the odor hit them first, stale and moist, like stinky feet mixed with a wet dog dipped in summer testicle sweat while baked in the sun—moldy—something must have leaked, popped, or drained, like a funky cyst underneath your leg destined to leave a scar.

"You're paying this guy's rent?" asked Sucio.

The living room was cluttered with clothes and fast food relics, bags from Checker's and Taco Bell, Chinese Food containers, a square pizza box, and a few plastic Coke bottles, a couple of plates with some remnants of scrap, candy wrappers, last week's *Miami New Times*, the Xbox was in the middle of the floor, its skinny black cord like a skinny long wormhole into oblivion, and there were games strewn about, and the glass bong was on the coffee table. No surprise.

Place barely resembled her home for the last four years. Good. Jimena thought it'd be worse. She'd imagined the experience like a POW returning to the cage in which they were once held prisoner, many years later, to make peace with the captive. This? Not even fucking close.

"Okay," she said, pointing around the room. "I want that coffee table and the rug underneath it. Just throw all his shit on the floor. Know what? Fuck it, now I want the dinner table and the chairs, he won't use them. Definitely want every painting on the wall, and the book shelf near the kitchen. Nothing from the bedroom. I don't even want to see that fucking room."

"What about the couch and reclining chairs?" asked Sucio.

"Anything I fucked that guy on, no, I don't want."

"Good," said Jackie, "that shit looks heavy."

They laughed and began to gather things as quickly as possible, in no particular order. Jimena went for the pictures: the framed photos she bought from a local photographer, images of the streets of Cuba, modern and destitute, old cars, stray chickens and children in narrow streets surrounded by decrepit buildings—her roots; the book poster containing the full text of *Alice's Adventures in Wonderland*; and the golden chicken, that lay on its own protruding shelf, she loved that golden chicken—art, from locals Mr. Somebody and Mr. Nobody—it was actually made of wood but painted golden bright, like Moses' golden calf, except it was a chicken.

Sucio and Jackie worked on the coffee table.

"You want to take his bong?" asked Jackie.

"The bubbler?" Jimena scratched her nose. He loved that pipe. She remembered buying it for his twenty-first birthday. Whatever. Lazy motherfucker. Find a job. "Yeah, take it."

They began what would only be a few trips up-and-down the old, slow elevator, carrying the remnants of a broken marriage from ground zero to the U-Haul truck, already filled with a bunch of her belongings from her parent's house in Little Havana, who again Jimena managed to avoid as they were both at some Saturday church retreat up in West Palm Beach. Inez called to witness the event by Jehovah, Eduardo reluctantly dragged by his wife of forty-plus years.

After emptying the kitchen of enough cutlery and cooking ware to fill a new kitchen (as if The Douche would even use any of it) all they had left to carry was the big wooden book shelf. Part of her could've left the bookshelf. The shelves were bare but for a few old coding books she once needed to pass a certification, but they were outdated, and some framed pictures of her and The Douche, one of them eating ice cream near the Fountain in Biscayne Park, another in costume, a gimmick from the Bayside Mall, Jimena a wench from an Old West saloon, The Douche a renegade cowboy, and a Bible, to which she would keep. That fucking Bible was hers for so many years it felt sentimental, she could leave Jesus at the door but not quite that particular book. Yet, the reason why she wanted to keep the bookshelf, besides from the fact that she bought it only a year ago, revolved around a desire to fill the shelves with college text books or novels required for some class, or books recommended to her, or books she came upon herself. When she first saw the bookshelf at West Elm it hovered over her like a powerful but unfinished tower, her tower, Jimena always hungered for knowledge, away from the Watchtower and her mom's religion, but what she didn't have was time. When she bought the bookshelf and had it shipped it represented a promise, one she didn't keep during the last year living with The Douche, but now, clearly a second chance, she could fill the bookshelves.

Leaving the pictures on the kitchen counter top, and the coding books on the floor, she tucked the Bible under her arms and helped Sucio and Jackie maneuver the light bookshelf out the door. This was it. She need not return. As her friends carried the bookshelf to the elevator, Jimena didn't even look around. Fuck it. She closed and locked the door.

On the way out, she scooped up the gnome outside 3C.

***

Little Haiti (33137) was as colorful as an orange, kiwi and a lemon. In fact, in the early days of Miami, when Henry Flagler built railroad tracks through the area, it was engrossed with lemon groves, and many still referred to the neighborhood as Lemon City. Those who prefer not to call the area Little Haiti may have a little bigotry in their blood, and there were many: real-estate developers, business and home owners in surrounding areas, those of Anglo and Caribbean decent who deemed Haitians a lower class of people. Was it possible to gentrify a location of its people? It's called Little Haiti for a reason. And even if

Little Haiti was one of the poorest areas in Miami, even if many Haitians have been pushed out or left to themselves, in the middle of the neighborhood, on Northeast 2nd Avenue, between 54th Street and 59th Street, the resilient heart of Little Haiti beat. In the widened streets and beaming, colorful storefronts, and in the foot traffic, light for a city, but flowing for Miami, the bright smiles of Haitian-Americans could be seen, *bonjour* outside the *bodega*, laundry mat, or nursery, *sak pasé*, by day, it was a beautiful Avenue, Northeast 2nd, *nap boule*, filled with proud, hard-working people, who dressed nice, ate healthy, and kept to themselves. The street vendors didn't sell hot dogs or pretzels but coconuts and sugar cane, wielding machetes to cut them open. Fruit trucks wandered the area like the ice cream man, selling fresh bananas, mangos, avocados, lychees, strawberries or whatever's in season, for less than the grocery store. A fleet of miniature buses called The Jitney roamed up and down NE 2nd Avenue picking up passengers who flagged them down. For a dollar-fifty, seventy-five cents cheaper than Miami-Dade transit, The Jitney transported people along the Avenue on a bumpy excursion, packed tight in a mini-bus with no air-conditioning and a radio tuned to Haitian talk radio. The Diaspora. If you wanted off The Jitney you yelled "bus stop" or "thank you" and the driver pulled over. Because of the colorful storefronts and houses, the sun seemed to shine brighter in Little Haiti. But at night, when The Jitney stopped running and the sugar cane venders retired, in the side-blocks, where chickens sang and stray dogs fucked, where the shadows were dark and the streets narrowed, in the side-blocks lay the secrets of Little Haiti.

***

Buena Vista (33127) was a neighborhood so small and intimate many in modern Miami referred to it as the Design District, but the charming little grove was older than Miami itself, and even more storied. Originally inhabited by Florida cracker immigrants, from North Carolina and Georgia — old frontiersman, colonial-era English and American pioneers who migrated to the area after Spain traded Florida to Great Britain in 1763 for control of Havana, Cuba, to which the British seized after the Seven Years War. Then, in the 1860s, the land was bought by William Henry Gleason, a New York born Skull & Bones member at Yale, who transitioned from banking to business around the Civil War era. The area from N.E. 41st Street to N.E. 54th Street between N.W. 2nd Avenue and N.E. 2nd Avenue was homesteaded by Gleason's son in 1892 and during the land boom of the 1920s Buena Vista was sold as subdivisions of the Biltmore and Shadowland development teams. Because of its proximity to a booming commercial area, many prominent businessmen built flashy and eclectic homes to match their rising wealth. However, developers also wanted to preserve the nearby marshlands and mangroves. With a half-expansion, half-preservation mindset, the neighborhood flourished from the 20s to the 40s. The houses today still reflected beautiful early twentieth century architecture, with examples of Mediterranean Revival, Bungalow and Art Deco, even more so with landscaped yards, and lush foliage hanging over the narrow blocks like an umbrella. The area was particularly sublime during June, when the Poinciana trees exploded with bright red blossoms. During the 1980s, the hood lost its esteem and roughened its edges, particularly to the west. Real estate was dirt cheap until the next boom and when the bubble popped in 2007, many of the old homes in Buena Vista maintained their values, although plenty of bargains existed two blocks to the west.

***

The Place, sandwiched between Buena Vista and Little Haiti, came with its own piece of history. Built in the 1940s as Air-force and Army barracks, they were constructed without style or flair, but more with a linear, mechanical monotony suited for quantity over quality, like horse stables. Abandoned in the Sixties, the apartments weathered into the late Seventies when they were cleaned up and converted into Section 8 housing for the lower income inhabitants of Little Haiti and North Miami. In the Nineties, The Place morphed into its modern state, bought-out, made-over, corporatized, spruced-up, manicured. With over five hundred units in the complex, many souls have been through the harrowed rooms to which Jimena Quintero prepared to move.

Only a fifteen-minute commute from her family's house in Little Havana, and a ten-minute drive to her ex-apartment downtown, it still felt like a world away. Her parents wouldn't try and control her social life with silly curfews and demands; nor would they worry when she stayed out late or forgot to call; out-of-sight-out-of-mind. It worked, okay, with her family. It did for the years she was married to The Douche. Speaking of whom, Frankie's fat ass would never venture anywhere near her new location, for there were no tanning tourists on the beach, or busty South American nubility perched on the golden steps of Brickell Village like hungry birds. Jimena was free. Goddamn it. Obstacles lingered, they always did, but she found freedom, rented a U Haul and moved. She wanted furniture in the apartment and texted The Douche to beat it for a few, no she didn't need his help, but thank you, and no they couldn't have lunch next week, and no, I'm not telling you my new address. The idea of meeting Frankie made Jimena see red.

***

Lacerations in coding terminology were used to describe wounds to organs or systems (liver, vaginal for deliveries, spleen, etc.) therefore, actual "lacerations" that occur via the skin were coded as "wounds." Also, hospitals code the actual injury first (example: wound to chest) since they usually treat the patient. Then, for reporting purposes they code the settings and causes as secondary ("E" Codes).

Places of Assault:
E849.0 Home
E849.6 Public building (nightclubs, courthouse, liquor store, etc.)
E849.8 Other places (woods, parking lot, pool, etc.)

Methods or Causes of the injury:
E965.1 Assault by handgun (not specific to number of times gun fired)
E965.2 Assault by hunting rifle

E966 Assault by cutting or piercing instruments (knifes, scissors, etc.)
E968.2 Assault by striking or thrown object (brick to head, or lamp, etc.)

Actual Injuries:

850.11 Concussion (head) with loss of consciousness (30 min. or less)
850.2 Same as above but with loss of consciousness (1-24 hours)
873.49 Multiple open wounds of face
875.1 Open complicated wound of chest
894.1 Multiple & unspecified open wounds of lower limbs (complicated)
884.2 Multiple & unspecified open wounds of upper limbs (complicated w/ tendon involvement)

Moving sucked, but not for Jimena, not that day.

PART II

Chapter 9—

The last Friday of the month meant Critical Mass, the community bike ride designed to promote eco-sustainability and sharing the roads with cyclists. Over the course of the last year, the event ballooned in size and now regularly attracted a few thousand participants. It was even rumored that a few members of the Miami Heat might ride. Since Critical Mass wasn't technically an event, they didn't need cooperation from the city of Miami or police. They met, as a group, at a certain area, during a certain time, and went on a bike ride. What's illegal? The fact that 4,000 riders (some of them lawyers and one possible MVP) complicated the logistics, for during the course of the ride, the cyclists owned the streets—they didn't stop at intersections or red lights—it would be counterproductive to the politics of the ride. Some drivers certainly felt annoyed at the monthly bike ride. If caught at an intersection, they'd have to wait on a Friday night (after a long day's work) for the mass to ride by, which could last twenty minutes. The police weren't fans, for they felt powerless and ignored—two adjectives Miami-Dade police did not desire in their description. But most people in the city supported the event. And for those inconvenienced in their cars, was waiting for a community bike-ride that much different than waiting for a boat at a drawbridge? Would you rather allow four-thousand health-conscious residents collectively ride in an eco-friendly neighborhood gathering attached with a political statement, OR, wait for one rich prick and his harem of whores to go by on a yacht? That was how Dolly put it, when justifying the traffic disturbance of Critical Mass. Of course Dolly was there in her lime green tank-top. As one of the queens of the Miami Bike Scene, what better platform existed to strut your single-gear fixie and knowledge of the biking community?

Jimena wouldn't call herself part of the Miami Bike Scene—more guilty by association. She saw them as an incestuous group of twenty-something rebels, yet also conscious, intelligent and hard-working, most with decent jobs. The Miami Bike Scene could handle their business. It'd been a few weeks since the Vilano thing, it didn't go anywhere, and one or two others already oiled her chains. Jimena's freedoms were hers and why not? Could you think of a more decadent city to enjoy your youth? That's so Miami, right? Pop-a-molly, bro. Miami-fucking-Vice-yo. Where the party at? Tony Sucio's favorite words, practically his catchphrase. He was also at Critical Mass. He came down from The Grove and met Jimena at the Government Center.

Critical Mass, to its credit, believed in punctuality, usually a misnomer in Miami. In Miami, almost nothing started on-time. Cubans and other Latin and Caribbean cultures were infamous for arriving more than fashionably late, per the phrase "Cuban time" which was what Miami operated on. The public transportation systems in Miami: Cuban time. The academic rigor of university classes and scheduling: Cuban time. Sporting events in Miami. Most plays, comedy performances and cultural happenings: Cuban time. If the word "sharp" didn't appear in a Miami invitation, it's safe to assume the event operated on Cuban time.

Except Critical Mass which left the Government Center on the last Friday of the month at 7:30 sharp. Rain or shine. And usually with a resounding cheer of the riders as they began their western jaunt as crowded and massed-up as they could be on tiny NW 1st Street. They crawled past the Clark Center, the main branch of the Miami-Dade Public Library, and the History Museum, all big buildings with a bland Sixties architecture, mechanical and impersonal. Crossing the first threshold of the ride always involved the bridge over the Miami River. It was a steep incline and some riders were better than others. Some were more fit. They had better bikes. This first test of the ride often splintered the mass of the group—for example, Vilano and Dolly were already way ahead of Sucio and Jimena, who labored to get up that first bridge, and they weren't alone. Many first time riders of Critical Mass weren't expecting such a challenge, especially so soon. Some walked bikes up the bridge, but when approaching the decline, staring into the part of Miami tourists hardly ever saw, its heart and soul—it added up to sublime.

The rewards of the hard-work paid off as riders flew down the decline. Many exceeded twenty-five-miles-per-hour. Some used precaution, like Jimena, who feared falling; she wasn't a strong rider, while others felt invigorated, like Sucio, who cruised with no hands, yelling into the summer breeze. At this point, as far as the eye could see, at least fifteen blocks, all were bikers. Once down the bridge, Sucio waited for Jimena. He didn't want to lose her (which was too easy). They reunited in the barren and impoverished area of Little Nicaragua.

"I like this," said Jimena. "It's different riding in it."

"You've come a long way," said Sucio. "You deserve this."

They rode west with the mass on Flagler until the road split to the left, at SW 22nd Avenue. It was at that intersection when Sucio and Jimena peddled by Dolly, yelling her name in the seconds they had before they passed. Dolly was corking the intersection for Critical Mass. Corking is a method "massers" used to ensure the safety of the ride. It involved directly planting a bicycle in the front of an intersection (usually at a traffic light). A car could not proceed unless they decided to drive through the corker, which was pretty much vehicular manslaughter. Corkers, like Dolly, always explained to the cars the details of the event. It's a community bike ride. Thank you so much for your patience. It'll only be a few minutes more. We're called Critical Mass. You're welcome to join us. Google it. Thank you, again. And when the majority of the mass passed by, the corker abandoned the intersection so the flow of traffic could continue. The corker then quickly caught up to the group, making their way to the front, usually to cork at another intersection. Corkers were more advanced riders and their participation was paramount. However, some corkers were more antagonistic. Some saw the road as theirs, and treated cars like a sworn enemy. Instead of thank you for your patience, they yelled phrases like what are you going to do? Are you going to run me over? Wait to the ride ends! Fucking wait! You might catch an antagonistic corker bang on a hood, if the car beeped. You might see a corker involved in a fight if someone stepped out of the car. These were the corkers you'd see at a neighborhood protest, wearing a creepy Guy Fawkes mask, the white-faced anarchist with an over-sized smile and red cheeks, with the upturned moustache. Every scene, especially with rebellion and traces of anarchy at its core, will admit to poisonous apples amongst its barrels.

Sucio and Jimena rode at a leisurely pace, closer to the rear than the middle. They moved along Beacom Blvd, a narrow and residential road that served as a shortcut into SW 8th Street, or Calle Ocho. Once they passed Miami-Dade College's Inter-American Campus they maneuvered onto Calle Ocho near the SW 27th Avenue intersection and headed west. This was Jimena country. They passed the Botanica Las Mercedes with its mysterious prayer beads and religious artifacts. They peddled by the 8th Street shopping center, and the bakery her mother and father frequented almost daily, the Don Pan International. And soon after that the Home Depot her father sometimes walked to, a store where some workers knew him by name. And of course the foreboding and cryptic Woodlawn Park Cemetery that always made Jimena think of her mother.

The bike ride continued west on SW 8th Street and briefly stopped on the corner of Ponce De Leon Blvd for a "mass-up." The concept of the "mass-up" was simple. It afforded the slower riders a chance to catch-up with the more experienced ones. Also, some riders, against the will of those in the Miami Bike Scene who organized this "unorganized" event, liked to turn the community ride into a race. There was no getting around it, some people liked to ride fast. The whole idea of Critical Mass was to stay together in a big clustered group, without patches or splinters. When people fell behind, or it turned into a race, it only put everyone else needlessly at risk, thus the "mass-up" on Calle Ocho and Ponce De Leon Blvd. By the time Jimena and Sucio approached the mass-up, the riders already returned to riding. However, there was still a huge back-log of riders and as Jimena slowed down the patch of people thickened. She began to feel nervous and lose her balance. The ride had crawled to a near stop and Jimena teetered from side-to-side. Too many people. She felt trapped by the density. She needed to stop but couldn't because of the riders behind her. The jam threatened her. The bike wobbled and it happened, she fell right on her side. Luckily those around her avoided the vacillating fall or they would've fell. Sucio rode a few yards behind and witnessed, but he couldn't help. The mass moved but Jimena was stuck on the floor, underneath her bike. Shouts of "rider-down" "rider-down" echoed, cautioning others to proceed gently. Jimena wasn't in pain but she didn't know what to do. The decision was made for her by a gentle giant. Dressed in the finest and most expensive bike gear, the large man leaned down and cradled both Jimena and her bicycle. He lifted them both up in one motion. The man didn't even stop riding. It was as if Jimena and her bike were a piece of furniture in the way, and this giant, muscular man, with tattoos on his arms assisted the situation and did so without exerting much effort while riding his bicycle slowly. A modernized African-American Ganesha removed the obstacle. Jimena felt taken aback by the man's arm strength. For a few seconds, she sat on her bike, carried along by a stranger. Quickly she regained her footing and balanced herself by peddling. The large man, three times her size, steadied Jimena until he felt her balance. Then he let go of her like a little kid off their training wheels for the first time.

"You got it?" he asked.

"Yeah, no, yeah," said Jimena. "Thank you."

"I-ain't-worried-about-nothin."

And then the man disappeared into the mass. With a few strong peddles, he passed like twenty people as if they stood still. Jimena back-in-control, moved slowly along Ponce De Leon Blvd, passing the blocks in Coral Gables with long apartment complexes—she remembered looking at this area as a possible place of escape from The Douche. The rent was surprisingly reasonable for Coral Gables, and conveniently located in the heart of Miami. All the Avenues had such beautiful names: Calabria, Santillane, Phoenetia, Antilla, Sedonia, Sallamanca.

"Are you okay?" asked Sucio, coming up from behind.

"Yeah, did you see me fall? How embarrassing."

"Bro that was fucking LeBron James."

"The basketball player?"

"So fucking cool."

"He was like really strong."

"What did he do?"

"He scooped the bike and carried us till I regained my balance."

"Oh my fucking God bro."

"He was nice."

"Your bike belongs in The Smithsonian."

"Whatever," said Jimena, peddling faster. "It's no big deal."

"I'm calling ESPN."

"Don't you dare."

"At least *The Herald*. That was news."

"Sucio, I don't want to be on no news."

"Whatever bro I can't believe you just met King James. He's not even on the Heat anymore. He must be in town meeting up with DWade or something. This is fucking huge bro."

"Stop with that."

"Why"

"*Dale*—shut up and ride. I'm getting thirsty."

Sucio grabbed the water bottle attached to his bike and offered Jimena a sip. After a few gulps, he put the water away and they rode in relative silence. "Okay, I'll shut up bro," he said.

The street lost its Miracle status and settled into its more humble codename of Coral Way. The ride was narrow and lined with overhanging foliage. They headed east towards tomorrow. What was left of the sun hung over them, clinging to the trees in a light purple haze.

***

They continued in silence, passing the Walgreens where Jimena used to pick up her birth control, before she moved and switched pharmacies. They rolled on past the Winn-Dixie where Jimena's dad loved to buy his churrasco, to which he would marinade in a homemade mix of orange juice, garlic, onion, oregano, and olive oil, while he made his own chimichurri sauce from vinegar, olive oil and cilantro. Her dad loved Winn-Dixie, nicknamed The Beef People. They did indeed carry a mean skirt steak. Growing up it was Jimena's favorite meal. He always cooked churrasco on Sunday, probably as a treat, or out of pity for his daughter. For Jimena, Sunday-funday meant church in-the-morning at Kingdom Hall with her congregation. Sitting in that vast, colorless auditorium, listening to the elders speak of the latest renewals of hope and faith, spewing anecdotes from the latest *Awake* or *Watchtower* publications sent down from New York. They looked like businessmen in their suits. The congregation dressed the same. There were no stained glass windows in Kingdom Hall, no robes on the elders, no frankincense or a crucifix, just long, boring speeches, sometimes re-enactments on how to handle rejection when preaching.

Jimena's dad never attended congregation at Kingdom Hall. Nor did he ever go preaching with them during the afternoon. From the age of three up until seventeen Jimena's Sunday consisted of Kingdom Hall in the morning and canvassing the city, preaching door-to-door in the afternoon. While her father stayed at home and rooted for the Dolphins, or the Baltimore Ravens, his second favorite football team because they had a strong defense. He liked a strong defense. While her father fell-in-love with American Football, Jimena reluctantly trailed her mother. If they knocked on a hundred doors, seventy-five to eighty didn't answer. Sometimes they weren't home, but often, they heard the whispers, mostly in Spanish, don't open the door, it's a Jehovah's Witness. Sometimes they weren't whispers at all, but loud shouts of instruction: *No abras la puerta— son testigos de Jehová*. And they moved on. If twenty-five out of a hundred answered, Inez had her spiel all ready to go. It usually involved some tragic incident in the news. Did you hear about the school shootings? Can you believe this happened? What world do we live in? But if you have faith, it all makes sense. Or, are you aware of all the crime and drugs that are in Miami? This poison can be cured, if you have faith. According to the Gospel of John…maybe fifteen people politely declined and cut-them off before the spiel fully blossomed. Another five would take offense and yell or curse or shoo them off their porch like an unwanted pair of raccoons. They were invited into five out-of-a-hundred doors they knocked on, and these consisted of usually old lonely souls who welcomed the company or chance to debate. Many perverts were more than willing to let two ladies into the house. Jimena saw a penis or two crudely whipped out. Sunday-funday. Once every other season maybe her mother would plant a seed that led to a conversion or a baptism. Maybe through all of their canvassing, Inez converted fifteen lost souls to the cause. Jimena never converted anyone, nor did she try, it wasn't her role, nor did she ever go preaching without her mother. Those Sundays were long. The years even longer. But, at the end of the day, when they arrived back at the house in Little Havana, exhausted and sweaty, they always found a marinated Churrassco waiting for the grill. And within fifteen minutes the backyard would smell like barbecued steak and goddamn if it wasn't the best meal she ever ate, voracious appetite or not, her dad could cook like a wizard. *Churrassco con papas* from the Beeehhf Peepol of Winn-Dixie courtesy of good-old-dad, his penitence for not being able to rescue his daughter from the throngs of his wife's kooky cult.

***

On Flagler Street, this time heading east, the streets opened up to four lanes. The city looked bigger and broader, especially since they explored so many of its unseen neighborhoods. Around mile ten, everyone felt the end of the ride approaching. They could taste that first cold beer at the after-ride social. All they had to conquer was one more bridge, back over the Little River and then they could cruise gently into the downtown corridor, into the city and the night.

The ride always ended at a bar a few blocks from where the event started. By the time Sucio and Jimena arrived, the street was sprawling with bikes and riders standing around. A beer vendor outside the bar popped open bottles and cans one-after-another. Inside the bar the line stood four deep. Vendors gave away promotional protein bars and muscle milk. One guy sold ice-cream out of a bicycle converted into a mini-food truck. The block just cluttered with chaos.

Jimena and Sucio had to lock up their bikes about 100 yards away from the heart of the action. As they walked past packs of bikers, hip-hop clashed with dubstep from competing speakers and boom boxes attached to bikes. Pandemonium would be an understatement when the bus driver of the Flagler Express explained to his boss why his route was twenty minutes late.

The first sip of beer, Jimena drank a cider and Sucio popped a PBR, felt like the orgasmic love child of gratitude and reward. They audibly let out sighs and scanned the area for room. Dolly was easy to spot in the middle of the street near the entrance to the bar.

"Hey guys," said Dolly, "Just getting here?"

"You're not even sweating," said Jimena, wiping her forehead.

"I'm on my third beer."

"How was your ride?" asked Sucio.

"Smooth, fast, yeah, it was fun. I heard Lebron James helped a girl who fell down, like he picked her up and carried her to safety. Isn't that crazy? Everyone's talking about it." Jimena issued Sucio a shut-up-don't-say-anything-stank-face. "What are you two doing after this?"

"Maybe head to Midtown," said Jimena. "Keen is playing."

"There's also a dance party in Wynwood."

"What kind of music?"

"Moombah-core."

"Someone tagged me about that party," said Sucio.

"Me too," said Dolly.

"I hate that shit, bro," said Sucio. "It's like I know about your event, you sent out a mass text, I saw a flyer in the toilet and outside my window a plane flew by with a banner. I get it, there's a party tonight. Don't tag my name on your flyer. Whatever. I ain't goin' to Wynwood."

"What's your problem with Wynwood?"

"Fucking hipsters, bro, what do you think?"

"I'll be right back," said Jimena. "Want a beer, Sucio?"

"What's your problem with hipsters?" said Dolly.

"I'll tell you —"

Jimena walked away in slight annoyance. Let them pick each other apart. Maybe they'll hook-up or something. Who knows? The clock flirted with a young nine, the night felt like a foreclosed condo recently on-the-market, ready to be owned. The Bank of America building hovering over the "massers" changed colors and the Metro Mover swiftly jutted along its electric rails. In line at the outdoor bar, Jimena perused the scene trying to decide if she liked it. Look at that clown, wearing an orange vest and blowing his whistle, trying to direct traffic.

The place was gridlocked. She kind of felt sorry for the people in their cars trying to drive through. When they beeped for the bikes to move, many of the riders booed and some threw empty beer cans at the motorists. Jimena definitely liked the ride. She enjoyed the exercise, fresh air, camaraderie, the synergy of rider and passerby, but all this *rah rah* social commotion she could do without.

Jimena was fourth in line when she felt a presence behind her. A man's warm energy, that's the best way she could describe it. Sometimes Jimena intuited darkness, creepy intentions, unwanted solicitations, she could *see* them coming, the streets of Miami her professor, but this human felt heated, like a calm Jacuzzi at night waiting for activation. She did not expect him to lightly frisk her skin at the hairline. The gentle touch forced her neck follicles to stand on end and a jolt traveled through her. Her shoulders quivered. The only anatomical organ not sweaty from the bike ride, her palms, moistened as she turned around.

He stood tall, almost six feet, with short, curly brown hair. His brown eyes sparkled in the street light. He looked tan and fit, not muscular nor fat, but not too skinny. From his brown complexion he looked Spanish, but not Central or Latin American. His had European blood, maybe Spanish or Italian. He looked handsome standing there with a big smile on his face. She didn't know what to do with this one.

"The girl with the balloon?" he asked.

"Excuse me?"

"I met you, in Wynwood, like weeks ago. You were on a bike sort of just staring at the Banksy mural of the girl letting go of the balloon—you looked a little fucked up, maybe on Molly or coke."

"I don't know what you're talking about."

"Please. I own a bar. I'm not judging."

"Sounds like it."

"Hey, I have mushrooms in my pocket, I'm not judging."

"You have mushrooms?"

"You don't remember the girl with the balloon?"

"I was fucking wasted that night."

They both laughed.

"I'm Alex."

"Jimena."

"This is my first Critical Mass."

"Me too."

It was Jimena's turn to order a beer. Alex cut in front of her.

"Two Magic Hats, you need anything else?"

"My friend needs a beer."

A beer for *a friend*, not *boyfriend*, Jimena revealed her availability.

"Make it three."

Alex grabbed the beers.

Jimena noticed the healthy tip he threw in her bucket.

"I heard LeBron James rode tonight."

Jimena's palms moistened more.

"That's what I heard."

"I like this. It's good to see the community come together. Miami needs more of that."

"Yeah, the ride was cool. This is too much though."

"You know, one of the greatest ironies of the twenty-first century is that the biker counterculture that started with gangs in the 1950s, greasers in leather jackets on motorcycles, portrayed by the likes of James Dean or Marlon Brando in *The Wild One*, or Danny Zuko in *Grease* or Fonzie in *Happy Days*, those cool, dangerous kids with the rebellious, authentic spirit of youth—the whole scene has re-invented itself without the power of an engine, the culture metamorphosed into a large, socially conscious bicycle gang, while aging yuppies ride hogs."

"Yeah, but most of these bikers are fucktards."

"How so?"

"They pretend to be conscious, sensitive to the environment."

"I hear you. They pretend to be socially aware. They pretend concern with big Government issues, like Monsanto and GMOs or income inequality like in the Occupy movement, but when in reality, they're just kids who want to get fucked up, like the rest of us."

"How old are you?"

He definitely seemed older, at least in his early thirties. He appeared schooled on current events. He revealed he owned a bar. And Jimena could see a gray hair or two, which she liked.

"I'm thirty-four."

"Eleven years older than me."

"Eleven, that's my favorite number."

They looked at each other until it became a little awkward.

"Go back to your friend, but I'd like to text you sometime."

So assertive and sure of what he wanted. She wouldn't resist.

"What's your number? I'll text you," said Jimena.

They exchanged digits across smart phone devices.

A simple text, only a name and a smile: Jimena Quintero ☺ Alex Lane ☺ All they had to do was "add" contact. She saved his info quickly, before forgetting. Neither saw this coming. Neither planned it.

Nor were they looking for it. Yet they both liked it.

***

Love is sillier than putty. Since the dawn of time poets and philosophers have tried to grapple with such simple questions: what is love? How do you make it stay? Where does love go when it leaves? You can't buy love. Can't tell it what to do. Love never comes when looking for it. And it hardly makes sense. Love can manifest itself in bipolar forms: carnal and physical love, spiritual and divine love, brotherly love, the unconditional love of parents and children. Don't forget the dark side—obsession, irrationality. How can love turn into hate? Love could be a monster. Love could be an angel and the devil in the same hotel.

***

Jimena sat alone at The Spot, a dark, brooding speakeasy off of 11th street, in the Park West district with the twenty-four liquor license. She was meeting Alex at the bar, it was jazz night and a quartet of post-grad musicians from the University of Miami crushed jams. It took all of thirty minutes before Jimena texted him. Yes. She texted him. Why not? Sucio lingered at the bike social, with Dolly, drinking. They considered going to see Keen. Jimena wanted something new. How many times could she see Keen? It's awesome that her friend was in a band, but, really, how many shows could she catch before it's like okay, been there, done that. They only possessed six original songs in their repertoire. Come on now. Jimena had a friend, Jose Zambrano, who used to be a Witness. Like many survivors who abandoned the religion, he rebelled and ran away. Jose followed some jam band around the country. He must've seen the band two hundred times. He tore across the states in marathon road trips, paying for the expense by selling pins. Pins. Little pins he designed. They referenced a venue or a song, an inside joke connected to the band. Jimena liked Jose but kind of felt he left one cult for another. And she never quite understood the charm in seeing the same band a hundred times, no matter how different or improvisational the sound. If Jesus traveled the country on a stadium tour, opening for the Almighty Father, proving the omnipotence and everlasting existence of God and heaven, Jimena would probably catch one show, maybe two. Really. Only one day previously Jose updated his social media status: *the journey is the destination*. At work, stuck in a cubicle, Jimena tried to understand the cliché. It's not where you're going it's how you arrive at the place, right? In other words, they have fun rolling along the countryside, through flat desert landscapes, up mountainous roads with no railings, stopping at quaint restaurants, meeting folks more foreign than Miami's foreigners, absorbing America's nuance, squeezing it for feeble wisdoms and hard earned truths. Meh. Jimena shrugged at her desk, commented: *throw me on a plane, with a Xanax, a glass of wine and wake me up when we're there*. Jose liked the comment.

She enjoyed adventures, wanted more. She felt fearless, if not totally neurotic. Why do you think Jimena texted this Alex guy only thirty minutes after they met? Was that not daring? Did she care he might reject her or judge it as a booty call? Maybe, but who cared? Anything to get away from the bike scene and the familiarity of friends. This constituted a journey onto itself.

***

Alex Lane walked into The Spot and approached Jimena at the bar. It was two hours after the bike ride and both had time to go home for a costume change. Jimena wore black leather boots, black fishnets, a red skirt and a vintage graphic t-shirt. Alex looked handsome. He'd combed his hair with some product and wore khakis and a flannel collared cotton shirt. Alex banged on the bar as if testing its viability.

"Coral," he said, 'not too shabby."

The bartender, a young bearded man, dressed in a blazer (neo speak-easy attire) approached Alex with a bottled beer, shook his hand and went back to work. Jimena noticed how Alex didn't have to order, the bartender knew what he drank, nor did he have to pay, hmmm.

"Let's go outside. Too loud in here."

Outside of The Spot looked mixed. Friday night attracted a crowd, even more-so after Critical Mass, but the clock only read eleven, early for Miami. Some people were leftover from the ride, others out for a drink before the club. The narrow sidewalk was littered with bikes. The Spot existed on the edge of the Overtown ghetto. Although the corner and surrounding area appeared well-lit, walk one block in the wrong direction, the shadows intensified and came alive.

Jimena and Alex found a table away from the fray.

"So you met Lebron James tonight, huh?"

"No," she said. Her eyes darted. "Who told you that?"

"It's on Vine. Someone filmed it."

"Ughhh, fuck my life."

"No one knows it's you," said Alex, "yet."

"Think people will see it?"

"Lebron James, the world's most famous athlete, scoops up a hundred-pound Cuban girl like cinnamon-vanilla ice-cream, and her bicycle, lifts them to safety, potentially avoiding a possible stampede, in seven seconds of blockbuster action. Nah, doubt it'll catch any traction."

"Fuck my life."

"Embrace the attention."

"Um, no."

"A Miami girl who doesn't want attention? I'm surprised."

"Surprise motherfucker," Jimena said.

"*Dexter's* my favorite show, you should know."

"Yeah? Who's your favorite killer?"

"Trinity," said Alex.

"Trinity's a sick-fuck, but not more than The Doomsday Killer."

"You can ignore the attention, if you want."

"I want."

"Why?"

"It's hollow and annoying."

"How would you know?"

"How could it not be?"

"Fame," he said, pausing. "Don't you want to live forever?"

"No," said Jimena, sipping her cocktail. "I don't."

She could tell he was testing her. Jimena didn't quite understand why exactly, but the coy, playful smile Alex wore definitely indicated a sense of sarcasm and irony in his questioning.

"What do you think of Miami?" he pressed.

"I have a love, hate relationship with Miami. I've been here my whole life, never really left. I'm hungry to explore the world, maybe even move away, but my family's here so—"

"Yeah, but what do you think about Miami culture?"

"What culture?" she laughed. "We're a bag of mixed nuts."

"See, that's where you're wrong. Miami is going through a cultural Renaissance. We are a relatively young city. Every ten years we grow ten to fifteen percent in population. Cities like New York, Philly and Chicago are shrinking. We're growing, especially in the arts. Miami has this stale reputation, formed in the 1980's, this old definition of look-at-how-weird-we-are—we're a cultural wasteland, just a place to party, a city with corrupt politicians and a diverse populace speared by a heavy influx of Cuban culture. And every major media outlet promotes and exploits this. Look at our tropical weirdness, our sex-and-strip-club definition. Our *Cocaine Cowboys* and *Scarface*—Miami: the closest city to America. The rest of the country looks at us like we're idiots. Every time something weird happens in the news. Look, hun, Florida, again—"

"Well, there are a lot of freaks and weirdoes here."

"There are freaks and weirdoes everywhere. Do you think San Francisco doesn't have just as many nut jobs? Or New York for that matter. Or, Austin, Boston, Cleveland, anywhere, really. But Miami lets the rest of the country define who we are. It drives me crazy. We'll let these writers from New York parachute in for the weekend and pen articles telling the world who we are, and that's bullshit. If anyone is going to define Miami, it will be defined from within, organically, by locals, for locals and the rest of the world. You'll see, Jimena. This is a great time to live here. We're growing. We're not just a fun-in-the-sun place to get all fucked-up—"

"Says the guy with a bag of mushrooms in his pocket."

Jimena liked what Alex said. It sounded refreshing to hear someone speak of her city with hope and intellect. She never thought about it, but she could drink this Kool-Aid. Miami represented home, how the city was perceived by the rest of the country seemed foreign.

"We can have it all, Jimena. This city has the potential to compete with any metropolis in the world when it comes to culture, achievement and significance. It will take a generation or two, but it will happen. Right now, we still lose our talent to New York and Los Angeles, but that's changing. There's a sense of circulation. We lose two All-Stars, but attract three promising draft-picks. When those All-Stars land in the big city, they bring Miami with them, spreading the flavor and misperceptions of our city like a virus. People see and hear that Miami isn't that bad, and it makes us look good. Thus more talent heads our way, plus many that leave return."

"You have a very glass-is-half-full look on our city."

"It's hard. Miami definitely does its best to prove we're idiots."

This Alex guy was easy to talk to and not burdensome to look at. She thought he was living on his own planet, but then again, what did she know? He could know more than her.

"Speaking of half-full," said Alex, pointing to their glasses.

"Yeah, sure."

Jimena watched Alex saunter towards the bar. The Spot had a service bar for outside patrons. She looked at his ass, firmly snuggled into the pair of khakis and she wondered when and where they would fuck. As far as her half-of-the-bargain, the deal was already closed.

Alex returned with drinks. He carried two cocktails, a whisky mixologist fusion concoction, a saucy blend of bitters and peppers. Spicy mixed drinks were the rage in Miami as of late; he also brought a glass of Riesling for Jimena and a Chimay for himself. They were set.

"Thank you," said Jimena.

"I-aint-worried-about-nothin," he said.

"Oh, boy," she said, laughing. "The attention's coming, huh?"

"I would ride that dirty whore to the highest media."

"I prefer not."

"I would tell the world that Miami has arrived."

"Yeah, well, I got news for you, Alex."

"What?"

"The world's brow isn't as high as yours."

"Your standards."

"What about them?"

"They're too low."

"So," said Jimena, sipping her cocktail, "you own a bar?"

"In Wynwood, yes."

"What's the name again?"

"Mecke."

"Is that like a Greek god or something?"

"Mecke was a horse."

"Why name your bar after a horse?"

"Because life is a horse race—"

"Life is a rat race, trust me, I work in the corporate world."

"Rats are ugly. Horses are beautiful, powerful, almost machine-like beasts. To label us rats demeans the human condition. I prefer horses. We've harnessed the power of horses for thousands of years. They've helped us transform society. And when they race, competitively, it's so regal and triumphant. There's a reason they call horse racing the sport of kings. Sometimes the races are so close too, like they'll run around this race track for ninety seconds, plowing over a course at forty miles an hour, to hit the finish line at the same time, literally a nose or a head apart. That's life. We're machine-like beasts, worthy of royal treatment, engaged in different classes and ranks. We start off green as Maidens and we rise up, with talent, training, good racing luck and timing. Can't forget the importance of timing. Some horses are expensive and royally bred; others underdogs who succeed with heart and grit. And they win or they lose. The winners are put out to stud to live an equine pornographic life until they die of old age."

"And the losers?"

"The losers aren't treated so well."

"Sounds like you've put some thought into this."

"Not really," said Alex, smiling.

"I've seen your place. It's not like a bar-bar—"

"We have a wine and beer license only. That what you mean?"

"You host events. My roommate Chito's mentioned Mecke."

"Chito from Keen?"

"Yup. The drummer."

"Miami, 90 degrees bring us together, one-degree separates us."

"Miami is pretty damn small."

"It's big enough to get lost, but small enough to manage."

"Why aren't you at work?"

"Because I'm here with you."

"Are you not open tonight?"

"I have employees."

"You're the bawse, huh?"

"Like a bawse," said Alex, laughing. "Should we order more?"

"Or, we can get a bottle of wine and go to my apartment."

"I like how your mind works."

"I'm not usually so forward," said Jimena.

"Am I supposed to believe that?"

"Believe what you want, but it's true."

"I don't want to rush things, or disrespect you, as a lady."

Jimena laughed and sipped the whisky glass for remnants.

"I'm not a lady."

"Then what are you?"

"I'm just a girl."

"Where do you live?"

"The Place."

"Should we take the jitney?"

"You're a mean one, Mr. Grinch."

"No, it's just funny. The Place. I used to live there."

"What the fuck?" said Jimena.

"At least you don't live on the beach."

"Where do you stay?" Jimena crouched forward and crunched her shoulders. She tilted her head and stared at Alex until the amber street lights sparkled off of her eyes.

"Near the bay," said Alex.

"I have a bike rack," said Jimena, aware he arrived on bicycle.

"I get the drift," said Alex, smiling. "Let's go."

***

On the way to the apartment they stopped at the Price Choice, a 24-hour market on NE 2nd Avenue and 19th Street. The market served wine and beer all night long. Late at night, the supermarket attracted Miami's underbelly, rogues and rascals, vagrants and vagabonds out for a middle-of-the-night stroll before finding a dry canopied corner to sleep under for a few hours; or a handful of late night industry folks, bus-boys, late night waiters, looking for some food or beer to take the edge off the day. During the day, the Price Choice largely attracted a lower socio-economic demographic, many immigrant families, most hovering rear the poverty line, people who couldn't afford the Publix only a block away. If the Walmart ever opened in Midtown, Price Choice would likely meet its demise. In the meantime, their selection of wine and beer far surpassed the gas station up-the-road on 26th, the nearest location you could buy beer all night. They both entered the supermarket. She didn't know what it was about this guy, but he seemed different. Of course she only met him, didn't know his secrets, but, there was truth when people say sometimes a woman just knows things. Like she could tell he was a little-shit, punky, rebellious, but he also seemed driven, intelligent, sarcastic, funny and a little dark. She liked dark and felt attracted to its light. She liked that he was older. She liked his filled-in frame. She wondered about his dick. Would he know how to use it? What a waste, if he didn't. Maybe the elders were right when they expelled her from Kingdom Hall for being a naughty jezebel.

"Are you hungry?"

"Not really."

"What do you want to drink?"

"Wine," she said, walking towards the section. "It's over here."

Alex grabbed a six-pack of Peroni and followed her.

"You're very pretty, Jimena."

"Awwww."

Don't grab my hands. Don't grab my hands.

"You're so skinny," said Alex.

In the alcohol section Jimena grabbed a bottle of Moscato. She liked sweet wines, a White Zinfandel or a Riesling, if she felt special. Anything too dry made her feel bitter, and most reds gave Jimena a headache. Moscato was her go-to, especially late night, even more-so for a first date nightcap. The supermarket was pretty empty and they paid the cashier. He was a young kid, no more than nineteen, Cuban, maybe Columbian. A bunch of sketches lay scattered near the register, an impression that he'd rather be out in the streets tagging up walls in Wynwood. Someone (probably his mother) instilled in him a work ethic, even if the job at Price Choice wouldn't last long, even if his classes at Miami-Dade didn't work out. Back in the car they drove the bumpy and beautiful late night drive up NE 2nd Ave, through Edgewater and the curvy roads into the Design District. Driving in Miami at-night radiated tranquility, the antithesis of the day.

They entered Jimena's living room, back at the apartment, quietly and without fear or reservation. One roommate was already passed out drunk and the other out playing a late night gig. Jimena felt relative ease around Alex. He made himself right at home, popping open a beer, turning on the television and turning to the Comcast Music Choice channel that only played Jazz. Jimena opened up her Yellow Tail wine, poured a healthy glass and joined him on the couch.

"Are you from Miami?" Jimena asked.

"Born and raised, third generation. We are very connected to the city. My grandfather was a judge, my father also. My uncle served on the County Commission, for a little while…"

She could tell he had more to say, but held back. Knowing Miami politics only a little, Jimena knew enough to assume his uncle probably left office in disgrace, maybe in a prostitution ring or drug laundering scam. She wouldn't push for details, they weren't important.

"It's good you want Miami to succeed."

"Miami needs definition by insiders, that's what I really want. I love our city, but it lacks definition. We're the 11th biggest media market in the country, which isn't *that* big. Dallas, Houston, Phoenix, Philly, Chicago, San Fran, Houston, all bigger than us. But I argue that next to LA and New York, the national media is fascinated by Miami. We're number three. We have a billion dollar film-and-fashion industry, we're the gateway to Latin America, which is the future face of America, and most Americans think all Latinos hail from Mexico and they have no idea what's coming their way. Our beaches and attractions are awesome. The news coming out of here is always large in scope, whether Elian Gonzalez and our Cuban refugee culture, the Recount election of 2000, the face eating zombie attack on Memorial Day, Trayvon—there's always something in our news. Without a doubt people care about Miami more than bigger media markets. People are obsessed with Miami. And only LA and New York are above us." Jimena sipped her wine and listened to Alex with ease. He could talk, maybe too much, but it was interesting and new to her, and quite frankly she wondered how this guy landed on her couch. "Now take LA for example. LA sucks. It takes three hours to drive five miles in LA if you're not navigating the time you're on the road. They have something like seven million cars in the area. You can't even stand outside in LA for more than a few hours without getting a sore throat. You can taste the air it's so polluted. Plus our beaches our better and our cost of living is decidedly cheaper so I argue fuck LA, we're better." Jimena opened up her Iphone to check her social media, a force of habit—*you know you want to, you know you want to, you know you want to*—she still paid full-attention to Alex, but a twenty-something in the digital era mandated a multi-tasking existence. "Compare us to New York. New York sucks. New Yorkers are miserable. Sure, they're the cultural and financial hub of the world, but it's a miserable, dirty, overcrowded hell-hole. The weather sucks. There's like three gorgeous days all year, two in the fall and one in the spring. The rest of the year is too cold, hot, windy, wet, humid, you name it—and the energy is wretched. Sure the pace is awesome, but New York can keep their overpriced pretentiousness. There's a reason why New Yorkers retire to South Florida. They want out from that hell-hole..." Jimena opened up her Facebook and quickly noticed an inordinate amount of notifications for a Friday night. "So, if you follow my logic, I firmly believe Miami's the best city in the U.S., or at least has the potential to wear the crown, but only if we define ourselves from within and represent what's good about Miami, our burgeoning culture, not the negatives."

"Fuck me."

"Here or in your bedroom?"

"No, fuck, shit, ugh," stammered Jimena, rolled eyes and a sigh.

"Lebron? It's out right?"

"I'm tagged in like forty posts."

"Embrace it."

"Fuck my life."

"Use the media."

"Okay, Radio Mambi."

Alex laughed. He knew he could talk. Jimena didn't want the platform, amplification, notoriety. He appreciated that -- most of the pseudo-intellectual hipsters around him would jump at the chance. He liked that she shied from it. In his heart, Alex didn't truly seek attention. He only wanted to embrace the future of Miami and help shape it.

But this was a different avalanche. A tidal wave of media that could crash on her shores with such power and brute force. And the media would definitely come-a-knockin. First from the *Miami New Times*, the alternative weekly, who always had its finger on the beat, especially the bike beat. She will ignore their emails, requests for interviews, and not pick up the phone. Then the *Miami Herald*, always a step or two behind the alternative presses, would seek her out. And NBC 6 Miami and ABC Channel 10 and CBS 4 and Fox News Channel 7 and 790 The Ticket. Producers from radio, television and print, from local markets up to the national media will all try to land the catch, but all to no avail, for Jimena will simply ignore the storm. She will turn off her phone, disable her Facebook and Instagram accounts, and stay off-line for a few weeks. The basketball player of course would address it, and when he does, he'll brush it off, play it down. He'll focus on the game of basketball, answer questions about the team tightening its defense next year, maybe by finding another strong rebounder in free agency or the draft, you know, make the proper adjustments, continue to execute the offense, he won't want to talk about a bike ride, so he'll laugh it off as no big deal, happy to help, girl felt as light as a feather, he's just glad she wasn't crushed.

Off-camera the basketball player will be happy to look like a hero. It will help his image and maybe add another multi-million dollar sponsorship to his growing portfolio. Deep, deep, down, the basketball player was simply annoyed at the small girl in his way. Really, the basketball player just protected his own health and progress forward. The basketball player had enough to worry about with the media. He operated under a microscope. He was already lucky the media didn't find out one of his sons needed stitches in a sketch the basketball player uploaded on social media a few months previous. He wanted to show his sons slam dunking like their poppa. Accidents happen, but if it got out that his son cut himself shooting the video, ooof.

Luckily, for Jimena, this wasn't *that* big of an avalanche. News trucks would not arrive en masse and camp outside The Place until the girl came outside. It wasn't news that'd last more than a couple of days. Jimena's plan: escape the spotlight with her privacy relatively intact.

"What are you going to do?"

"Ignore it."

"Lebron can't, but you could."

"I don't want to think about it."

"What do you want to think about?"

"Anything other than national attention."

"You know," said Alex, moving towards her. "I've never fucked a celebrity."

They both laughed.

Jimena purred like a cat, an indicator of her twirliness.

"Ever get your dick sucked by one?"

"Can't say I have."

"Well if you stop talking about this shit."

"What shit?"

"That's better."

She grabbed his hand and led him to her tiny room.

"I hope this turns out well," said Alex. "I kind of like you."

"Right, first hook-ups could be so awkward." Jimena began to set a mood. She lit unscented candles and a stick of Palo Santo, a wooden chip carved from special trees in the Amazon. "Like what if it's just not a good fit? Or what if you cum like super-fast because you're nervous? You're older, but you never know." The incense smelled potent, crisp and refreshing, like the combination of a fresh night where a fire burned in the distance, mixed with a deeper, relaxing aesthetic, not as strong as sage, but jarring, yet in a sweet citrusy way, with a hint of mint; much better than some cheap incense. Jimena clumsily looked for the Aztec like-calendar of her birth control on the dresser, to double-check. "Or what if this is a one-night-stand?" She pushed Alex onto the bed so that he fell onto his back. She pounced, grabbed the side of his head and kissed him. They're first kiss, drunk, in the largest room in a cheap apartment in Little Haiti, with the fresh spicy fragrance of Palo Santo bouncing off the shadows cast from the candles, was less awkward than passionate. Memories. She came at him like a tiger and he received it, kissing her with engaged energy. He bounced up, trying to flip the hundred-pound *latina* on her back. He wanted control but Jimena wasn't having it and quickly threw him down, displaying strength and tenacity beyond her tiny body frame. "Stay right there, on your back."

She began to kiss him, a second round of succulent mortar shells from her artillery, some soft and low-flying, others like bombs dropped from a B52. This wasn't romantic. They could do romantic. This was combat. And the first stages represented a sloppy inflamed battle, one that would quickly turn its direction as the plane navigated its course, riding a tailwind south, taking his shirt off in the process as tiny shell kisses planted themselves along the coast of his round and hairy chest and abs. The happy trail lead to an even happier trail as Jimena seamlessly ripped his boundaries right from his legs and thighs and tossed them onto the war-torn floor, taking her top-off in the carnage. Down to his last defense, white boxer-briefs from Hanes, her eyes lit up.

"Merry Christmas! You're smart and have a nice cock."

Before he could open his mouth, her mouth took a shot at his commander-in-chief, directly halting all communications. Coherent arguments and snarky statements melted into a nuclear goo of *oooohhs* and *aaaahhhs*. Her mouth quickly sedated his salty commander, who still stood hard and upright, even in recognition of his helpless defeat.

She slowed her bombardment, using her tongue to explore the surface area, like a scout, examining the curves and bumps of the field, listening for secret spots, her sonar attached to his moans. Her right hand stroked the top of his chief, rubbing her mortars all over his battlefield.

He pushed back wiggling in retreat. He weighed double her. He wasn't as weak as this, just caught off-guard. Alex wanted to fire his own mortar, to drop his own shells across her field.

"I want some."

"No, not tonight."

"I want it."

"You're not going down on me."

"Why?"

"I haven't showered from the bike ride."

"It's okay. I want it. I want to."

"No, not tonight."

"Okay."

"You can have it. Just not tonight."

"Okay."

"You want this pussy?"

"I don't have a condom."

"Shit. Me neither."

"Should I go to the store or something?"

"Fuck." She sighed. "Fuck it."

"Fuck it?"

"Fuck it."

"Are you sure, Jimena?"

"I want on top," she said.

Jimena licked her fingers, coaxed her juices, and hopped aboard like a thirsty pirate, now transferring the battle to the seas. Strike your colors. No quarter given. She plundered the plank. The ship was at full-mast as it set sail for an adventure both could not anticipate. The waters were rough but easy to navigate. Waves crashed against their sterns and the booty below rattled with every movement of their bow. Starboard bound. The boom. The rudder. The hull slammed up-and-down against the rough seas. Keep a weathered eye open matey! The spot was marked by an X. X Marks the spot! Land ho! Land ho! Wet me pipe! X Marks the spot! X marks the spot! "It's building, it's building," Jimena said, her ass moved up and down with the speed and gears that ignited her engine. "I'm close, yeah, yeah, yeah, fuck, I'm cummin. I'm cummin."

She yelled so loud light-sleepers up the street turned over in their bed, crumpling lonely and stained sheets, jealous and completely turned on. Alex flipped Jimena over and muffled her face into the pillow. There was a lull, a moment where Jimena could barely catch a breath, before he raised her ass and mounted her from the back. Sliding in with ease, the roller coaster shot through the tunnel. Through the twists and turns, the drops and free-falls, through the darkness and into the light, the gyration and gravity turned upside down, until the camera went flash, catching them both with a stupid look on their faces as he fell, limp-less beside her on the bed. "Oh my god that was fucking crazy."

"I've never cum so fast."

"You were so wet."

"You were so hard."

"That felt amazing, Jimena."

There lay two fallen warriors, drunken pirates, conquered, numb. Better to fall into a post-orgasmic slumber from a mighty passion than to fade into it with a whimper and a whiff.

"I need some water."

Jimena hopped out-of-bed. She skipped naked into the kitchen in search for two bottled waters. She saw Alex noticing her tiny frame, firm and skinny. What types of women did this man conquer? Maybe tall and long-legged women, cold and aware of their stature and beauty, of whom he never quite fit into properly, like two pieces of a puzzle that looked like they could connect, but no matter how hard they tried, the pieces didn't fit. Or big-boned, gentle-hearted women, who gave themselves fully, as often as he wanted, but whose vivaciousness eventually decayed, slowly, like rust on a car, tearing through his metals. Or women with fake breasts, who seemed to him awkward, insecure and potentially a hazard or liability, like an asset one wished they didn't have to insure, or register, because it wasn't worth the time or expense.

And finally girls like her, Jimena, small, awkward, tight-skinned, natural, with small breasts and a ribcage you could see. Time blessed this body type kindly. Yeah, she imagined he had a body type. But her body was different. Hers came with an ass that could break a speaker.

Jimena returned to the bedroom.

"Why are you getting dressed?"

"I have to go."

"Really?"

"I'll text you."

"Don't go. That was just round one."

"I've stayed out too late already."

"You have to work or something?"

"No, it's not that," said Alex. "I'm married."

Jimena dropped the water bottles.

"Now you fucking tell me."

PART III

Chapter 10—

Send me a picture.
I'm at work.
Come on, send me a picture.
A picture of what?
You are so beautiful, it hurts sometimes.
Shut up.
If you were a smoothie, I'd be your blender.
You're so stoopid.
The moon lives in the fiber of your skin.
You sir are NOW making me blush.
Your flaws make perfection blush.
What's with all the sweet talk?
My subject is a walking poem.
Are you making these up?
I'm looking at a picture of you and they are coming out-of-me.
Maybe I should send you more pictures.
Your contagious happiness is the only disease worth catching.
You are too much.
Your lips are a sugar factory.
Okay. Here. Enjoy!
THANK YOU! YOU MADE ME DAY!

***

The beeping sound of Jimena's phone led Claudinette to rise above the partition of the gray cubicle. Each time her coiffed head appeared on the horizon, the eyes below the forehead, and the brow surrounding it, seemed tighter and each squint cast a dire judgment.

"Ooo-meeny-dimes-dat-ding-goin-to-beep."

"Sorry, Cleo—I'll put it on vibrate."

A stack of charts lay scattered in Jimena's area. Her computer had twelve windows open. Four medical keeping software platforms: MD Flow, EMR Dashboard, Vitera and Sage Intergee; these databases were what coders used to digitalize medical records and charts. Also open on the computer were Facebook, Google, Instagram, Craigslist, StubHub, Pandora, Gmail and Orbitz (Jimena always had a vacation on her mind. Although she hadn't been on a plane in years, she perused one-way flights to San Francisco, New York, Paris, London, Tokyo.)

Jimena felt tired and the day stalled around three-thirty.

"I have a secret," said Jimena.

"Do-it-have-to-do-with-awdi-dexting?"

Jimena laughed. "I have several secrets."

"G-a-a-a-wn."

"I'm leaving Perez Medical."

"Sheet, gurl—take-me-wit-cha."

"I can't do this bullshit anymore."

She rustled the paper on her desk.

"I put my notice in last week."

"Whatcha-goaawn-tah-doo?"

"I don't know, Cleo. Maybe go to school."

"Maybe-shake-ya-Cue-ban-ass-at-Tootsies?"

Jimena laughed. "Maybe."

"Mmmm hmmm."

"Anything but this."

"You-a-yung, gurl—live.."

"I'll miss the top of your head, Cleo."

She issued Jimena a stank-face straight out of North Miami.

"Figured I'd tell you. No one else knows, just Mrs. Perez."

"Wah-da-misses-upset?"

"She understood. Annabelle said I could come back if I changed my mind. She said she understood I was young and that all these codes could be a lot on a mind. Ain't like she offered me more money or nothing. She made a joke that I was leaving because of Obamacare."

Claudinette sucked her teeth in disgust.

"Why you frying eggs? You love Obama."

"Fook Ooo-bah-ma."

The Affordable Care Act had the office divided—of course bosses (like Mrs. Perez) didn't like it because she felt her health care premiums would rise, the doctors (mostly conservative to begin with) saw it as socialized healthcare which would bring down the level of services provided. If doctors normally saw ten patients a day, they felt the new legislation would force them to see forty a day to earn the same amount of money. Nurses saw it as morally acceptable and perfectly fair. Receptionists and billers were indifferent. Coders felt confused. The ICD-9 code manual was changing from 13,000 to 70,000 codes for diagnoses. 57,000 more codes to decipher. It had nothing to do with Obamacare but more with a general tightening of the Medicare system for efficiency, but the timing seemed awkward. When it came to the Affordable Care Act, to Jimena, the office often seemed misinformed and biased.

"Keep my secret on the hush, okay, Cleo?"

"No-par-tee?"

"How long we work together? Three years? You know me well enough to know I definitely don't want any fanfare. I ain't walking out with a marching band behind me playing 'When the Saints Come Marching in'—although that actually sounds like a cool fucking idea."

Claudinette sucked her teeth, walking away shaking her head.

***

Sucio and Jackie have been spending a lot of time together in The Grove. They had a complicated on-again / off-again intimacy that revolved around a strong friendship, which was always a good foundation, but, the nature of their renewal inevitably became strained and manifested similar and silly patterns. Jackie wanted to have a family and Sucio did not. The vasectomy he underwent a few years previous after his heart shattered into a million particles from the wizardry of his ex was the proof. Between the ghost of an ex-girlfriend past, and the barrenness in the ghost of the boyfriend future, sooner or later Jackie would wind up in the arms of another, and Sucio and her would fall back into the comfortable zone of friendship, unless Jackie's current boyfriend didn't want it, which was collateral everyone understood but hurt Sucio. However, as the seasons changed, and the world revolved on its axis, certain people, in certain geographic areas, with similar lifestyles, tend to find themselves re-united, in the form of a Congress, like now, with Jackie recently single from a jealous and macho brute.

Jimena loved when two of her best friends were flowing together. Regrettably, she wasn't around as much as usual, with her living in The Place and spending most of her time in Midtown and North Miami. Grove rats didn't leave The Grove, so, it'd been awhile. This felt good. The three of them chilling inside Sucio's house, the 58-inch flat screen silently broadcasting a marathon of *Shameless*, a bottle of wine open on the living room table, a stacked bar nearby.

"So this guy is married, huh?" said Jackie.

"He says it's over, or in its last stages, like he's over it."

"Bro, I don't know, bro, he sounds *sucio*," said Sucio. "Like you're his number three."

"We haven't done anything since he told me. Like we've been talking and texting and whatever, but I don't know, I believe him, and I like talking to him, he's kind of different."

"He owns a bar in Wynwood?" asked Jackie.

"Yeah, so?"

"So, he's like a hipster, bro," said Sucio.

"So?"

"Who cares if he's a hipster?" said Jackie. "I'd be worried about trusting a bar owner."

"He's not even a hipster. I mean, he's definitely smart, which I like, but he's kind of goofy too, and he has this fire and spirit and passion that I kind of like, I don't know. It's fresh."

"Sounds like you're chasing a waterfall, bro," said Sucio.

"And what's wrong with that?"

"Okay, okay, *ehh-coo-me*, Left-Eye Lopes," said Sucio, smiling.

"Everything's changing. I don't even care. I mean I do. I like him. I'm not even closed-off to being with a married man, but I believe him when he says it's ending. Why lie? Either way, I still feel like I'm living in a brave new world and for the first time in my life I don't feel tied down, like no strings attached, and it doesn't matter because I'm young and free. The Douche moved to Jersey and rented the apartment, which is now his anyways so I don't have to pay for his chump ass, I'm leaving Perez in less than a week, and I'm meeting new people—"

"Wait," said Jackie, "you're quitting your job?"

"Yes."

"As a medical coder?"

"Yes."

"Oh shit, that's strong," said Sucio. "You hated that job."

"What are you going to do?"

"Make us a round of shots to celebrate, bro."

Sucio hopped up off the couch to head to the kitchen.

"Not you, idiot," said Jackie. "Jimena?"

"We're young," said Jimena. 'We can do anything."

Sucio returned with three shots.

"These are called bling blings," he said, "in honor of Jimena."

Sucio was a bartender and could make a thousand shots.

"Where the party at?" he said.

"What's in this?" asked Jackie, who learned to ask first.

"Stoli Raspberry and butterscotch snaps."

"It tastes bittersweet," said Jackie.

"Doesn't everything?" asked Sucio.

"God you know what I really want to do, and tell me if I'm being too impulsive, because if I am, you know, I'd like to know, but I want another tattoo. I've been thinking about what I want...I keep seeing the image in my mind. It's nothing crazy. Want to come with me?"

"Like now?"

"Yeah," said Jimena. "Like right now."

"The Fountain Pen is open," said Sucio.

"Next to The Reef," said Jackie. "We can drink before or after."

"*Dale*," said Sucio, "Let's watch Jimena get a tattoo."

***

Yoga in the park? Maybe a walk and talk first?

If I do that, the rest of my plans will no longer be plans, feel me?

Jimena, I swear, sometimes the things you say just make my blood rush, like wild. The blood rushes from my heart to my groin. Like right now I can feel the blood rushing.

Wait, wait, wait--explain what I said that made your blood rush from your heart to your groin. I said nothing, at least to my knowledge that could make you feel that way.....but I like that it did.

How do I explain? Just the whole "I know if I do that with you today, the rest of my plans will no longer be plans" like the way you say "if I do that with you" makes me feel like it's something more than just meeting in the park. And "my plans will no longer be plans" feeds my imagination to think that all of this other stuff will happen. It's like all this sexual innuendo, you might not be doing it consciously, and maybe I'm projecting nuance into it, but, I swear, you do and say things like this all the time, in the little time we've met. I like it. I really like the blood rush feeling too.

Sorry if this might seem weird, but the way you explain things is hot.

You don't even want to know what I'm imagining.

I do now.

Sorry if this seems weird, but I'm picturing myself kissing your smooth legs and working my way up to your thighs, slowly, staying there, until moving up your groin, and planting little kisses so close, so close to your pearls, like right on the edge, and your toes are curling, and your back is leaning backwards on the bed, and then I lick you, and you're very wet and I love the way it tastes, and I just start slow, and lick it all, your clit, your wet pussy....I better stop..

Geez, have you ever considered writing an erotic novel?

Does my muse find amusement in my musings?

You flatter me too much.

I can be an asshole, if you prefer.

No, I prefer the guy you're being now.

Can you send me a picture? I know, I know.

My neighbor at work is giving me that look again LOL
Send me a picture and I'll leave you alone
Why do you want one? Just say you want to see me!
I want to see you, very much. In many ways.
In how many ways?

I want to see you:

1. *sideways*
2. *from the bottom up*
3. *topless in a bathroom mirror*
4. *in a bathing suit selfie*
5. *naked*
6. *laying on your side*
7. *happy*

I like number seven, Alex.
I like seven, five and two—I can't stop thinking about your legs.
Five is hot, two sounds kind of hard, to shoot.
Be creative. Send me a picture. I want to see you.
Geez. Let me fucking work. I only have one more day here :) . . . xo

Chapter 11 —

The sun faded over the raised WYNWOOD signage on Miami Avenue and NW 24th Street—a large white billboard, homage to the HOLLYWOOD sign in the hills of Los Angeles. It was a fairly new prop that many tourists would appreciate. Second Saturday in Wynwood was the neighborhood's art walk and the busiest day of the month. It was arguably one of the hippest areas on the globe, and on nights like this, at peak time, or during the week of Art Basel, it certainly appeared to be not only a breathing, living outdoor museum, but a thriving metropolis.

Jimena rode bike with her roommate Chito and his friend Alberto Suarez, who knew everything about street art. Alberto, a Cuban-American in his early-thirties, was a Wynwood ambassador. When big name artists were in town to paint, like the Invaders and Shephard Faireys of the world, he provided them guidance and valet service. Alberto wasn't very social. He had no patience for hipsters, scenes or any of the "it." He'd say fuck "it" in a Miami minute with a rebel streak many street artists respected. Plus he knew the area like few others.

It was early for art walk as they rode bike. Most people showed up after sunset when the event became less about galleries and more about partying, which was what Jimena had in mind.

"That's Atomik there," Alberto pointed out. "Nunca, Phibs, Ron English of course—"

"Of course," said Jimena.

"This is En Masse. They are a group from Montreal that allows other artists to collaborate on their walls. This piece must have thirty different artists on it from all over the world."

"That's sick, bro," said Chito.

"Wynwood's a wild, wild west," said Alberto. "Some walls are on un-tenanted buildings, some abandoned, other walls are leased or being built. Sometimes you'll see idiots like this tag up some dumb tag, fucking teenager idiots, this pisses me off. They tag right over fine art."

"I'm skeptical of Wynwood, bro," said Chito. "It's my favorite neighborhood and I want it to succeed but I see what's happening. Everyone's moving. What you see during Art Basel is not Wynwood. What we will see tonight during Art Walk is not Wynwood. There's nobody in Wynwood during the day. There's no foot traffic like they have at Lincoln Road or Brickell."

"Who cares," said Jimena. "The art is cool, well, some of it."

They rode bikes past Wana Wynwood Production Village, a full-scale, three football field sized studio with amazing light and sound. A string of birds lined the wires above their heads.

"Look at this studio," explained Alberto. "It was recently built with the mantra if you build it, Hollywood will come. Hollywood has not come. For most of the year the production village sits empty. There's very little production. I'm telling you, there's plenty to be skeptical about, bro. Within a few blocks of this, on the outer edges of Wynwood, three other production warehouses exist, all of them ready to host huge corporate events, or video shoots, modeling shoots, and movie or television production," Alberto pointed out. "Plus, the city of Miami recently offered ten million dollars as a tax incentive for a hungry producer to buy a building they own that belonged to the Department of Education. They bought it for peanuts. Sometimes, in Miami, if you want to get to the real dark truth, all you have to do is follow the real estate."

"I never heard you sound so negative," said Chito.

Alberto laughed.

"Wynwood is not what you think it is," said Alberto. "The reality, or should I say realty, of Wynwood is this. It's a small, aloof neighborhood, five blocks long, two avenues wide, surrounded by intense ghetto to the south, like *The First 48* ghetto, and less ghetto to the north. It's a neighborhood owned by a few visionaries with last names like Lambadi and Feldman and one of them is dead. It's a hood losing its local soul and the neighborhood faces serious issues trying to evolve into the future. I'd bet on the Downtown corridor before Wynwood. And believe me, I love this area, I can rattle off every artist on the walls, their bios, back stories, one can only hope for the best, or enjoy it while it lasts, in case it goes away like 5 Pointz in New York."

As was the case when Jimena hung out with Chito it was only a matter of time that they ran into someone else he knew and had to engage in conversation. Turned out Alberto knew the person as well. They were standing there, balancing their bikes with their feet. Jimena met many cool people through Chito, and she was always grateful for the encounters and introductions, but quite honestly, she didn't feel like hanging around, hovering over conversations that didn't belong to her. It's hard to keep a group together, especially at an event with a lot of people. One person will see someone they know and slow down the group, or one person will grab a drink or go to the bathroom and then everyone else was waiting. It's freaking selfish to go out in a big group. It's better to have a base, do your own thing, stay in small groups or roll alone, and then meet up as the night flowed. Jimena's modus operandi has always been no more than three, and hanging with Chito was like hanging with ten because he knew so many goddamn people.

"*Oye*, bro, I'm going to hit The Timber and get a drink."

"Not a bad idea."

"Art walk's starting to blow up," she said.

"Okay roommie, I'll catch up to you."

***

NW Second Avenue in Wynwood was Shakedown Street. The roads were packed with a river of people moving north to south and vice-versa. Earlier in the evening, aficionados moved like art-frogs from gallery to gallery, bouncing from opening to opening, perusing a handful of galleries who used the event to launch the showcase of their latest installation or collection. For the galleries, Second Saturday ushered in buyers, especially during the early evening, but that changed with time as the event transformed into a block party for philistines (like Jimena) who considered art nothing more than vaginas and breasts and some weird shit they didn't understand. Most of the reputable galleries closed their doors by 9pm, even 8pm, wanting nothing to do with the throng of drunkenly people entering in-and-out of their establishments like a Macy's door during the day after Thanksgiving. Some of the more moustache-twirling high-brow galleries didn't even bother to open their doors during Second Saturday, instead offering previews the Thursday before the Saturday night art walk. Ninety percent of those in attendance at Art Walk knew not of the politics and egos of those behind the neighborhood. Many encountered their first experience with the neighborhood during this occasion and liked what they saw. The colorful graffiti murals plastered everywhere, art everywhere, vendors in the streets selling art and crafts, street artists performing, dancers, drum circles, live music, and freestyle hip-hop battles. Homeless people sold lukewarm beer for five bucks a pop out of Styrofoam coolers, not a bad hustle. $30 for six beers sold. Cost $6 up the block. Even less if bought in bulk. They're looking at a minimum 300% profit to share ratio. Attention Wall Street headhunters, Jimena thought, comb the streets of Wynwood, Miami on the 2nd Saturday of the month, that's where you'll find talent, maybe not in the business schools of Harvard or Yale.

Some galleries stayed open and welcomed the ebb-and-flow of the large crowds. They served wine and beer or whatever liquor sponsor they could secure for the evening. A coalition of the swilling. For some mysterious reason, Becks and Grolsch loved to sponsor art events. Could anyone truly understand a German's motives? Never disregard the French at an art event who loved to dispatch its bubbly Perrier. Bacardi, whose U.S. headquarters were spread across numerous buildings in Miami, including a defunct video production warehouse in Wynwood, owned not only their rum empire, but also Dewar's scotch, Bombay Sapphire gin, Kettle One vodka, and a minority share of Patron tequila, so it was never a surprise to encounter these spirits at an art soiree. The galleries that stayed open late were local, but none of them sold blue-chip art. The main attraction of Wynwood was undoubtedly the Wynwood Walls, a series of monster outdoor murals, curated and updated yearly, featuring the world's most famous street painters.

Jimena started off at The Timber and had a drink. She moseyed to another bar, popping into a gallery to grab a wine for the walk. She stopped to watch some Latin hippies dance and pound the worn leathered skins of djembe drums. The streets were alive and packed. It was past ten o'clock and she never saw so many people in Wynwood. Even by the food truck ally, where at least 15 trucks looked very busy serving hungry cavaliers looking for a respite from walking. On her way back to The Timber, she entered Mecke to catch a glimpse of Alex.

He hustled the counter, with two other employees, serving a packed house beer and wine. She caught his attention with a wave. He froze in his tracks, held her eyes across the crowded room and smiled warmly. His stressed, tired body language indicated he needed a break. A deejay maneuvered a Mac, transitioning from 50s crooner Del Shannon's "Runaway" into early 90s Miami Bass with DJ Uncle Al's "Hoes in the House" which set Jimena into a mild frenzy.

Latina and black girls born and raised in Miami know how to shake what their mamma gave them. There's a reason why the Miami Heat dancers were voted the best dance squad in the NBA year after year. There's a reason why the Supreme Court of the United States refused to hear Broward County's appeal of 2 Live Crew's *As Nasty As They Wanna Be* as being obscene. *this ain't nothing but a Wynwood party* . .

Jimena wanted to dance. A wave to move hit her shores like it had been at sea too long. Jimena wanted to lose it in music. The deejay transitioned into a dubstep song and inside Jimena went, entering the rabbit-hole just at the very pinnacle of a {{{BASSS}}} beat that DROPPED. She closed her eyes, licked her lips and felt the {{{BASSS}}} pick itself up from the echo chamber all-sloppy until the {{{BASSS}}} started to climb and ascend, rapidly, redundantly, in sixteenths, distorted, building to a crescendo, right there, the {{{BASSS}}} reached THE SPOT and HUNG only to DROP AGAIN even harder and sloppier and dirtier, for this party occurred in the South and in the South the {{{BASSS}}} was always dirtier. Jimena licked her lip and let go, moving near the front of the dance floor, where the deejay bounced along to the tweaks and turns of his fingers along with the Mac computer that glowed like a cross at an alter. Jimena bowed at this pagan alter, and opened her mouth, ready to receive the body of {{{BASSS}}} and it dropped over her, onto her, inside her—and she moved with it, inside of it, all over it, every inch of her body covered in the sloppy {{{BASSS}}} and it felt fine. And she looked fine. And she wasn't alone, the whole dance floor was filled with a group of kids getting sloppy, dropping and nodding to the {{{BASSSS}}}} Flying, really. Alex noticed Jimena's moves for she stood out. Her contortions were a little deeper than anyone else's, her foot work faster, and her drops just a little LOWER and longer than those around her. Jimena, to her credit, lost it. She lost time. Lost space. She lost everything but the {{{BASSS}}} which kept her captivated, mesmerized and locked-in. She felt good, without molly or any drugs. It was an awakening of sorts. Her breathe felt good, the taste of sweat dripping into her mouth like taffy. Sometimes she found a flow of air-conditioning and allowed it to chill her firm and loose body. She surrendered to the {{{BASSS}}} to the movement and accepted whatever it offered, with gratitude. It could have been ten minutes, or four hours, she had no idea how long she danced, until finally the need for water overtook her. She danced for about fifteen-minutes non-stop. She still wanted to dance but craved water and hit the bar. Once at the bar the sacred temple of {{{BASS}}} weakened, crumbled, sounding old and antiquated, like she'd heard it before. *come on and have a ball, ain't nothing but a party y'all . . .*

The Most-Eclectic-Deejay-In-the-World doesn't always spin 60s retro, but when he did, he sometimes transitioned into Nancy Sinatra's "These Boots Were Made for Walking." Jimena made her way towards the rear of the venue, near the restrooms and exit to the back door and outside patio. Alex greeted her with a glass of water. "Let's go outside."

They exited the crowded interior. The back patio looked just as packed but they could talk. Jimena drank the water in gulps, for she had worked up a quick thirst and a hard sweat.

"How are you?"

"Good," said Jimena. "Catching a buzz."

"Did you see anything worthwhile?" asked Alex.

"Like in the streets?"

"No," said Alex, laughing. "Like in art. Like in the whole purpose of art walk—to peruse fresh art. There were some interesting openings tonight. I wish I wasn't stuck in here."

"I heard Pharrell was around."

"Blurry lines," said Alex, "blurry lines."

"What do you mean?"

"Art is not supposed to be celebrity sightings and partying."

"Do you believe in Wynwood?" asked Jimena.

"What do you mean?"

"I mean does it even exist or do we just really want it to exist?"

"Of course it exists. There are multiple art complexes, dozens of galleries, a handful of salons, performance spaces, movie houses, event and production venues. There are at least twenty restaurants and bars and these numbers will increase over time." Alex lit a cigarette, a Camel Light. "Don't you see what's going on tonight? It's off-the-hook, Jimena."

"Yeah, but how many businesses are truly profitable?"

"Look. Rents are increasing, sure, but there's steals here too, you just have to hustle. And yes, a lot of people have left, but plenty have stayed and more are coming. Plus, organizations, both political and philanthropic, are getting more committed to the area. We finally have a Business Improvement District. And we at WADA are doing things."

"What's that?"

"WADA is the Wynwood Arts District Association. It's a non-profit putting unity into this community. We're making the streets more secure, promoting businesses from within. I'm actually on the Board of WADA and I can tell you first hand, Wynwood's not going anywhere."

"Ugh, I love hearing you talk sometimes."

"I love watching you dance," said Alex, tossing his smoke, entering back inside. "I need to get back to work." He kissed her cheek. "Let's talk soon. And be safe out there." Jimena smiled, watching him walk away. She exited out the side, making her way to a final resting bar.

Chapter 12—

Subject: Re: Who Got Game??
From: jimena.quintero@gmail.com
Date: Tue, 15th Jun 20xx 18:14:51 -0400
To: miamiisnotsouthbeach@gmail.com

Haha seems like you had a great night!
And yes, I'm so relieved to be away from Perez Medical.
And no, I don't have a job just yet.
But, I did pick up some side work, and I have some savings, so
I'm okay for now. What are you up to? What were you drinking?

Sent from my iPhone

From: miamiisnotsouthbeach@gmail.com
To: jimena.quintero@gmail.com
Subject: Re: Who Got Game??
Date: Tue, 15 Jun 20xx 18:34:27 -0400

I'm in my room, sort of potskying around.
Was drinking beer, but I never ate yesterday, that's why I'm
feeling off today. I have the house to myself—so nice.
BREAKING NEWS: she's moving out this weekend. It's over. I'll
be divorced in a month. ☺

Subject: Free at last, free at last . . .
From: jimena.quintero@gmail.com
Date: Tue, 15 Jun 20xx 19:15:59 -0400
To: miamiisnotsouthbeach@gmail.com

Thank God almighty!! Wow. Are you for real? That's awesome.
You must be relieved. I know I was happy to leave. But I was
also the one who left. Do you know the divorce rate is hovering around
75%? Isn't that crazy? Fuck it. I mean who knows what the fuck love is
anyway. There's no formula and who even cares I mean, whatevs.
So did you check me out when I was dancing at your bar the
other night?

Sent from my iPhone

From: miamiisnotsouthbeach@gmail.com
To: jimena.quintero@gmail.com
Subject: Re: Free at last, free at last . . .
Date: Tue, 15 Jun 20xx 19:34:27 -0400

Of course I checked you out.
Why do you make me repeat it?? ☺
I've never seen a sexier dancer in my life. You're wild. Even in
the busiest circumstances, it's impossible to not keep an eye on you.

Subject: And the beat goes on . .
From: jimena.quintero@gmail.com
Date: Tue, 15 Jun 20xx 19:58:25 -0400
To: miamiisnotsouthbeach@gmail.com

Lol I wanted to hear you say it again, to be honest ☺

It makes me feel good.
Thank you, you are very sweet. ☺

Sent from my iPhone

From: miamiisnotsouthbeach@gmail.com
To: jimena.quintero@gmail.com
Subject: RE: And the beat goes on . .
Date: Tue, 15 Jun 20xx 20:14:27 -0400

You little vixen . .
What else do you want to hear me say??

Subject: Re: And the beat goes on . .
From: jimena.quintero@gmail.com
Date: Tue, 15 Jun 20xx 20:26:51 -0400
To: miamiisnotsouthbeach@gmail.com

Vixen is actually one of my favorite words. I don't know why.
I've just always liked it. I like the way the word looks and I like what it
means. It's nice hearing the way you describe me. I guess I was just
fishing for compliments lol so feel free...... ☺ I'm in a good mood right
now for no reason. It feels good to be happy and not have a reason for it.

Sent from my iPhone

From: miamiisnotsouthbeach@gmail.com
To: jimena.quintero@gmail.com
Subject: RE: And the beat goes on . .
Date: Tue, 15 Jun 20xx 20:37:03 -0400

Main Entry: **vixen** [vik-suhn] Show IPA

Part of Speech: *noun*

Definition: foxy person

Synonyms: Xanthippe, cat, dragon, harpy, harridan, hellcat, she-
                 devil, shrew, termagant, virago,

Compliments, hmmm.

Okay, I'll give you three . . .

You're intelligent; wise beyond your years, but like street smart and that's sexy to me. Your hair and bangs have so much life they could be used in a Pantene commercial. And your breasts are exquisite . . . lol

I'm glad you're in a good mood. That makes me happy...

Alex

Subject: Re: And the email goes on . .

From: jimena.quintero@gmail.com

Date: Tue, 15 Jun 20xx 20:42:43 -0400

To: miamiisnotsouthbeach@gmail.com

This email might be my favorite email you've sent me so far.

Everyone tells me I'm not allowed to cut my hair anymore. They say it's what makes me ME. Haha I just say it's really good shampoo and conditioner. When have you truly seen my breasts? That night was dark.

Sent from my iPhone

From: miamiisnotsouthbeach@gmail.com

To: jimena.quintero@gmail.com

Subject: Vixen, yes
Date: Tue, 15 Jun 20xx 20:52:27 -0400

No, there were candles, remember. But hey, you're right, I need to see more. Still, with your body type and height, I'd bet my paycheck they are exquisite. Gawd-You are a vixen, you're making this room and my blood feel kind of hot . . .

l o l

Subject: RE: Vixen, yes
From: jimena.quintero@gmail.com
Date: Tue, 15 Jun 20xx 21:02:47 -0400
To: miamiisnotsouthbeach@gmail.com

My breasts are pretty exquisite, if I must say so myself lol...
Maybe you're just hot-blooded ;)

Sent from my iPhone

From: miamiisnotsouthbeach@gmail.com
To: jimena.quintero@gmail.com
Subject: RE: Vixen, yes
Date: Tue, 15 Jun 20xx 21:14:27 -0400

Vixen, vixen, vixen . . .
You're making it hot.
You don't know what I just did. You would never guess.
And I'm not telling.. ☺

Subject: RE: Vixen, yes
From: jimena.quintero@gmail.com

Date: Tue, 15 Jun 20xx 21:23:24 -0400
To: miamiisnotsouthbeach@gmail.com

You HAVE to tell me now.

Sent from my iPhone

From: miamiisnotsouthbeach@gmail.com
To: jimena.quintero@gmail.com
Subject: RE: Vixen, yes
Date: Tue, 15 Jun 20xx 21:34:27 -0400

Okay, maybe.
But first. You have to take three guesses, which you will never get, but that's the process..You can also ask for hints, if you want.
I will give you one hint now: I've never done it before . . .

Subject: Re: Vixen, yes
From: jimena.quintero@gmail.com
Date: Tue, 15 Jun 20xx 21:48:23 -0400
To: miamiisnotsouthbeach@gmail.com
There can be thousands of things you've never done before.

I need more hints because I have no idea...

Sent from my iPhone

From: miamiisnotsouthbeach@gmail.com
To: jimena.quintero@gmail.com

Subject: RE: Vixen, yes
Date: Tue, 15 Jun 20xx 21:59:27 -0400

Guess
Come on, use your imagination . . .

Subject: Re: Vixen, yes
From: jimena.quintero@gmail.com
Date: Tue, 15 Jun 2oxx 22:07:36 -0400
To: miamiisnotsouthbeach@gmail.com

I literally have no idea. I'll try.
Ok, so we were talking about the word vixen and my breasts and hair and then the room got hot.
Don't think I'm a crazy freak cause of my guesses, k?
So you:

1. Made out with yourself lol
2. Played with yourself (even though I know you've done that)
3. Jacked off to the picture I sent you

Sent from my iPhone

From: miamiisnotsouthbeach@gmail.com
To: jimena.quintero@gmail.com
Subject: RE: Vixen, yes
Date: Tue, 15 Jun 20xx 22:24:27 -0400

I like your guesses and definitely don't think you're a freak...

1. I wouldn't know how to make out with myself.

2. Yeah, that's not a first.
3. Hmm, no way. Don't give me any ideas tho lol.

I will admit I have your picture open in a separate window. But that's just because I like to look at your little vixen face... Okay, I'll give you some hints:

What I did was not an action. It was an idea (creative, brilliant, naughty) that could lead to an action. It would be mysterious yet fun to execute. But you would probably never go for it. And I wonder if I myself would go for it. Any ideas? Is this getting old yet??

Subject: Re: Vixen, yes
From: jimena.quintero@gmail.com
Date: Tue, 15 Jun 20xx 22:42:40 -0400
To: miamiisnotsouthbeach@gmail.com
Omg I'm so embarrassed lol.. Did you want to make me feel vulnerable? I'm sure that email made you crack up. For the record, you can always make out with yourself in the mirror lmao! I have no clue what idea you came up with that you're not even sure you'd go for.
Just tell me...

Sent from my iPhone

From: miamiisnotsouthbeach@gmail.com
To: jimena.quintero@gmail.com

Subject: RE: Vixen, yes
Date: Tue, 15 Jun 20xx 22:53:27 -0400

Don't be embarrassed. I liked your answers. You can feel safe. I was trying to get you to head in that direction, actually..

Okay, I'll tell you. I just got this idea, to get a hotel. And I went to Hotwire where you could choose an area, but they don't tell you what hotel you get, which seemed mysterious to me, and I was like fantasizing having you meet me there, a rendezvous, to talk in person, get away from it all, do who knows what exactly. In my mind, I was about to get the hotel, and just the fantasy and allure of doing something like that was new to me; I've never done something like that, and I was feeding the tone, and it was hot, and I kind of like the idea, but I know you wouldn't go for it. And I wonder if I would actually have the courage . . .

Subject: Re: Vixen, yes
From: jimena.quintero@gmail.com
Date: Tue, 15 Jun 20xx 23:10:45 -0400
To: miamiisnotsouthbeach@gmail.com
That sounds really hot. It sounds like a cool scene for a movie or a book. Did you imagine a conversation between us if that were to happen? I've never done anything like that either.

Why don't you think you'd have the courage to do it?

Sent from my iPhone

From: miamiisnotsouthbeach@gmail.com
To: jimena.quintero@gmail.com
Subject: RE: Vixen, yes
Date: Tue, 15 Jun 20xx 23:16:27 -0400

Yeah, I imagined us kind of laying around, talking, like we've been doing all day, naturally, with a smooth flow, getting to know each other, slowly, like no rush, just feeling safe, yet someplace exotic, new, strange, private, removed, yet in our own city; we wouldn't even have to stay the night, or we could, it doesn't matter, and sometimes there would be silence, but not a tense or uncomfortable silence, just a relaxing, peaceful silence; we might become intimate, but again, it doesn't really matter, but if we did, it would be slow, real slow, and gentle, new, fresh, ours. I've never done anything like that; so it makes me nervous; I question if I could go through with it; it makes my hands sweaty, yet my dick is rock hard. omg

Subject: Re: Vixen, yes
From: jimena.quintero@gmail.com
Date: Tue, 15 Jun 20xx 23:29:12 -0400
To: miamiisnotsouthbeach@gmail.com

That all sounds really sexy

Sent from my iPhone

From: miamiisnotsouthbeach@gmail.com
To: jimena.quintero@gmail.com
Subject: RE: Vixen, yes
Date: Tue, 15 Jun 20xx 23:34:27 -0400

Do you want to? Could we? Should we?

Subject: Re: Vixen, yes
From: jimena.quintero@gmail.com

Date: Tue, 15 Jun 20xx 23:35:44 -0400
To: miamiisnotsouthbeach@gmail.com

Sounds tempting but you're still living with someone
and it just doesn't seem right. ☹ Jimena

From: miamiisnotsouthbeach@gmail.com
To: jimena.quintero@gmail.com
Subject: Vixen, no
Date: Tue, 15 Jun 20xx 23:38:27 -0400

	biddy [bid-ee] Show IPA
Main Entry:	
Part of Speech:	*noun*
Definition:	fussy old woman
Synonyms:	battle-ax, beldam, crone, fishwife, fussbudget, fusspot, hag

Just kidding, jk jk....LOL...just kidding...

Subject: Fuck you, dick head . .
From: jimena.quintero@gmail.com
Date: Tue, 15 Jun 20xx 23:40:12 -0400
To: miamiisnotsouthbeach@gmail.com

JK. ☺ Fuck it. Surprise me.
Choose at least a 3-star hotel . . .

Sent from my iPhone

***

Secrets. Everyone's familiar with them. Everyone has at least one. Some need secrets to survive, others hide from them. Some live in denial, burying secrets in masks and illusions and layers of tumbling lies. Most of the time secrets come out into the light. Some confess to a variety of sources, a psychiatrist, priest, parent, teacher, counselor, detective, best friend or lover. Others take their secrets to the grave and the Lord knows the dead don't talk, most of the time. Secrets make the world go around. People spend the most important hours of their day shrouded in the dark safety of their secrets, living two lives, one for all to see, the other, and more interesting, under the cover of secrecy. Secrets? What's yours, Inez? Do you have a gambling problem nobody knows about? Do you sneak away to the Flagler casino under the false pretense of venturing out to preach? Jackie? Have you betrayed your lover again? Will they forgive you this time? Will they ever know? Chito? Do you have an inclination for prostitutes or massage parlors hidden in dark strip malls? Sucio? What's your secret? Keep believing you're only harming yourself with the cocaine habit. What about you Alex Lane? Mr. Perfect. What does your web search browser know that no one else does? Maybe it's not so dark. Maybe it's small. You breaking a law as we speak? Is it fiscal, legal or moral? Fraud? Cheating on your taxes? Everyone does it. No, they don't. It's fine: keep your secret, it's all yours. Secrets. The constructs of our civilization couldn't handle everyone's secrets brought out into the light. We need our secrets right where they are, in our hearts, in our conscious, and in our darkest dreams.

***

Secrets was a strip club located out west, near the nomadic culture of the airport. Tonight constituted Jimena's tenth and last night working as a dancer. Strip clubs in Miami-Dade needed qualification. The venues were not like other states, cities (including Las Vegas) or even other counties in Florida. In Miami-Dade, strippers were allowed to undress completely, no pasties, thongs, just down to the bare skin. They were also able to make contact with patrons in the form of friction;

if a patron wanted to touch the stripper, and the stripper was okay with it, *no problemo*. There absolutely was sex happening in the champagne room, if the stripper was okay with it, and many of them would happily oblige the request. Raw. Strip clubs in Miami were raw.

From a human resources and employment point-of-view, they were also efficient. Jimena was hired immediately at Secrets and did not have to fill out any paperwork. It would be off-the-books, not the usual practice by Florida law, but in a field with such a high turnover rate, and in clubs with a less than reputable corporate reputation, it was an easy obstacle to bypass. So, no taxes, or W-2 forms for Jimena, at least not at Secrets, not yet. She also could start work the night she was hired, which indeed impressed her, again, from a human resources point-of-view.

Furthermore, there was no training. She lied, saying the gig wasn't her first rodeo, and they allowed her to jump into the mix. From a moral perspective, Jimena felt little confliction. She'd been to strip clubs many times, her ex-husband had an affinity for them, and so did she. The woman's body carried a tremendous form and there was no shame in displaying it. She considered herself fit and firm and she loved to dance so why not give it a try? After medical coding at Perez for three years, this honestly felt like a relief in comparison to the endless paper.

The job didn't require a degree or much effort. Every two hours she would have to strut along the stage, dance in her panties, take them off until nude, use the pole, if desired. This dance would last either one or two songs—she could pick the tracks from a deejay. The deejay was an innocent huckster type, with brown teeth from smoking cigarettes and weed. He sported a Mohawk with a shaved head and a maroon shirt and black tie. Jimena picked a few songs for him to choose: "I Touch Myself" by the Divinyls, "Where is my Mind?" by the Pixies, "Push It" by Salt n Pepper and "I'm In Love with a Stripper" by T-Pain. All the songs were under four minutes. You'd have to be crazy to choose a long song like "Voodoo Child" from Jimi Hendrix, which clocks in at almost fifteen minutes (maybe in a bar and you wanted to get value from the jukebox you would choose such a track but not when stripping on stage).

Dancing on stage was the least favorite part of every stripper's job, whether a newbie or a vet. Multiply vulnerability by sleaze and divide it by the least amount of money you make all night. Plus everyone can see you. You're playing up to a crew of men who are too cheap for a lap dance and can touch you for the price of a dollar, and then after the five to eight minutes, to stack shame upon shame, you have to pick up the scattered dollars and fives. Some girls were really good on stage. They used the pole to their advantage, spotting high rollers who dished out twenties rather than fives and ones, and maybe someone would make-it-rain like a Florida thunderstorm all over the stage, which was an easy $50-$100, maybe a lot more if some big shot celebrity was in the house but Secrets was not the house. The dancers could pay a bouncer to pick up the money, if desired, but nothing in the strip club came for free.

Strippers made most of their money off of lap dances. The standard lap dance lasted one song and cost a patron twenty dollars. If you could take a guy into a private room, keep him there for a few songs, it was very easy to make $80-$100 in about 20 minutes. The key was spotting someone who looked too drunk to notice time, yet innocent enough to respect boundaries, in other words, a tourist or businessmen. Most tourists weren't familiar with Miami-Dade's leniency and most businessmen weren't spending their own money so why give a fuck.

Most of the night a stripper just hung around, especially when slow. The girls walked the room, like a purring cat rubbing along a friendly leg, eventually landing on a warm bar stool.

Jimena knew all of this before she danced her first song. Her first night at Secrets was a Saturday and the club was busy enough so that she could do her own thing without ruffling any other girl's feathers. She wasn't there to make friends, and most of the other girls ignored her. They viewed her as a newbie. An alternative small-framed cunt with a few tats and not an ounce of plastic did not pose a threat or carry much intimidation among the sea of South Florida silicon.

She spoke when spoken to, to the girls, customers and managers. She tipped the gentlest bouncer a twenty before she earned a dollar and spoke to him in Spanish, asking him kindly to keep an extra eye on her for she was new to the game. That smart alliance provided her an extra shield against other girls, as well as any knucklehead patrons who wanted to cross the border without the proper documentation. But her borders would remain secure and well-guarded. She had one self-made rule going into the gig: no dick—not near her mouth, hand or pussy.

She called herself Jaguar, if anyone asked. That was also the name the deejay shouted when it was her turn to walk the stage. The first Saturday night went smoothly. It didn't take long to pick up the game. At first, when on stage, she kept distance from the few that sat nearby and found refuge in the music. Jimena used a lot of hip gyration to attract bills thrown her way, as opposed to allowing patrons to slide them into her strings. But by the end of the night she didn't have a problem allowing men to slip cash in her garments. It's not like she picked up twenties with her vagina or latched onto fifties with her anus. Men liked her body type, she was definitely the tiniest girl in the pool of fifteen others, so it wasn't too difficult to land lap dances.

Without going into a private room one time, on her first Saturday night, from 8pm to 4am, she walked out of the club with a stack of crinkled and musty bills that she didn't count until she laid them out on her bed in The Place at 5am with a glass of cold Moscato. She cleared four-hundred-and-fifteen-dollars, after tipping the deejay, bouncers and house. Before falling asleep that first night exhausted, as the sun began to come in from the east, she did math. She had to work 3 ½ days at Perez to make the same and they taxed her 20% for the honor.

She would work at Secrets three days a week, Thursday through Saturday and stack money, that was the plan and it unfolded accordingly for almost a month. No one knew. Lying wasn't that hard. Her roommates, family, friends and Alex provided interchangeable excuses. Over the course of working at Secrets the experience began to broaden. By her second shift she started to allow patrons to buy her drinks, mojitos or vodka and cranberry were her choice. She was never a heavy drinker and it didn't take her too much to reach a buzz. Drinking at work made the job more fun at first, but it also allowed her to let her guard down. She had less internal opposition when gentlemen began to grab her at her breasts and ass. She made more money but felt dirtier the next morning. By her third shift she balanced the drinks with bumps of cocaine offered to her by gentlemen in the back room during private lap dances. The coke helped her tremendously as she was able to drink more and still maintain a firm disposition. Cocaine went really well with stripping. She worked harder, faster and with more confidence. By her fifth shift she bought her own coke, bringing it to work, sharing it with other girls in the back dressing rooms and bathrooms. It was fun. She began to fit in, make allies, not friends, but stripper comrades, girls who liked her generosity and slightly dark alt style. Not the black girls, but some Spanish girls, not Cuban, they didn't understand her cultural shift, and definitely not Colombian who trusted and cared for only themselves, but Dominican, Venezuelan and other Spanish girls, from Latin America, like Costa Rica or Nicaragua. There were no white girls, count them, not one single white girl worked at Secrets by the airport.

Jimena learned the stripper way, to stay away from men or women who smelled bad, or didn't shower. The girls warned her that the dudes in the tee-shirts and worn shoes were bad news, cheap, but Jimena preferred them to those who dressed nice, even if they weren't her most lucrative clients. They were easier to talk to, more her type, if she had such a thing. Too much cologne definitely turned her OFF, like a bug spray. As did bad breath; how hard was it to purchase a piece of gum from Jean-Paul, the bathroom attendant? The freaking guy had the worst job in the house. Show some compassion. He could use the dollar and the customer could definitely use the refreshment. She hated guys who tried to haggle about the price of a lap dance. The best customers were the ones who paid in advance, with a tip. If a guy coughed up a fifty and paid for two dances out front with a ten dollar tip, that intrigued her, opening up boundaries—he could touch her breasts and maybe high along her thighs and ass, as long as he wasn't too drunk or aggressive, it was not altogether business, a sense of sensuality indeed sparkled. All the girls liked it when a man approached them, Jimena included, for not even strippers enjoyed cold calling to close a sale. She never gave her real number out, although some girls did. Jimena had no interest in hooking-up with anyone she met at Secrets, and no matter what, no matter the offer, (on one occasion a patron, a pharmaceutical rep from St. Louis in town for a convention, issued the indecent proposal of one thousand dollars for sex), no matter how inebriated or out-of-her-senses, she never fucked or blew a guy, and she was definitely in the minority when it came to that standard of service at Secrets. Some guys played grab ass, others pretended to be high rollers, while others broke promises or refused to pay. Some assholes sat by the stage and didn't tip. And some were perfectly polite and fun. A lot were insecure, more than she could imagine, like they never saw a naked body or talked to a lady.

The fifth and sixth shift were probably the peak of her jaunt as a stripper, after that the routine started to tap the circular waist of redundancy. There were a couple of negative instances that dampened whole evenings. Once with a patron who managed to pin her down and stick his drunken and chubby fingers inside of her in a back room. She had to scream and it didn't take long before the cavalry arrived and the pervert was not arrested but quickly escorted out of the club and barred. Jimena did not like that and needed to leave early and find a bottle and a friend to lose herself. Another night some alpha-stripper tried Jimena for no reason other than to exert some sort of weird catty dominance. Jimena had never engaged the girl once, a tall and busty black woman, closer to her thirties than mid-twenties. She called Jimena a coke whore devil with her tattoos. Jimena ignored the bully but it only escalated so eventually she yelled back until the bouncers had to break it up and both were written-up in the manager's back office and forced to apologize. There were no other problems with the girl but the whole event was needlessly dramatic and strange. No one ever knew Jimena worked as a stripper for one month. And no one would ever know. She left for a few reasons. After her tenth shift ended, her manager informed her that if she wanted to stay on, she would need to make it official. She needed to fill-out all the forms, a W-2, pay taxes, and claim the job on her taxes, the whole nine. That rubbed her the wrong way—exotic dancer—it would likely follow her forever, if probed. She also started to develop more feelings for Alex, their relationship was blossoming, and it began almost overnight to feel morally wrong to appear nude in front of others, even more so without him knowing. Alex was probably progressive enough to be open to the idea, but the argument didn't feel worth defending, especially when she looked around her environment. Secrets was a tacky eco-system, from the plush maroon décor, to the Mongoloid bouncers and security, to the decadence of her lifestyle, and most offensive the smell. The whole place had a horrible wretched odor, it stuck to the money she brought home at night and filled her room so that she had to burn sage in the morning. She smelled it in her car and she drove with her windows down but it didn't help. It was like an odor of stale smoke, mixed with bad perfumes and colognes, marinated in sticky sweat and sex. She couldn't escape the smell, even after a long shower. It smelled dirty. *Sucia, sucia.* Jimena was dirty but not that kind of dirty. So she quit or rather never returned. Threw the paperwork into the garbage back at her apartment. After ten shifts at Secret's she was able to save five thousand dollars, which she could live on for a few months, if necessary. Although, traveling seemed like a real good idea. She needed a vacation. Japan sounded possible. The Japanese men she encountered at the club were always the most polite and generous. And she heard about certain cities in Japan being like a Disneyland of sex, S&M, rope bondage. She didn't know where she would go, but she did know where she wouldn't.

Chapter 13 —

Alex Lane lived in a beautiful sky rise on the Bay in a part of Miami that blurred jurisdictions between Downtown, Edgewater and Club Row. His condo stretched high into the sky, forty-plus stories, where one could see a storm come in from the east, off the water, slowly, like an ominous gray nothing, where rainbows bounced off the water after a light rain, where turkey vultures indigenous to Florida flew in packs, circling the condos hungry for what? Condo cougars. His place had a million dollar view, facing both east unto the bay, and south, onto an ever expanding downtown littered with cranes and construction, buildings erect enough to serve as toys in an orgy for Greek gods and goddesses. From Alex's balcony one could clearly see Miami was a city going up, not down. In fact, every time Jimena visited Alex, when she entered the elevator, a calm, mature voice reminded her that she was "going up" which seemed to create a subtle psychological effect of satisfaction and positive re-enforcement. The same voice articulated the antithesis upon descent but for some reason she never heard it, probably because her mind felt disoriented always trying to make sure she didn't leave anything behind. Her trips to Alex's condo increased in frequency. His wife no longer occupied the space nor did her energy. Alex did a fine job converting the apartment into a bachelor's pad. He had an extra bedroom he considered renting or subletting but for now he'd keep the space as a guest room. Jimena's presence was appreciated and regularly welcomed. She slept over more often, but still maintained her apartment in The Place and intended to do so. Their relationship was at a stage where she had her own "toothbrush" at his place, that's it, but it began to reach a plateau where maybe soon she'd have her own "drawer." Neither felt compelled to force the issue. So far their relationship seemed healthy, although immature. They were still getting to know each other.

***

Tell me the story of being expelled from the Witnesses.

I had just turned fifteen. I was dating Eddie, a Chilean—

How old was he?

Older than me, like 22—

Right there that's trouble.

Ha! You're eleven years older than me.

Every rule has an exception, besides—you're not fifteen, yuck.

--And he was crazy, like psycho crazy. We dated for a few months before I broke it off; he was too possessive. Shit got stupid from there. He would show up at my work uninvited—

Where were you working?

I had some stupid retail job in The Gables. He'd show up and stare at me. He wanted to make sure I wasn't lying about my whereabouts. I'd already broke it off but he wouldn't leave me alone. It started getting even crazier. Like he'd hack into my email account and my AIM messenger to see who I chatted with. He was so fucking jealous. He actually wrote a letter to three of my friends, the only friends I had in the church. He imitated me and accused them of being horrible whores and all this other shit going against the way of Jehovah—

Was Eddie even a Witness?

No, that's the fucked-up part.

So what does this have to do with you getting kicked out?

That motherfucker went to Kingdom Hall and pulled aside one of the elders and confessed for me. There's two ways a person is kicked out, either you confess, or someone snitches and confesses for you. Then the elders convene, like a trial, to decide if you can stay. Eddie rolled into the congregation and pretended to be interested in becoming a Witness. Then he told an elder I was committing sin against Jehovah by fornicating. I remember the day, it was creepy. I showed up to Kingdom Hall with my mom and there were a group of elders, like six of them—

Who are the elders?

Like the leaders, kind of like a preacher, all men of course.

What do they wear, like robes?

Suits, they wear suits. About six of them, all way-y-y- older than me, and behind the elders there stands Eddie, with this shit-eating grin on his mug, like I got you now, you crazy bitch. And then the elders took me into a back room and started asking me all of these questions. I'm still mad at my mom for letting this happen, like she could've been in there with me. There were no women, just me, barely fifteen, and a group of six men who started asking these personal questions. like how many times did you have sex, did you engage in oral sex, anal sex, how many partners did I have, did I enjoy it, was I able to reach a climax

Get-the-fuck-out-of-here—

Yeah, it was so personal and creepy. I honestly thought those perverts were going to drop their pants and start jerking off—

What did you do?

I stopped them in their tracks. I said, you know what, this doesn't feel right, you can expel me, do whatever you want, but I'm not answering any more of your questions. And I left the room.

And what happened?

They said they had enough information and would convene to discuss and also share the info with the Watchtower up in New York who ultimately would make the decision. And sure as shit, at the next congregation, like a week later, in the middle of the sermon, they made an announcement, we regret to inform you that our sister in the name of Jehovah, Jimena Quintero, has sinned and by the guidelines as dictated to us by the Watchtower is expelled from the order..

No-o-o-o, how embarrassing—

I totally sunk down in the pews, like fuck my life.

Did they announce the nature of your sin?

No, but everybody fucking knew.

Well at least that was the end of it.

I wish. Jehovah's Witnesses are a weird fucking religion. Once you're disavowed or expelled or whatever, they give you a chance at redemption, but you have to go through all these hoops—

Like what?

For starters you have to attend every assembly. Jehovah's Witnesses change their religion with the times, it's weird, but when I was in it, in our congregation in Little Havana, there were three meetings per week. One meeting took place in the house of an elder mid-week and it felt like a book club where everyone discussed the latest publication released by the Watchtower, whom are based out of Patterson, New York. Then on Sunday there were two sermons, the first one focused on how to deliver the word of Jehovah, how to preach. As you probably know, a big part of the cult is trying to recruit others, so they would hold workshops emphasizing successful ways to preach. Sometimes they staged dramatic scenarios, with actors pretending to say "no" to a Witness's preaching so we learned how to respond when faced with rejection. And then the main sermon in Kingdom Hall which was pretty much like any Christian sermon, emphasizing scriptures and certain themes, blah, blah, blah, except since I was expelled I had to sit in the back in a special area where mothers with newborn children were kept.

Wow, you must've felt like you were in *The Scarlet Letter*.

What does that mean?

It's a book.

Babe, I was homeschooled. I don't know about no scarlet letter.

I'm saying, everyone must've thought you were a little slut. Boys probably gave you attention.

Exactly, boys would hit on me because they thought I was easy, and the girls hated me. Ugh.

Your mom made you do this, huh?

Yup, and they reinstated me, after six months. I was the fastest person to be re-instated in our congregation's history. Everyone hugged me and welcomed me back. And the day I turned eighteen and could legally stand on my own I said fuck you to all of this and never returned.

Whatever happened to Eddie?

Fuck that needle-dick prick. We should've thrown him in jail but we didn't want to make a bigger scene. He disappeared after successfully expunging me from the church. Sick fuck.

Wow, that's so interesting to me.

Really? I think it's a miserable story.

***

The condo life was strange to Jimena. She felt awkward driving up to the valet in her jalopy and considered buying a new car just for the mental security, but she felt without a steady job it wouldn't be prudent to kill her savings on such a wasteful endeavor. The goal was to drive less, not more. So to avoid the judgmental stares of the valet people she parked in the streets and took her chances with parking tickets when staying overnight. Maybe one out of three sleepover nights she acquired a parking ticket. They took turns paying for them. Jimena didn't want Alex to pay at all. The feminist in her felt firmly that she didn't need a man and Alex tended to agree. However, if a woman was to have equal rights as a man, if the patriarchy truly has evolved, not into a matriarchy, but into a form of Egalitarianism, which they both believed was the natural order of the times, then it would only be fair if Alex paid half the parking tickets, which he insisted, and she agreed fair. The alternative would be for Jimena to rent a parking spot in the garage across the street for only $65 per month, but that too felt rushed and brazen, and neither dared suggest it, not at least until the relationship was at the "drawer" level and definitely not the "toothbrush" faze, a rush to action like that really could sabotage a relationship, as if there really was a formula for any of this stuff. But conversations like this filled their hours, over dinner, or after sex, before sex, there was always a lot of sex.

The concierge at his apartment issued her mixed feelings. On a good note, she didn't have to call-up when she arrived. She'd visited Alex enough where they all knew her face and destination, both the day and night crews. But the idea of a concierge seemed overblown and unnecessary, at least from the perspective of a *latina* from *Calle Siete*. Although, as a women the concept of a toll or gatekeeper provided an extra sense of security she could get used to. Some of them held judgment in their eyes, either thinking she was "the other girl" or not knowing that Alex had another girl now, but most of them knew. It wasn't brain surgery to comprehend. There would come a time when she would have her own clicker or FOB and could walk by them without engagement. There would also come a time when Jimena would know all their names, ask them if they wanted anything when she ventured to the supermarket, a soda or candy bar, but at this point, she only knew the name of one: Dharma, a Trinidadian woman who always smiled when Jimena sauntered towards the concierge desk. Dharma was easy to remember due to her contagion. She never failed to smile and always carried a sparkling glimpse in her dark eyes. The bellmen, on the other hand, Jimena didn't like or trust. They were all men, like the valet, they roosted in front of the building, and there was nothing they could do for her. They always had a look in their eye that suggested their attitude went beyond cordiality into a subtext of misogyny and creepiness. They raped her with their eyes. She could park her own car, carry her own belongings; Jimena had no interest in that flock of peddling rascals.

Speaking of peddling rascals, some of the people that lived in the building were the most pretentious one-percent maniacal tyrants she'd ever come across. Sounds judgmental but without knowing how they made their money, it smelled dirty. Old, South American money poured into the towers of Miami bay with a nip and tuck plastic and an east coast silicon valley in the elevators. Some of the men were too groomed, too old and their body language too stiff. They didn't hold open doors or say thank you if you held open a door or held an elevator. Jimena felt surprised Alex lived in such a building, some younger people loitered but the majorities were blue-haired, blue-blooded Latin fogeys. They actually ate at the in-house restaurants that served an entree starting at twenty-five dollars. Alex's apartment was awesome, once you made it into the Ivory Tower. The apartment was also a gift from his deceased grandmother. He had no mortgage or rent, other than maintenance fees (exuberantly priced at $800 per month). To live practically rent-free in such a part of town was worth the elites, he explained. And some of the tenants were very cool, mature and professional. He explained one of his neighbors worked for the White House press core, another a popular actor in *telenovelas,* and another an ex-Miami Hurricane running back and yet another a current Heat player. You have to see the glass as half-full, even when you're stuck down in the dredges, he explained.

***

Jimena, you have to understand my point of view.

From this Ivory Tower, not everyone has your view, babe.

Yes, there is a lot of corruption, economic disparity and problems with education in Miami. But that's not the whole story here. Why do we always have to focus on the negative side?

Because it exists. We can't deny it or run away from the truth.

Yeah, but why exploit it?

That's what the media does, babe.

Let me tell you a story. This is the Miami I see, and it's not South Beach. This is a typical Monday for me. I enter the elevator of this "Ivory Tower" on the Bay and I descend down 39 floors, with my bicycle, to hit the streets of Miami at rush hour. Moving faster than gridlocked cars, I pass a historical church, an arts and entertainment complex, and a huge construction site for Museum Park. I ride past the AAA arena where they recently hung another championship banner. I pass the Port of Miami now housing a Disney cruise ship that will deliver joy to tens of thousands of children. I arrive at the Tina Hills Pavilion for a FREE community yoga class to which two hundred like-minded beautiful people of all ethnicity, sexual preference and socio-economic status practice under the sunset skies for 90 minutes. I take my shirt off, it could be December, and I feel the bay-breeze tickle my stretched skin. I notice the low hanging thick cumulus clouds hanging in the horizon like a pack of roaring Arabian white stallions. And after the practice, I ride my bike back home, passing the Bayside mall bustling with retail. They are preparing to construct the largest building in the city, an Epcct type of entertainment complex. I look at the Freedom Tower, illuminated in a dark purple. It's a symbol of our immigration, a landmark that's property of one the largest and most diverse university in the country.

Miami-Dade?

Yes, Miami-Dade College.

Go on, babe, I'm listening.

Before entering my apartment I choose to take a stroll around Pace Park, the same place where 15 years ago hookers were washing up on the rocks, now the tennis and volleyball courts are packed, condo dogs enjoy their second and final walk of the day, in the soccer field a group of children are engaged in a scrimmage, fit and firm adults train in Cross-fit, others practice Tai-chi. On the other end of the park the basketball courts are packed, with a gallery watching. I sit on a nearby bench and stare into the sea until I swear I witness a pack of dolphins. I'm not making this shit up. A little later I look at a Poinciana palm tree and through the fronds I see a green parakeet; in the rocks along the bay an iguana emerges, and I think, as the sun has turned the clouds into this cotton candy machine, a pallet of divinity, I think, yes, Miami is the best city in America. Despite the homeless vagabonds I passed squatting on the church steps, despite *The Herald* building being demolished, despite the museum being named after a Philistine, despite the cops who were arresting a man for stealing at Bayside Mall, despite all the economic disparity I think as I enter my condo, smiling at Dharma, picking up the mail, I think, besides the church, mall, Freedom Tower and college, none of this was here fifteen years ago, and yeah, as the elevator closes, I think to myself Miami is definitely the best city in America.

Babe, beautiful, you should work for the Chamber of Commerce.
Shut up, stupid.
I kind of want to leave Miami.
For good? Like move away? Or do you mean for a vacation?
I'd like to travel with you.
Okay. Let's go to New York. See some plays. Visit the Guggenheim or Whitney. I know people we can stay with in Brooklyn. They run the *Brooklyn Rail* and this is a nice season. Or maybe San Francisco. We can wander around the Bay. It's such an odd time there.
I was thinking something more fun, but, don't get me wrong, that does sound interesting, and I love how you are so cultured and know people everywhere, but I kind of want to really let loose.
What do you have in mind?
Bonnaroo.
Bonnaroo is awesome. I've been three times.
See? That's what I mean. You've been everywhere, twice. I've never been anywhere.
How old were you when you married?

Eighteen.

Right after you left the church.

The fastest ticket out-of-my-house was a marriage—so predictable, huh?

Not really. Your life is very interesting. After growing up in some religion you had no choice or core belief. It makes perfect sense to marry at a young age. Luckily you escaped, childless.

Ha. I ain't having no babies.

Ever?

For a long time.

I like that answer.

Too young for that shit.

You never traveled with your ex-husband?

No. That guy was the worst. He used to take pictures of girls tanning naked on the beach and hide them in a folder on our house computer. And as far as traveling, Disneyland was a vacation to him. I'm telling you, babe. I've never been so hungry for something in my whole life. I want to live—to live and travel and try everything not once but twice. So much is really new to me.

That's what I dig about you, Jimena. You're like this ripe fruit. So supple and raw and organic. And it's like you fell from the tree just as I was napping underneath it. You landed on my head and woke me up. I'm not old, you know, thirty-four is not old, but I've seen a lot, my wanderlust is corroding, acquiring rust like a Cadillac near the ocean, but you, you afford me an opportunity to come alive, and I can share the things I know, the culture, experiences, mistakes, epiphanies, and hard-earned truth. It's inspiring, and you're so fucking hot, at least I think so.

I like the way you explain things.

Yeah, let's do Bonnaroo. It's this weekend, no?

Too late?

No, it's just right, babe.

Chapter 14—

Spontaneity was an important ingredient in the recipe for adventure. Making plans of course had its merits, but being able to commit to a journey or event at the last minute, without knowing if all the logistics could come together, was exciting and nerve-wracking, both feelings that tickled and fueled the spirit of life. They didn't even have tickets. But, Alex knew well-enough 100,000 people attended Bonnaroo, there'd be at least two or three percent that wouldn't make it, someone sick, maybe a couple were fighting or recently broke up, people changed their mind, shucks, tickets appeared all over Craigslist and Stubhub. Alex solved the ticket issue with a single Facebook post. Anyone have any extras to Bonnaroo? In less than thirty minutes his phone buzzed with a text, someone in the community, a foodie who ran a popular food truck, Freddy Amaya, a friend whom Alex had hired more than once to cater events at Mecke's. Turned out Freddy was working Bonnaroo and had extra production bracelets. Two of them? No problem. Boom. Ticket dilemma solved one hour. Alex and Jimena now had two production bracelets to Bonnaroo. Know what that meant? They were in for free, they'd have unfettered access to VIP, as well as back-stage, side-stage, on-or-under the stage. Wherever they wanted to go. Plus, they wouldn't have to wait in lines. They'd have their own separate campground and entrance to the festival. Free drinks. The whole kit and caboodle.

But if they were going to head to Tennessee, they needed to quickly execute logistics. Question one: should they fly or drive? A fourteen-hour drive from Miami was a lot. Alex wasn't twenty years old anymore, once you crossed into your thirties you fly, if possible, and you didn't ask people for rides to the airport either. A nice plane ride sounded right up Jimena's ally but she was so excited it didn't really matter. Unfortunately, flying to Nashville, the closest port to Bonnaroo would be out of the question due to the lack of space on flights and the jacked up prices. Atlanta was an option. The capital of the South was only three hours from the music festival, they could rent a car, but unfortunately the flights were also expensive. As Alex maneuvered through Orbitz and Expedia it became apparent they were driving. Besides, they could use the car to transport other festival necessities: a tent (Alex had one), fold-up chairs, quilts, pillows, backpacks, suitcases filled with clothes, and most important, a cooler loaded with water bottles and canned beer. Other necessities, if needed, they could acquire at the festival's outposts or markets, objects like sun block, toilet paper, Gold Bond powder (no chafing please), baby wipes, aloe, a bandana (it gets dusty like Afghanistan), rain boots (just in case), and food

It all came together really fast. Jimena was not working. Alex's business could survive a few days without the boss. It's not like mid-summer represented peak season for Miami or Wynwood. It might serve as the best time of the year for locals to earn their stripes and come together as a community, but hey, Bonnaroo was the biggest and baddest music festival in the world. Everyone needed a little road trip now and then. *Good-bye*, like the antiquated computerized voice when you log off of AOL. They were out, logged off, unplugged. The kind of out that would let them in. Like the ghost of Jim Morrison crooning the ceremony's about to begin. Florida Turnpike bandits raging across the middle of a state that takes eight hours to reach the border. They didn't know where they were going except for the festival. Who knew what might happen after? Maybe they'd stop off at a state park or hot spring or rock quarry and lie down on a quilt blanket. The white noise wouldn't be an air conditioner or that jazz Alex loved. It would be a running creek and some crickets and birds. Summer will stick to their skin, but the breeze will let them wear the heat with comfort and fashion. In the car, the windows were already down and the wind played masseuse. It wasn't all-good. Jimena complained about the sheer quantity of anti-abortion signs along the bible-belt. One image of a baby after another: **My Heart is Beating 18 Days After Conception. All Life Is Sacred from conception to natural death. Take My Hand Not My Life.** And other signs: **Pray the gay away. Dusty bibles lead to a dirty life.** Jesus Christ, Jimena thought—is this the state I call home? There's no jurisdiction in the union so divided as the chasm between North and South Florida. Shit. She'd never even seen a Cracker Barrel. Now she'll be hearing southern drawls, seeing different license plates. She thought of her friend Jose, the ex-witness who traveled extensively around the country following the jam band. For the first time she truly understood that the journey was indeed the destination. To alleviate the dogma, they listened to satellite radio and found a station playing music from the bands that would perform at the festival. The grooves filled them with anticipation and energy.   Jimena broke a cycle, escaped a routine, demolished a wall. It felt like she was going home. On the road in America, there's no better place to be; the best part of all, the whole thing was free.

***

After driving fifteen hours, from late afternoon Thursday all the way through the night, with a few stops for gas, a couple of shift changes while resting, some bathroom breaks, and three fast food take-outs, they arrived in Manchester, Tennessee, home to the 100-acre farm that hosted Bonnaroo, around eleven in the morning Friday. Because of their production bracelets, they had to check-in at a facility a few miles from the farm, along with other venders and artists.

Check-in occurred at the Coffee County Central High School, in a lunchroom. They entered the old brick facility with a content eagerness for making it so far. It was a beautiful summer's day, early-eighties, not a cloud in the sky. The weather called for clear skies all weekend. They planned to rage the event Friday and Saturday and then begin the trek back south on Sunday, maybe detouring somewhere. While Alex waited in line for credentials, Jimena explored the high school, looking at glass containers holding football and soccer trophies. Pictures of student athletes lined the cases. They wore the school's colors, a crimson and black, not unlike the Oriole, such dark colors for such a white team. The first thing Jimena noticed in Tennessee: few people of color. It's easy to forget Miami-Dade's populace was only 16% Caucasian, and most of them Jewish. In Coffee County, Tennessee: 89.6% were white people. She stood out. The rest of America must accept and understand the Latin infusion. How clueless was the United States when it came to Latinos? The collective American consciousness regarding Latinos in the early 21st-century was arguably stuck somewhere between: reckon-all-Latinos-are-Mexican and check-out-the-curves-on-dat-dere-Sofia-Vergara.

In the Super Walmart located in Manchester, Tennessee, a town with a meager population of ten thousand (there would be ten times that at the festival) Jimena felt like she was looking at America for the first time. And what she witnessed bordered on terrifying. There seemed an epidemic of obesity as she encountered sixteen (she counted) women or men too fat to walk so they sat in mechanical wheelchairs and skirted the gigantic aisles. These people were not old and decrepit, but in their forties and fifties, the scene harrowing. She held Alex's hand, sweaty palms and all, as they made their way to the back corner and liquids.

Alex had a way of avoiding her sweaty palms when Jimena felt nervous. He understood she needed comfort, but to avoid the balminess he slid his hand up and held Jimena by the wrist, walking her around like a child, which made Jimena laugh so her palms stopped sweating.

"This place makes you nervous, huh?"

"Does it make you nervous?"

"Yes."

People who live in the Downtown corridor of Miami rarely visit a country Walmart, just like people who frequent a country Walmart rarely venture to the Downtown corridor of Miami.

***

Entering Bonnaroo at such a ripe time, early afternoon on Friday could pose serious issues with parking and traffic. Most people were looking at a couple of hours waiting just to enter the farm and find a parking spot, but not Jimena and Alex whose production bracelets offered them a private entrance to a separate camping facility. Alex made sure to point out to Jimena the difference because one of the things he loathed most in life was waiting in any line. Their destination was a little camping area off the beaten path, near the first aid tent, which was occupied by three registered nurses and two tending physicians, in case of any health issues like dehydration, sun fatigue, severe sun burn, broken bones, and of course, any potential drug overdoses. Bonnaroo didn't play around when it came to covering all of their bases.

Almost two in the afternoon and the day was just unfolding. The first thing Alex did when he parked the car at their home for the next 48 hours was pop open a cold beer. He bought two cases of canned Magic Hat. Alex felt surprised to see his orange little buddy's at a country Walmart. Forty-eight beers might seem like a lot for two days, but you never know, not having to drive, surrounded by a hundred-thousand party people, music all-day-and-night, forty-eight appeared better than twenty-four. Jimena, on the other hand, couldn't wait to settle. Staking land in the camping grounds (in her imagination) equated to frontiersmen laying their claim to a lot. And Jimena wasn't going to waste a minute's time. She wanted to explore the festival grounds.

"Are you going to help me?"

"In a minute babe," said Alex, unpacking the folding chairs from the trunk, as well as the cooler. He busied himself filling the cooler with beers and organizing the car. Afterwards he sat down on a folding chair. "I need a couple to relax. That drive, *oooof*—it's just nice to kick back."

"You don't know how to pitch a tent, do you?"

"Haven't the slightest."

"Have you used this tent before?"

"Me? No. Well, once—but I paid some hippie to pitch it."

"Where did you stay the other times at Bonnaroo?"

"We rented RVs."

"You spoiled little sprig, ugh—"

"Not a big outdoorsmen, bae. I turn into Woody Allen camping. Panic attacks about mosquitos. Weird sounds in the night -- hence, self-medication." He reached for his bag and grabbed a prescription bottle of klonopin and shook it like *cha-cha-cha*. "The goal is to pass out, not gently fall into a Walt Whitman trance on the deeper meditations of nature."

"Well, you're going to help me here."

Jimena was remarkably deft at assembling a tent. She had the canvas spread out, with the dome off to the side, and almost all the rods connected. She didn't even look at the directions.

"Let me find a garbage bag first."

"Are you serious?"

"Yes, it's important. Relax, babe. I'll be right back."

"Ugh."

Alex grabbed a fresh Magic Hat from the cooler and sauntered off to the information booth not too far away. There were about eighty campgrounds at Bonnaroo spread across the 700 acre farm. The campgrounds were broken into twelve districts, each one named after a pop culture movie like *Rocky*, for example. Then in the Rocky district, the camps were named after characters like Camp Apollo Creed, Camp Ivan Drago, Clubber Lang. This helped people find each other's camps as well as a way home. Other homages included: *Zoolander, James Bond, Pulp Fiction, Star Wars, Sixteen Candles, Ghostbusters, Ace Ventura* and more.

Alex needed a map and a garbage bag and he knew where to find them. Bonnaroo was an extremely well-produced, world-class music festival. Within a few minute walk of every camping district one could access an information booth, a taxi stand, bathrooms (cleaned and emptied multiple times per day), food vendors and an ice vendor. Closer to the main entrance existed more food and retail vending and even more vendors were located inside the grounds.

At the information booth, Alex picked up a few maps and two large plastic garbage bags, courtesy of the festival. The less mess you made, the less they had to clean up so they had no issues handing out free garbage bags. Alex also inquired about purchasing two bracelets for unlimited taxi rides throughout the weekend, a service he found indispensible. Taxi service on a farm consisted of privately hired festival goers who worked and were paid in shifts to transport people around in a golf-cart for ten dollars a head. Unlimited taxi service assured them maximum efficiency, expediency and comfort when it came to moving around the 700 acre farm and navigating numerous tent cities. If they needed to rush back to the tent, for some beer or a nap, taking a golf-cart taxi would save hours of walking and ensure tons of relief on strained feet. It was a worthy investment that most festival goers wouldn't even think about if it was their first time at the event. Alex knew better.

He explained all this to Jimena when he returned with a taxi-bracelet. She felt giddy as ever and couldn't wait to explore the grounds. It was okay that her man didn't know how to build things or couldn't fix a car. He was one-better, he knew how to get it done for a cheap price, and he comprehended through his hard-earned experiences the fastest way from Point A to Point B. She loved that about him. After attaching the plastic garbage bag to the bumper, he helped her finish up the tent. She did most of the connecting, lifting, attaching, sliding of rods into buckles, and hammering, but he helped hold the habitat together and soon it rose: a humble four-person tent, erected in the Vendor campground. That was the name of their area, according to the Bonnaroo map, not something cool like the grounds across the way from them, Camp Pussy Galore, but simple and bland, Vendor Camping, fine by them. They had access to free, private hot showers, unlike everyone else who had to pay and wait in a line if they wanted to freshen up.

By the time they threw the blankets and pillows in the tent and locked up the car with most of their valuables, it was about three o'clock in the afternoon and the day was in effect.

"What should we do first?"

"Center Roo, babe," he said, pecking her lips. "It's showtime."

***

Taxi-drivers wore bandanas wrapped around their faces to limit inhaling dirt. With the pristine summer conditions the farm was dry and the golf carts kicked dust into the air. Alex and Jimena sat on the back of the cart strapped with smiles and they zoomed past the pilgrimage of heads who journeyed towards the entrance of Bonnaroo. They drove along a long wooded shadowy road for two hundred yards and popped back into the sun near the VIP and RV camping. Up 1st Avenue and west on East 2nd Street they ventured, tent city not an exaggeration, until they arrived on Main Street which was the closest the taxis were allowed to drive since the terrain became too dense with people. Along Main Street were a slew of venders selling a variety of hats, shirts, dresses, posters, art, drug paraphernalia, and all types of food, veggie or meaty.

When Main Street converged with Broadway they could see the entrance to the main grounds, a large arch with the words BONNAROO in big white letters, not unlike the Gateway arch of St. Louis cross-bred with the HOLLYWOOD sign on the west coast, just like in Wynwood. Again, like the city they arrived from, they passed a slew of street artists painting the outside walls of the venue. But Jimena couldn't take her eyes off the huge sign. She'd made it. For Jimena it looked like the yellow brick road to Oz and Alex was the lion that delivered her.

"I'm so happy," she grabbed his hand.

"It's special," he nodded.

"Grateful I am." She kissed his cheek.

"Are you Yoda now?"

She slapped his arm. Alex always knew how to ruin a moment.

***

They had a great time and did what most do when attacking Bonnaroo. They followed the schedule and attended as many bands as they could both agree on. One of the first tasks Alex insisted upon was meandering to Food Truck Ally to find his friend to thank him for the bracelets. Music may surround the idea of Bonnaroo, but as you pulled back the layers of the festival at its inner core you find diverse culture, not just music. It's more than just music but film, fashion, comedy, politics, food, the healing arts, the theater, all represented in a gonzo buffet to diversify a day. They laughed it up in the Comedy Tent. Caught a flick in the Cinema Tent. Jimena shopped for weird knick-knacks like rings and patches and art prints, souvenirs to take home. They drank craft beer from the homebrew tent. Jimena signed petitions while Alex argued with anti-fracking activists. Around sunset they ventured back to the tent and drank from coolers. While kicking back on lawn chairs, resting, they chatted with neighbors and passers-by.

There were no strangers or Grinch's or grumps. They met people from all over the country, and everyone had the same contagious smile and demeanor. After a nice rest, they headed back to Center Roo for more of the same, but now with the moon as their guide. They danced and sang and ate and played. Their vibe centered on drinking mostly due to free beer in the VIP area, plus all the alcohol by the campground. Jimena also brought a couple of grams of cocaine from Miami (from a secret source) which she was more than happy to share during the course of the weekend. The cocaine balanced the alcohol. Near midnight Alex ran into someone he knew from Miami who happened to have molly for sale. They both said why the heck not?

And that's how it went. From "This Tent" to "That Tent" to "The Other Tent" to "What Stage" to "Which Stage" they explored the music until they couldn't anymore, around four a.m., when the bands finally stopped. With no music they caught a cab back to the tent and Jimena passed out with a thud. Alex needed two klonopin and a couple more beers before he found solace. He crawled into the tent with Jimena as the sun began to crack the eastern horizon with a taint of dark blue. They were lucky to sleep until eleven with the sun roasting them like peanuts.

But they did and Saturday was born. They both needed coffee and showers. There'd be no time to wallow in serotonin levels or holes-in-the-soul at the devilish hands of La Cocaina. Go, go, go, wash, rinse, repeat. They groggily freshened up and headed directly back to Center Roo for a yoga class. Alex insisted they partook in a yoga class and then eat a well-balanced meal before they began to party, but after yoga and lunch, go, go, go, wash, rinse, repeat. It started with a beer and a trip back to the car because the party favors were all alone with only the cooler of beer for company. They had more drinks, rested for awhile, and then go, go, go, wash, rinse, repeat, back to Center Roo. Saturday was almost the same thing. They met and engaged interesting people from all over the country. They danced and screamed and sang and laughed. They learned of new music and bands. Around sunset on Saturday they both jumped into the huge water fountain in the center of the festival grounds. It looked like a giant red and white mushroom that spewed water from its Smurfy mushroom cap and served as a sprinkler for hot and sweaty kids, and as a shower for a few of the more stinky ones, go, go, go, wash, rinse, repeat, back to the campgrounds for a few drinks and a costume change into evening attire. Jimena had bought a new dress and wanted to wear it and Alex stuck with some khaki's and some ironic t-shirt he picked up at Urban Outfitters. They both wore sandals, *pata sucia*, Jimena must have said the phrase fifteen times during the festival, but whatever, go, go, go, wash, rinse, repeat, back on a taxi to Center Roo for the evening festivities, wash, rinse, repeat. Alex ran into a couple of people he knew from Miami and they shared time and space and drugs, go, go, go, wash, rinse, repeat, molly, coke, dancing and drinking like a rock star. What? Were they supposed to just smoke a joint? Or, even worse, stay sober for the weekend? Yeah, right This was Sodom and Gomorrah on a goddamn farm in Tennessee. Freaking Rock and Roll, baby, in the middle of nowhere, summertime in America, goddamn it all, don't judge the kids let em live while they're young.

The highlight of the weekend happened late Saturday night, after two in the morning. They'd just left the Silent Disco tripping on the concept of dancing with a group of people without audible music. The participants heard sounds from headphones as a top-notch deejay blasted tracks into earlobes of those in attendance. From the outside looking in, people looked possessed. There was no audible music yet everyone shook like an avalanche of James Brown.

Behind the Silent Disco stood an old school ferris-wheel, there was nothing incredibly thrill-seeking about the ride. It was just an old, well-lit, five-story ferris-wheel on the horizon. Jimena wanted to ride it.

Alex felt hesitant because he hated lines and thought it childish.

"Please, babe."

"I mean, if you really want to."

"I'll wait in-line, go grab us a beer."

She handed him a twenty.

"Okay."

He didn't mind so much waiting in line for a beer, if the line was relatively short. By the time Alex returned with two craft beers, Jimena was considerably closer to the front of the line. "I feel so good."

"Me too," said Alex.

"When was the last time you rode a ferris-wheel?"

"Gosh, as a little boy maybe."

"The colors are so vivid."

"Yeah."

"I like the blinking red lights."

"Weird."

"All the patterns in the lights are crazy."

"Crazy."

Alex was fucked-up enough to a point where words could hardly escape his mouth. He stood firm, without sway or vacillation. He stood with swag, just his gift-of-gab left for a swell.

Soon they found themselves seated in an old blue ferris-wheel cart. They moved backwards, slowly, so the next cart could fill. "I've never been on a ferris-wheel." Truth serum.

"Crazy."

"My mom, you know. Witnesses believe thrill rides and places like Disneyland or Busch Gardens are temptations from the devil. Anything fun was a message from the devil. It sucked, babe. She'd throw away my dolls. I have a lot of bad memories. I couldn't watch television."

"Kill your television."

"What?"

"Crazy," said Alex.

They moved higher and higher, backwards, until they reached the top and stood there. They could see over the wall and into the campgrounds. They could see a panoramic view of the 100 acres of madness. People were scattered everywhere. They could see the fragmented grid of light from within the festival grounds, especially in the music tents where light shows exploded at full throttle, but the light also spread across the campgrounds, in patches and bursts. They could also see on the horizon in all directions the pitch darkness of the land outside of Bonnaroo. The darkness was not far away and in the darkness there was absolutely remotely nothing. "Could we stay here forever?"

"Crazy."

"Babe?"

"Yeah?"

"I love you."

"I love you too, Jimena."

Yes of course they were beaming on molly and fueled on cocaine and uninhibited by lots of alcohol, but they meant it, unequivocally, and naturally. They were also positioned atop of the world they currently conquered. They couldn't rise any higher if they wanted. It was the first time they uttered those words to each other. Alex grabbed Jimena's hand, looked at her and smiled. Her hand wasn't sweaty. She smiled back. The ferris-wheel suddenly turned bright neon blue. It bounced off their faces and they began to move in circles for the duration of the ride.

***

Sunday morning, maybe they slept two hours. Go, go. go, go, wash, rinse, repeat mutated into no, no, no, no, ouch, fuck, deplete.

Jimena stumbled out of the tent and walked like a zombie to the toilet for a pee. She grabbed two bottles of water from the cooler and climbed back into the tent to snuggle with Alex. It felt hotter than a pre-heated oven at 420 degrees and all they could do was bake together.

By eleven the heat was too hot to bear and they escaped their tent-cave-sauna. The world was a mess. The only thing that made the mess a little organized was that everyone around them felt the same. Sunday mornings and musical festivals weren't compatible companions.

"I guess it starts with a coffee."

Jimena mumbled something incoherent as Alex walked to the nearby vendor to purchase iced-coffees. He knew Jimena liked a million sugars so he sweetened hers up to her liking. Back at the campsite they both sat down on the fold-up chairs and enjoyed their Sunday coffee.

"Are we leaving today?"

"In a couple of hours."

"Can you drive?"

"Unfortunately," said Alex.

"What's next?" said Jimena.

"Death."

"Death sounds reasonable."

"Need to charge your cell phone?"

"Yes."

"Just turn the key so the battery is on and use the adapter."

"Oh my god," she rubbed her temples. "I feel like shit."

"But was it worth it?"

"The emptiness I feel is better with you here."

"Awww, that's sweet, babe."

He leaned over, kissed her and almost fell from his chair.

"Do you want to go back to Center Roo?" she asked.

"Not really. Two days was enough. There's nothing I need or want. I couldn't do a yoga stretch other than maybe cracked-out Monkey Pose. I say the earlier we leave the better. We have a long-ass drive. We should use as much as the daylight as possible. Sound okay to you?"

"We can go. I just want to shower first."

"Go shower, I'll start packing-up."

"You don't want to shower?"

"No, I will, when you get back. I feel like Pigpen from Peanuts, you know the dude with all the dirt following him like a storm. I keep forgetting you have limited pop culture references."

"I know Snoopy, ding-dong."

She proceeded to whistle the theme song to the show, but half way through the rendition she lost the rhythm and her breath trailed off to a gothic crawl and she couldn't finish the jingle.

After a few minutes of not moving, they began to stir like a medium chili simmering for an hour or two at the lowest possible temperature. Jimena gathered the necessities for a warm shower like soap, a wash cloth, some shampoo, and a towel. No, no, no, ouch, fuck, deplete. "Try not to take your traditional forty-five minute shower."

Jimena shot him a stank face. "I'll be back in ten." The bathroom water held traces of sulfur worse than The Place. It created a rotten-egg smell so she wouldn't take a normal shower. Meanwhile, the coffee started Alex's engine. He looked motivated to hit the road. Since he'd be driving most of the way, or at least the first few hours until Jimena felt more human and less zombie, he wanted to get going so he started to clear the tent of all the pillows and blankets and packed them in the car. He emptied the tent of litter and food wrappers. He dumped the water from the cooler. Fifteen Magic Hat beers would live to see another day. That's thirty-three beers they drank in two days, not counting all the free beer inside and some beers they paid for. To his credit, as a functional alcoholic, Alex dished out several beers to neighbors while they chilled at the tent. With the cooler packed in the car, and the tent empty, he began to break it down, which even he could do. He only had a problem with putting the tent together. By the time Jimena arrived back at the car, with wet hair, wearing only a towel, Alex stuffed the tent away.

"I'll be back."

"Let's boogie, babe."

"I need to get dressed. I forgot my clothes."

Jimena grabbed clothes and slowly trekked back to the bathroom to dress in privacy. She moved at a snail's pace, but hey, they had a crazy weekend. By the time she returned in clothes, Alex, wearing sunglasses, had the car running, with the AC on. Their garbage bag had been thrown away. It looked like they were never there, which was the point.

"We're on the road, babe."

"Okay, okay, okay." One of the few phrases Jimena popularized that actually held hints of her Spanish accent and *Calle Siete* roots.

They left Bonnaroo around the same time they arrived, early afternoon, approximately forty-eight wild hours later. Alex maneuvered them out of the farm through the vendor's entrance and had them on the parkway heading east five minutes later. He hit the road in haste.

"Babe," he felt like talking. "Indulge me. Say hypothetically, because of the proverbial candle we just burned on both ends, let's pretend those forty-eight hours raging at Bonnaroo meant we would live two weeks less, and if the choice was ours, you know, not like it is, but if it were, what would you rather have? Two more weeks to live, even as an old and decrepit life force, or those forty-eight hours at Roo?"

"It's not even close."

"Another 48 hours?" He laughed. "You want a sequel."

"Don't you?"

"I'm okay for now, but I'm not sure it was worth two weeks."

"Babe," Jimena leaned against the window, snuggling on a pillow. "I'm faded."

Alex turned the radio on, finding a station to catch up on news. Jimena barely had enough energy to do anything so she grabbed her phone from the charger and opened Facebook. Pretty soon they'd have no signal so she might as well check-in with the world. The service at Bonnaroo was spotty, except for the media tent which they stayed away from. So many Iphones in one place in the middle of nowhere will always corrupt and confuse a satellite. It was pretty refreshing to not have a cell-phone. She imagined what it must have been like living in the nineties, or even earlier, in an old antiquated world when people talked rather than texted. And looking at her Facebook account was a bad idea.

"Oh my god."

"What happened?"

"Is this for real?"

"What?" Alex lowered the radio.

"My roommate Dolly," she said.

"What did she do?"

"She was hit by a car on her bike."

"Is she okay?"

"No babe," Jimena leaned up. "She's dead."

Chapter 15—

The four most dangerous cities in the United States for walking or riding a bicycle are located in Florida: Orlando, Tampa, Jacksonville and Miami. According to Chito's status, Dolly rode along NE 2nd Avenue around one in the morning when she made a right turn onto a street and a huge Freightliner semi-truck heading towards the Port of Miami plowed into her head on. Dolly and Jimena were friends, not best friends, but friendly. They did share the same space, the same bathroom and toilet, the same refrigerator chilled their juices and beers, the same oven baked their potatoes and fish filets. They were often passing ships in the night because of schedules, even more-so when Jimena started spending most of the week at Alex's place, even more-more-so when Jimena soured on the Miami Bike Scene after the Critical Mass debacle.

But this was the first time the fickle fingers of death touched Jimena's environment and she felt cold and empty, hollowed out like a pillow without its stuffing. Working in a hospital, surrounded by depressing medical codes and eternal illness, and fighting for her own mother's mortality in her battle with cancer, of course afforded her a deeper understanding and context of death, but experiencing it felt different, especially when you didn't see it coming. After Bonnaroo, a dark cloud hovered over her. The drive back was quiet and depressing. Jimena didn't want to talk, instead she begged her boyfriend for two klonopin to sleep the hangover away, bury the sad, unbelievable news at least for the duration of the road trip. Alex understood and obliged Jimena, who fell asleep within thirty minutes and stayed asleep for the whole drive. Zonked-out and faded, Alex stepped-up and drove like a bandit to get them home quickly. Through Chattanooga and Dalton, Atlanta and Macon, Ocala and Gainesville, past Orlando and the home stretch, he blazed the 850 miles in 11 hours fueled on Red Bull and spirit.

As soon as they arrived in South Florida they encountered rain. It had been raining for two days. Summer storms. Very little sunshine. Heavy and low cloud covers with humidity like an oven. Dark, gloomy, gray. Perfect weather for a funeral. Jimena felt groggy and sad. Simple emotions. No sense of inquiry into anything existential. No connection to a higher being. She possessed no "why" questions—no why did this happen—why are we alive—why do we suffer?

Groggy and sad. She didn't want to talk. Eat. Fuck or drink. She turned off her phone. No texts. Facebook. Instagram or blogs. Sleep sounded good. Maybe some television. Nothing funny. No sitcoms. Laughs. Smiles or smirks. Maybe a few episodes of a Showtime series.

Alex had to go to work but she stayed in, lounged around.

The funeral was in two days. She hesitated about going back to the apartment but the next day she needed to see for herself and headed over to Little Haiti. The place smelled like spicy incense. Chito probably burned some sage. He was home, in-the-shower, fortunately, because she wanted to see him. The door to Dolly's room was closed, not locked. She turned the knob. It would've been better if she walked into a room ripped and torn to shreds, the bed burned with holes and ashes, the desk and chairs turned over, with dark blood splattered across the walls in different and chaotic patterns, indicating a fight and several lashings, a victim trying to put up a resistance, with bloody smears and smudges and Dolly lying on the floor, in pieces, her intestines wrapped around the ceiling fan dripping blood onto Jimena's terrorized face.

Instead of a crime scene Jimena stared deadpan at a room that looked alive. It felt warm. The same spicy incense had been burned, but she could still smell taints of Dolly's odor, sort of a musty coconut, it lived in the pink carpet, bed linens and pillows. Dolly never made her bed, no surprise it wasn't made now. In fact, her room always looked dirty, not super dirty because she didn't have a lot of stuff, but disorganized. Disorganized and minimal, that was Dolly. She liked to ride bike. Drink beer. Work. Screw. She ate out a lot, left dishes and to-go containers in her room. There was no art on the walls. No pictures of family, although they were around South Florida, up north in Broward.

She came to Jimena with a kind attitude, willing to share, and she left in-a-flash, leaving behind a room of clothes, bike swag and some secrets.

Jimena knew if she poked around, dug through the closets, the dresser drawers—that's where Dolly's secrets lied. Maybe some fetish or drug paraphernalia? Maybe a picture? A letter? The boy that got away. Jimena didn't want or need to know. They weren't that close, even now.

"You're home," said Chito.

"Holy shit you scared me."

He stood frigid in the living room, leery, almost afraid to enter Dolly's room. "Did you hear?"

Jimena walked to Chito and hugged him. He was wet, shirtless, wrapped in a towel fresh out of the shower. "I saw your post online."

"I didn't want to ruin your trip to Bonnaroo."

Jimena took a deep breath.

No tears. There would be no tears, not yet.

"This sucks," she said.

"Dolly is here. It's natural for her to want her bed, comfort, and spare bike." He pointed to Dolly's spare bike near the kitchen. "She's here. I burned some sage in case she's mad."

"Why would she be mad?"

"Because she was on her way to see me."

"Oh, Chito, she's not mad at you, sweetie. Maybe she's mad that she had to fucking die so young, but she's not going to take it out on us. We loved her. We were her friends."

"It's just . . . too weird."

"What about her things?"

"Her father and younger sister are coming to collect her belongings. Her mother lives in New York, re-married, but her dad and sister are making all the . . . arrangements."

Jimena rubbed her eyes. They weren't wet, but tired. She felt extra faded. After a strong binge, especially one like Bonnaroo, she always felt the most faded two days after the fact.

"I don't think I can live here anymore," said Chito.

"I don't blame you."

"You don't?"

"No."

"What are you going to do?"

"I don't know."

"You know they burned down the school where all those children were killed."

"They tore it down," said Jimena. "They didn't burn it down."

"We can get another place, maybe."

"Go get dressed," said Jimena. "We'll see how this shakes out."

***

The night after the funeral Alex decided to let the Miami Bike Scene hold a memorial / fundraiser for Dolly at his establishment. It was a nice gesture. Jimena didn't ask him; in fact, it wasn't even his idea. Someone from the Miami Bike Scene, in collaboration with Merge Miami approached him. Merge was an organization that united progressive activists across a various spectrum of social issues important to the city. Bike Safety was one such cause and losing the Queen of the bike scene, quite frankly, was an opportunity to get some attention on the issue.

They wanted a venue where people could talk, drink and maybe watch a movie or a video presentation. A place with a sound system. They didn't want a loud party, or a deejay. A place without a liquor license but close to an establishment that did so after they could let loose.

Mecke's was the go-to-venue for such events.

The event was packed with people. Both *The Herald* and the *New Times* ran stories in-print and online about Dolly's tragedy and both previewed the fundraiser on their blogs. Alex's place was converted into a bike store of sorts as a plethora of local shops agreed to donate a variety of biking equipment and gift certificates for a silent auction. The Miami Bike Collective donated a re-assembled custom Cinelli fixed gear bike for a raffle. Before items would be given away, there was a monitor playing videos from Dolly's Facebook page. She loved to post videos, whether of bike polo or the sunset-ride that she coordinated every other Wednesday afternoon or of everyone hanging around The Spot or the Collective just hamming it up. A few people spoke up in memory of

Dolly, including Vilano, who started to cry and couldn't finish telling a story about how Dolly visited him every day when he was hit by a car.

The funeral showing itself was less dramatic. Held up in West Broward, a little out-of-the-way, the crowd was sparse compared to the Miami memorial (after-all, most of these kids only had bikes as a means of transport and riding thirty-five miles to see a closed-casket held little appeal). Out of respect, Jimena and Chito dropped by the Serenity Funeral Home but they didn't stay long. There was nothing to see. They knew no one. They found out one piece of information that wasn't too shocking that they could deliver to the event in Miami. Dolly's remains would be cremated and her ashes held in an urn at her father's house.

Jimena didn't want to attend the memorial at her boyfriend's bar. He had to convince her while almost insisting that she attend. She reluctantly agreed but swore not to stay for the whole thing, and under no condition would she eulogize Dolly or say even one sentence publicly. Others at the event spoke about the bigger issues the bikers were concerned with. The platform consisted of two simple requests: more bike lanes and to widen existent bike lanes. To make this happen they needed organization and leadership to lobby the County Commissioners or the mayor who had the authority to make such a request a reality. Any donations accrued would go to the pursuit of lobbying, through advertising, petitions and speaking up at public transit meetings. Their goals were attainable. Most Commissioners as well as those in Law Enforcement and Public Safety agreed that Bike Safety was an important issue. It was just "a matter of keeping the pedal to the metal," said one activist, unaware of the mixed metaphor.

For her part, Jimena sat in the back corner, hidden behind the shield of dark sun glasses and a bottle of Merlot. Dating a guy who owned a beer and wine bar had many advantages, and a bottle of Louis Jadot Beaujolais definitely ranked among the best perks. Surprisingly, meeting young up-and-comers from basically every facet of Miami's emerging cultural world didn't rank higher than the free wine; on the contrary, Jimena was not educated like these book people. They made her a little uncomfortable. The whole scene. She also viewed them as carpetbaggers, or non-locals, newbies hungry to capitalize on the future of Miami. She didn't always see it, or necessarily believe in it. Sometimes when listening to Alex she felt glimpses of hope. He certainly believed in the future of Miami, and she respected his passion and willingness to participate rather than speculate, but all of this seemed too good-to-be-true. The Miami she knew didn't include a rainbow at the end of a grant proposal. The only silver lining produced for her so far was Alex.

The more she listened and watched the more she drank. Like one of her father's favorite pastimes, drinking wine had a domino effect, making her emotional and then angry. Her fucking roommate Dolly was dead. What could pandering accomplish to bring her back? The apartment was over. Chito didn't want to live there anymore. Should she start from scratch? Begin the roommate search again. Did she even want to live in The Place? Damn, Dolly. Why did you have to die? Why couldn't you have just moved to New York or LA like everyone else?

All this conjecture amongst bicycle and transit advocates was bullshit. They could go fuck the No Walmart in Midtown coalition of Independent Thinkers consumed by a Green Mobility Network, all hoping for philanthropy so they could paint dollar signs on their dog and swim in a pool of gold bullion. Save This and Abolish That, just pay us for the cause. That's what it seemed like to her in-the-moment and she couldn't take it. She finished her glass of wine and stormed out of the memorial's front door. Alex, busy behind the bar, noticed and followed.

Outside, Jimena looked across the street at a car that just pulled-up to valet at a new trendy restaurant in the district. The car was bumping loud House music into the early evening.

"Hey, babe," Alex tapped her shoulder. "Are you okay?"

"I can't take it here anymore."

"If this is too much, why don't you go back to my place?"

"No. I can't take it here anymore, Alex. This city is a fucking nightmare. Between these wannabe glamorous slicked-back douchebags, in their expensive cars, their Audis and Benz and Beamers, with their fake-ass silicon Barbie Doll girlfriends, blasting all this House music, ugh, this city and its EDM—god forbid you say their music sucks—an angry raver mob will attack. It's so annoying, Ultra and Fontainebleau and Club Space, ugh, ugh, ugh—" Jimena started to yell at the couple exiting their valet car across the way. "Go back to South Beach. Take your music with you. Miami isn't South Beach, motherfuckers."

"Jimena, hey, Jimena," he grabbed her arm. "Where is this coming from?" She jerked away from the grip and looked him in the eye.

"Everyone in this place is so fucking phony, Alex. People say one thing and do another. They'll talk about you behind your back. And they root for you to fail. It's like there's literally Hater aid in the clouds and it rains down upon this city with wrath and envy and jealousy—"

"Jimena, calm down, babe—"

"Don't tell me to calm down. This is the most disloyal city ever. Unless it's Cubans being loyal to Cubans, or Jews looking out for Jews, or Haitians or whoever. I can't take it here anymore, babe. There's a good reason why everyone moves to New York or Los Angeles."

"Why are you so upset—"

"And the people in Wynwood. Your people, you think these hipsters are fucking better? They're more fake and phony than the douchebags on South Beach. They think they're so ironic and witty and creative but they're all followers. There's no originality, loyalty, love. This place is broken. Miami people are broken, shattered like a broken mirror stained with fucking cocaine resin. You're crazy to think there's hope in this city. The only hope a person has growing up here is maybe, just maybe, they can move the fuck out. And I'm not even talking about the large majority of this city that is so uneducated, impoverished and crunked on some ratchet style and culture. Ratchet! And what about our corrupt leadership? Alex, you really think Miami will ever change?"

"Jimena, you don't see Miami like I see—"

"You're so fucking delusional, Alex. You really are."

"Are you drunk? Don't talk like you are if you're not drunk."

"My glasses are off and I can see clearly."

"Jimena, what's going on?" His voice indicated little patience.

"I just don't want to be here," her voice softened. "Not tonight."

"I understand."

"I love you, babe. I really do."

"I love you too."

"If you weren't here, I'd leave in a heartbeat."

"Is this about Dolly and your apartment?"

"It's Dolly. It's the apartment. It's work. It's a whole bunch of—"

"Because I was thinking. I wanted to talk to you later, but, I don't know, maybe now's a good time. Let me just come out and say it."

"Say what?"

"I want you to move in with me."

"Shut up."

"I'm serious."

"No, you're not."

He wiped her eye. "I am."

"Why?"

"I love you," he said smiling. "Number two, we've been getting along great and I want to take it to the next level. Number three, I spoke to Chito, you know, and I can tell he doesn't want to live in that apartment, he thinks ghosts haunt it, and I'm sure you feel the same. Number four, you're over my apartment more than yours. Number five, my rent will go down even more." She smiled and hit him in the arm, not because she expected to live rent free. They already shared all costs, and Jimena wasn't a gold digger. She hit him for that diabolical smile he cracked when ruining moments like only he could. "And number six, if it doesn't work out, you know, no biggie, you'll just get your own place."

"Awww, babe," she wiped her eyes. "You thought about this."

"I have," he looked inside. "Need time to think about it?"

"No baby," she said. "I'm in."

They kissed on the lips before he went back inside. Jimena looked around Wynwood feeling a little happier. A lot happier actually. Alive and happier. Again, simple emotions carrying no sense of inquiry into anything philosophical. No connection to a higher being. No "why" questions—no why do I feel happy—why did Dolly have to die to make me feel alive at this moment—why is love so dang impossible to predict?

Happy and alive. She didn't want to talk. Or go back inside. Maybe eat. Fuck. She texted Jackie the news. No Facebook. Instagram. Relaxing sounded okay. Maybe some television. Something funny. A sitcom. Laughs. Smiles or smirks. Maybe a few episodes of a HBO series.

Jimena Quintero simply longed for a place that felt like home.

PART IV

Chapter 16 —

Television On . . . we're live in Lake Worth, as you can see the waters are starting to pick up, there are a few crazy surfers . . . *click* . . . in South Beach Hurricane Catherine has cleared the beaches . . . *click* . . live from . . . *click* . . . LIVE . . . *click* . . . as you can see from the Doppler . . . *click* . . . the latest satellite images concur . . . *click* . . . two o'clock advisory puts the hurricane at seventy-six degrees . . . *click* . . . the five o'clock advisory is expected around five o'clock . . . *click* . . . the Future Track . . . *click* . . . as the outer bands creep closer and closer . . . *click* . . . we're live at Home Depot where the story tonight in South Florida is one of preparation . . . *click* "Jesus Christ," said Jimena. "It's on every channel."

"There's nothing else to do. It's Chicken Little sensationalism."

"I don't know, babe, this one looks weird."

"It's the same every year. It's the biggest way for a network or meteorologist to make news. Hurricanes sell. They get so many clicks. They sell generators and aluminum shutters. They sell out supermarkets and Home Depots. They keep viewers glued to televisions."

"Yeah, but, this is like forming almost right on us."

"The sky is falling," he said. "The sky is falling."

"Ugh, you're so fucking stubborn, Alex."

"Know what we should do? Let's wait till it gets really bad and go to the beach and look for television reporters. Those poor dudes who get the short end of the stick. We'll find one from CBS or NBC and fuck with them. I'll have a microphone. Tell them we're doing a documentary on sensationalism in the media. I'll ask the reporter what they think about scaring the public during a natural occurrence. The reporter will be so confused to have a microphone in his face. He'll mumble about safety. Maybe you can video bomb the interview. Take your shirt off and show the world those perfect titties. The whole thing will be on someone's Tivo, we wouldn't even need a camera. We'll use their camera. It'll be gonzo. It'll go fucking viral. The weatherman, when they cut back to the studio, they'll call us something reckless, like we're troubled miscreants. We'll entertain hundreds of thousands because everyone will be glued to their television. I can turn it into a short film, a meta-documentary and submit it to the Potage Festival, who knows, maybe get it into Sundance or Cannes. What a brilliant idea, babe."

"That's the dumbest idea I ever heard."

"I can wear a hat that says Kill Your Television."

"Babe, you have a business. Shouldn't you prepare for this?"

"You're right," Alex popped out of bed. He opened the blinds to see a dark and wet landscape. Stumbling around, he found slippers and underwear. "Last minute hurricane party."

***

Hurricane Catherine came to life with a sudden furor off the eastern coast of Cuba at approximately 2 a.m., less than forty-eight hours previously. Tropical Depression Eight formed into the Category 1 hurricane in a bizarre series of meteorological circumstances. The storm formed off of the remnants of Tropical Depression 6, which had lingered near the Bahamas for a few days but weakened due to a trough in the upper troposphere. A new tropical wave formed off of Cuba at the same time the trough weakened in the Bahamas, so a new tropical depression formed off of the old one, and alas the third named Hurricane of the season was born: a little bitch named Catherine. Hurricane Ashley and Hurricane Billy failed to cause a stir as they dissipated on that long journey from off the coast of Africa across the pond towards the Eastern seaboard and Caribbean. Catherine was a different bitch altogether. She came out of nowhere, her eye born in the warm waters north of Cuba. Anatomically, she moved extremely slowly with a west-by-northwest pace of six miles per hour. Wind gusts already clocked in at over seventy miles per hour and with the gulfstream unseasonably warm the intensity of the storm would easily reach Hurricane 2, maybe Hurricane 3, status before it hit Florida. The cone of uncertainty looked pretty fucking certain that this storm would make landfall somewhere in South Florida directly by the next evening. The effects of outer bands with tropical storm winds could be expected that very night. All the computer models projected little multi-colored spaghetti lines right at the Tri-county area. The meteorological graphic looked like a nappy headed George Clinton when he had rainbow dreads. This was some funky shit. Whether landing in Dania Beach, Lake Worth, or North Miami, the storm would undoubtedly tussle with all of South Florida, as well as Monroe County in the Keys, and even the Gulf Coast and possibly Central Florida. Catherine was an average size hurricane, with a width of about 100 miles, which meant South Florida would feel the effects the greatest. After South Florida, the storm was projected to turn east and then north heading off the coast, over Bermuda, and then likely lose its potency somewhere far off the coast of the Carolinas. Basically, Catherine had her bitchy eyes on South Florida and mainly South Florida. Residents were definitely aware of the situation but this storm's formation was very sudden. It had been raining for awhile. Usually in South Florida a storm was tracked for days as it slowly crept towards the Caribbean and usually fell apart or altered its course. Ninety percent of the time hurricanes were anti-climactic. This little bitch was different. Hurricane warnings were already issued for all of South Florida and the Northern Keys, with Hurricane watches across the Gulf Coast. Residents of the beaches were under mandatory evacuation and state toll roads were suspended. Schools and colleges announced closings for the following day. The financial and business sectors of the community announced closings. Basically all of South Florida would be closed. A hurricane in South Florida was very much like a snow day for Northerners. Ninety percent of people take snow storms and Nor'easters as serious and dangerous occurrences likely to have effects for days, maybe weeks to come, the other ten choose to embrace the storm and go play in it.

Most residents scurried from the supermarket to the Home Depot to the hardware store, programmed to find the necessities for their checklist. Remember Andrew in '92' and the '05' orgy of a Hurricane season that produced a three-some between Dennis, Katrina and Wilma.

Power outages seemed inevitable. Cell phone towers could fall. There'd be no internet or Wi-Fi. The food could go bad. Lines at gas stations were around the block with the very real possibility of the area running out of fuel. People filled their cars and whatever containers. ATMs ran out of money. Whole aisles of supermarkets laid barren, stripped of water by the truckloads, and canned food. It became impossible to find a flashlight. Batteries suddenly seemed more valuable than gold. Families panicked. Are all the bases covered? What about the first aid kit? Is it adequately stocked with sterile gloves and dressings, antibiotic towels and ointments, bandages, aspirins and other non-prescription drugs? What about prescription drugs? Is everybody covered? What about scissors? Scissors? Do you have scissors? Tweezers? Eye wash? Check. Can opener? Check. Wrench to turn off utilities? Check. Whistle? Wait, a whistle? Yes, do we have a whistle? Are we refereeing a game? No sarcasm, McDougal. Sorry, hun. Antibiotics, check. Fire extinguisher, check. Pet food, check. Sleeping bags, check. Are the insurance documents in order, flood insurance? Check. Electric generator? Maybe next year, hun. What? But the Jackson's next door have one? Well, the Jackson's next door don't have a seven year-old girl and a two year-old boy, now do they? Speaking of which, do we have enough baby formula? Check. What about games to keep them busy? Board games, coloring books, crayons, playing cards? Check, check, check. We need bleach and a medicine dropper in case we have to dilute our water. Great idea, McDougal. We need to do our laundry as well. Again, great idea. And you need to border up the windows! Plywood, check. Hammer and nails, check. Drill, even better. Duct tape? Of course we have duct tape. Everyone has duct tape. Matches and candles, check. Paper supplies, plates, cups, utensils? They were all out at the supermarket and pharmacy. Damn it, McDougal! Prepare for the worst.

While the rest of South Florida scrambled like runny eggs, Alex, in a whim, decided he would host a Hurricane Party. His lackadaisical attitude was somewhat surprising to Jimena, whose own family took Hurricane preparations a lot more serious. Alex assured Jimena that their building was hurricane proof. They wouldn't lose power. They had emergency generators, a perk that came with a maintenance bill hovering around eight hundred dollars a month. They needed to bring all the furniture and foliage from the balcony indoors and that's it.

"Yeah," said Jimena, "but what about supplies?"

"Like what?"

"Fucking food, water, shit like that."

"Babe, people are overreacting. There will be restaurants open selling food and water. Our building will not lose power because of the generators. Our windows are at an angle where the wind shear cannot shatter the glass nor can debris take out our windows. We're good."

"But what about your business? It's on ground level."

"This is not the end of the world, babe. A storm is perfectly natural, especially this time of year. Our college football team is called the Miami Hurricanes. We can handle this. It won't be that bad, trust me. Everyone's off of work with nothing to do, let's have a hurricane party and fuck and dance. Nine months later they'll be babies named Catherine in Jackson Memorial."

So instead of boarding the windows of his business, like most of his neighbors, Alex busied himself with accumulating large amounts of beer, wine and cigarettes, while also taking to social media to promote his party. The following Facebook invite blasted to the 8,667 people who "liked" his page: HURRICANE PARTY AT MECKE'S IN FULL EFFECT. Come out and celebrate nature's wrath with friends and family. Kill your television and dance! We will party till the lights go out and then party more with candles. Join us for the following drink specials:

Catherine the Terrible
12 cans of Narragansett and a bottle of Merlot. $49

The Cone of Uncertainty
6 Magic Hat # 9's, 6 Cigar City Jai-lai IPAs and a bottle of Beaujolais and two packs of American Spirits. $89

Low-Pressure System
6 cans of Narragansett, 6 PBR's, a pack of American Spirits. $39

The Dissipation
12 Magic Hats, 12 PBR's and two bottles of champagne. $99

The Storm Surge
12 Magic Hats and a pair of American Spirits. $49.

Plus our regular selection of beers, wines and nibbles.
Stretch your outer bands. Come dance! See you tonight!!

Chapter 17—

Hurricane Catherine made landfall in South Florida at approximately 7:30 pm. as a Hurricane 2 storm carrying winds of 100 miles per hour, with gusts clocked at 120mph. Imagine being plummeted by a series of fastballs thrown by some of baseball's strongest pitchers: Nolan Ryan, Randy Johnson, Roger Clemons, Goose Gossage, Stephan Strasburg, Justine Verlander, Bob Feller. Imagine their fastballs were everywhere and expansive like a wide cloud. These fastballs were not little tiny stitched balls but wind like the breath of God with wide dark cloud. Imagine the cloud threw water with the same amount of speed in a counter-clockwise direction. Imagine being pounded by these fastballs for a few hours, off and on, and then on again, but with a slowly deteriorating speed, proceeded by more rain, and then a resurrection of fastball. Every object in South Florida faced these continual fastballs for five hellish hours. What a horrible day to be a tree. The tall ones most vulnerable—Gumbo Limbo, Southern Magnolia, Sand Pine, Sycamore, Laurel and Live Oak. How many limbs lost? How many roots uplifted through the cement and city streets? And what of the palms, the poor palms, whose fronds were stripped with ease, landing everywhere. Mr. Royal. Mr. Sabal, Mrs. Thatch. Mr. Loblolly Palm. How many friends did you lose? Some bent, others broke. Poor foliage, fruit, herbs and spices.

Sharks, marlin and most large breeds of fish felt the pressure change and instinctively swam away from the trouble. Dolphins were too smart to get stuck in shallow waters or beached. Iguanas and other ground animals burrowed in their secret hiding places, little coral caves that have survived the Florida landscape for thousands of years. Most of the birds and parakeets had the instinct to migrate. Some pelicans and seagulls were blown half way to Alabama. They'll find their way home to an environment with less trees to nest in and berries to munch on.

The city could not force residents to evacuate, unless the state or city declared martial law, which hardly happened in America's history, and never during a hurricane, the great Chicago Fire the closest thing to a natural disaster to warrant such circumstances. Floridians were seldom rattled in the face of a hurricane. There have been so many instances when the storm just misses them, or dissipates, or changes directions at the very last moment. After years of hurricane desensitization, the logical reaction for a few was not to take to the highways and migrate under pressure, like the birds and sea animals, but the alternative, stay put.

Alex's establishment Mecke's was the only bar open in Wynwood. Other bars operated throughout the city and beaches, but only one in the art district. In fact, Wynwood looked eerily abandoned. All of the galleries were boarded up with thick plywood. The retail and coffee shop also boarded with plywood. The restaurants boarded with plywood and stacked sandbags. Most of the businesses in the neighborhood prepared the right way, with plywood and sandbags.

Alex did not. If up to Jimena, they would've hopped in a car, raced up the Florida Turnpike to Interstate 4, then west, forecasted to miss most of Catherine. If up to Jimena, they would've grabbed a hotel in Ybor City and played around with the buccaneers of Tampa Bay.

***

The party started off decent. They had more than enough beer and wine. They stocked up on board games, adding more to a collection they already had which now included Connect Four, Trivial Pursuit, Jenga, Chess, Checkers, Scrabble, Clue, Life, Battleship, Pictionary and Taboo. In the early evening, before night fell, while the storm came and hit in rough and tumble outer bands, more than a handful of curiosity seekers ventured through the neighborhood and doors.

Alex had two bartenders working, Jordy and Liz, and his security guard, Jerome. Expectations were not super high, but by the time night fell he began to realize the "party" idea wasn't the brightest. The storm roared, whistling every time the doors opened. Debris spiraled around the landscape, mainly palm fronds and branches, but also junk, garbage wrappers, twigs and leaves. You didn't want to stand outside for too long. The wind shook people sideways attacking eardrums with a deafening reminder that nature was not humanities bitch, but definitely the other way around. At times, street signs vibrated so violently they seemed inevitable to fall. It was more than harrowing.

The twenty or so patrons dedicated to riding out the storm inside Mecke's were still in positive and playful spirits, in awe of the storm but also committed to drinking, laughing it up, and occasionally venturing outside for an entertaining kamikaze type of thrill experience.

A deejay played music but not for too long. The power went out in Wynwood around 9:30p.m. They tried to stay positive and quickly lit candles and gas lamps to keep the place adequately lit. To ward off the ominous sounds of the storm, Alex always planned on providing live music. He hired a jazz band, drums, a stand-up bass and brass. And for about fifteen minutes the vibe in Mecke's felt pretty damn special. Beer and wine were flowing over the mellow continuity of brass and light drums and unplugged stand-up-bass, all in conjunction with soft ember lighting from the candlelight bouncing off the walls. They had a groove and for awhile Catherine seemed to approve, almost accompanying the musicians in a howling duet that could be described as abstract acid jazz or freestyle squealing be-bop or something avant-garde. But this storm was no member of a band. She clearly controlled the scene and illustrated authority with a stroke of her maestro's baton by propelling a flying piece of metal debris through the front window of Mecke's, shattering the glass in several different directions, luckily hurting no one.

It was a metal mailbox torn off the door of a neighboring gallery. Catherine took a rocker-step back, made a small turn to pivot, then lifted her high winds into a balanced position and delivered the metal mailbox at 100 mph with a full wind-up and no runners on base.

A collective gasp and yell of legitimate fear filled the room at Mecke's and even that sound collapsed as the howling winds now freely entered the small little bar in Wynwood. It happened fast, within a couple of seconds. All the candles on the table extinguished. And the winds blew the board games and menus on the ground. Rain entered through the front window that was broken, and everyone, including the security guard by the front door, made their way towards the back of the bar, away from the window, swirling glass and incoming water. The light was limited to a few gas lamps and two powerful Ironton LED flashlights Alex owned. Outside the streets were ominous and dark but not pitch black so as not to see. Telephone wires were ripped from poles and dangled in a few separate areas within eyesight of the venue.

"We need to get out of here," Alex said, turning his flashlight on. He issued his other flashlight, which could easily be a weapon, to his bouncer. "We need to get out of here now."

"Do you have a generator?" asked Jordy.

"No," said Alex, trying to remain calm. "We have nothing. We have a broken fucking window and a few hours of storm left. Gather your belongings, get to your car and go home." Alex moved to the front of the room and yelled over the storm. "We're going to put down the outside shutters so no more glass breaks, but I don't think this place is safe to ride the storm out."

"You heard the man," yelled the security guard, using his flashlight to point towards the front door. Evacuating the patrons happened very quickly. The musicians needed a little longer.

"Don't worry about tabs," said Alex. "Let's just get home safe."

"Watch out for fallen telephone wires," yelled Jimena.

Within three minutes the only people left in Mecke's were Alex, his workers and Jimena. Alex and his security guard quickly took to task the closing of the aluminum shutters to the front of the establishment, essentially locking everyone inside, with the back door their only exit.

The winds could be heard outside like a swarm of bees or wasps, omnipresent and angry. Sometimes they sounded loud only to retreat and then return with a wicked and scary vengeance.

Something fell onto the roof and resounded with a loud thud.

Also, water was entering through the front part of the building.

"Fuck this shit," said the security guard, Jerome.

"Seriously, what are we going to do?" asked Jimena. Whatever fell onto the roof did damage. Leaks began to drip from the ceiling.

"We need to go home," said Alex. "Fuck, I'm such an idiot." Alex rented this building, he did not own it. He honestly did not know exactly how up to standards and codes the owner kept the building. For the rent he paid, considering his location, it wouldn't be surprising if the building wasn't equipped to handle the storm that fell upon them.

"Does everyone have a way to get home?"

"We came together," said Liz.

"I need a ride," said Jerome.

"We'll take you," said Jordy.

"Let's just get the fuck out of here," said Alex.

"The back door?" asked Jerome.

"Run for it. I'll lock up," said Alex.

Alex opened the back door and his three friends and employees dashed out of the business right into the whipping and howling wind and the rain of the storm. Catherine wasn't at her harshest and they made it out fine. Before Alex closed the back door, he noticed damage to the wooden deck he recently built in the outside courtyard. The roof he hired some locals to build a few months ago partially fell onto the floor. Was it his fault for hiring illegals practically off the street rather than using consummate professionals? Or would it have mattered? Whatever the case, he now had a serious feeling that they were in trouble.

"Babe, we need to go."

"Oh, Jimena."

"It's okay."

"No, it's not."

"It's just stuff, babe."

"No, it's more."

"We need to go."

Alex and Jimena stood in the middle of the room. They both held flashlights. She shined hers on him, while he looked around the place trying to figure out what they could do. Mecke's had a warehouse style air-conditioner with highly efficient industrial HVAC equipment. What if the roof fell in on it? He had no insurance for any of the things he installed. What about the art on the walls? He had a decent and respectable collection of contemporary art from locals, some of which he bought, others were gifted. Was he supposed to leave it on the walls and hope for the best? What about the two computers in the back office? He didn't have any data related to the business backed up. What about the books and the magazines he sold in the front of the store? Some of them were already blown over by the winds and ruined in a growing pool of water that filtered through cracks he didn't even know existed. A lot of those periodicals were expensive collectible art magazines, or exclusive editions of reputable and hard to find 'zines and books. What about all the food and beer in the back cooler? What about the chairs and tables?

"Babe, we need to get the fuck out of here."

"I can't leave."

"Do you fucking hear this shit? It sounds like the roof is going to fall, not to mention the hell that is raging outside. Not to mention there's nobody in the hood. We're alone. Let's go." Alex just stood in the middle of the room. "I'm going to hit you with this flashlight, Alex." Jimena grabbed his hand and tugged him towards the back. She opened the door and ventured outside into the vicious howling storm. He followed her, locking the entrance with an empty, hollow feeling in his gut that locking the door wouldn't really matter. They ran around to the front of the building, heading towards his car. Catherine howled in surround sound. The rain fell on them in blinding sheets. The street signs that were still standing shook violently. "Let's go, baby," yelled Jimena. "Let's go."

Alex couldn't hear her but they made it to the car. He unlocked the passenger side door and ran around to the driver's side. Once in the car they booked towards the condo. Not many trees in the warehouse district, but definitely live wires fell down, and a lot of debris. Catherine was a terrible storm whose damage wouldn't be known for a few days.

***

Hurricane Catherine was not the strongest or most intense storm to make landfall in Florida, not even top ten, but she turned out to be the costliest. The President of the United States declared a state of emergency for the state of Florida, thus freeing up FEMA to flex its administrative superhero powers to deal with emergency situations, allowing Congress to set aside federal assistance. The exact figures wouldn't be known for weeks but billions of dollars in property damage incurred; original estimates put the costs ahead of Hurricane Andrew.

Catherine's problem was she decided to pick on a heavily-populated portion of the state, linger only in that area, and then go about her merry way as if nothing happened. The day after the storm one could've tanned on the beach (even though half the beaches eroded) — one could've caught a wicked tan, and enjoyed a calm and refreshing ocean. But, there were bigger fish to fry. For example, a manatee was found swimming along a side street in Brickell. The sea-cow was safely returned to the Bay by the Florida Wildlife Commission. Some parts of town experienced ten inches of rain, causing flood damage to thousands of homes. Tens of thousands of houses, boats, businesses and cars were damaged or destroyed. There were deaths. Trees on cars and people, lost surfers at sea, elderly collapsing under stress, live electrical wires.

The lack of electricity during the peak summer months would be grueling. Alex was right, his apartment never lost power, but by the end of the destruction at the costly hands of Catherine, over 80 percent of Miami-Dade would be without power, some a lot longer than others. Power grids connected to schools and other social service areas, like police and fire stations, were turned on within a couple of days. More affluent neighborhoods were turned on next, with the poorer areas having power returned last. No matter how adamantly Florida Power and Light stood by their statement that there was no bias to returning power, Coral Gables, Key Biscayne, Miami Shores and Doral all had their power on within a week, while Little Haiti, Opa Locka, Allapattah, Overtown and Liberty City had to wait two weeks before their power returned. Everybody in Miami was affected by Catherine and, like most disasters, instead of the city turning on itself, people made the best of the situation and relied on each other for comfort. Alex's business was no more. Mecke's was damaged beyond repair. In a matter of hours, wind, water and poor architecture ruined his business. The wooden roof collapsed entirely on the inside and what once represented his pride and joy now turned into a huge pile of debris. There appeared very little to salvage. Obviously his spirits would need a lot of spirits for salvaging.

***

The day after the storm, Jimena and Alex surveyed the damage.

"Motherfucker," said Alex.

"Holy shit," said Jimena. "I'm not sure about this, babe."

They'd brought thick carpenter's gloves, prepared to dig through the rubble. "You might be right."

"Nothing's recognizable."

"All I have is junk."

"You have me," said Jimena. "And Miami will support you."

Alex looked at Jimena.

His eyes watered but he managed a smile.

"This isn't safe. Look around, Mecke's received the worst of the storm and now everything needs to go. This is a threat to public health and safety. I already spoke to the landlord. He said it's my call. Either we can dig through the rubbage and debris, or he'll arrange for the bulldozers to come." Alex walked over to the pile of his dreams, now splintered and demolished. He took a few steps as if to try and climb his mountain of dismay. The rubble was too jagged and coagulated to maneuver. "The choice is obvious." He bent down and picked up a picture. The frame was cracked and the picture inside a little wrinkled but not destroyed. It was a picture of a character from a movie, the Butcher from *The Gangs of New York*—Daniel Day Lewis sported a moustache in that movie that Alex felt represented the spirit of his business. If not for the thick carpenter gloves he would have cut himself saving the one relic he rescued. Part of Jimena wanted to say *I told you so* but she knew that would've been the worst thing in the world to say at the worst possible time. But Alex could handle such a criticism.

"I told you so, babe."

"You did."

"We should've dipped."

"It happened so fast."

"Come down from there."

"What do we do now?"

"What do you want to do?"

"Get drunk."

"Babe," Jimena reached out her hand and helped Alex walk away from the pile of dangerous debris. He held onto the picture of the actor from the movie. "You're not alone. Remember that. You. Are. Not. Alone. I was doing research the day before the storm, when we still had the internet. I read that forty percent of businesses that experience a disaster never re-open, and another twenty-five percent close down within two years. It's called hazard mitigation. I thought we'd have a chance because we're not that close to the water, and this isn't a flood zone, but we got fucked. And now it's up to you to decide what's next. But you're not alone. The whole city's fucked. Old and poor people have to live without air conditioning or a refrigerator for who knows how long. It's whatevs, babe. What do you always say? 'Under the great strains of stress character is revealed.' Make a move, babe, it's on you."

"I will rebuild, start from scratch."

Alex had small narrow eyes, stretched to the side by wide lacrimals, but his pupils were like a perfect black marble ball and the same with his iris, like a perfect brown marble ball. His eyes could roll on and on. They had life and rhythm and a pulse. His sclera looked knuckle bearing white and alive. Alex's eyes usually had a light to them, a glowing pulse—they were like high beams on a dark country road, providing guidance and direction; the road wasn't always smooth and it curved and had its bumps and detours, but at least one could see on it.

"I'll help you—"

"Mark my words."

"I'll work full-time, help around the house."

"This place will re-open."

"You can move to a different neighborhood, like Downtown—"

"No way. I'm not leaving Wynwood. Everyone else is already moving Downtown, but not me. No way. We'll find another spot here and start from scratch," he said, pointing at the debris. "From all this shit, garbage and trash, we'll rise. We'll call the new place The Phoenix."

"That's the attitude."

People from the area approached the site where they stood. Alex knew a few of them, some neighbors, scenesters. The whole city had a story to tell, three and a half million stories in this collection; some short stories, others longer, some poems and odes, maybe a few novels; three and a half million ways to look at loss, suffering and redemption. Alex and Jimena's story would unfold according to their own convictions and will power, in combination with a community more open than it appeared from the outside. Their story might turn out just fine.

***

Over the next three months, a perfect storm of positive circumstances transpired and disaster turned into opportunity, as it often does. While Alex exhaustively researched the real estate market in Wynwood looking for a space to re-open, he was awarded a $250,000 grant from the King Society, the city's largest philanthropic organization. The King Society poured tens of millions of dollars into Miami and represented one of the biggest reasons for Miami's cultural renaissance. Most of their grants are issued as "matching" funds meaning the recipient needed to raise an equal amount on their own. For example, if the indie film theater operating in Wynwood was awarded a $100,000 grant to build a second viewing room, to receive the money they had to raise or produce $100,000 as well. The King Society funded specific ideas from organizations or individuals with matching grants. But, the coffers of the King Society ran deep, with over two billion dollars in the kitty, and every once and awhile, they offered grants that did not require matching. In other words, they could do whatever they wanted with their money. And they wanted to help out Alex. The King Society was a foundation started by Lawrence and Brett King, two brothers from Ohio who moved to Miami in the early part of the twentieth century and opened a highly successful construction company. They were once the biggest and most influential builders in the history of Miami and towards the end of their lives they decided to create a philanthropic foundation with most of their life's savings. The main goal of the King Society was simple: foster the growth and development of Miami through education, art and community engagement. Alex, who knew the vice president of the King Society, received a phone call shortly after the hurricane and was told by the same gentleman that he would receive the grant, if he wanted it, and that it would not require a match. Basically, about one week after he lost his business, he was given two hundred and fifty thousand dollars to re-open, with no strings attached. The King Society was very interested in Wynwood for its artistic appeal and they decided to invest in Alex when they realized what happened to his business. Like most philanthropic organizations, the King Society had a board that convened to decide who received what, and after the storm, they felt it imperative to the community to help out as quickly as possible. Alex was not a stranger to the King Society, having once received a $25,000 matching grant for an idea of creating a monthly seminar, featuring a mix of Miami artists, as well as guests from out of town, lecturing on process and craft in a variety of artistic disciplines. The series was well-received and promoted in the press and the board members of the King Society were happy with it. Alex was one of four recipients of the $250,000 rebuilding grants, but he was the only individual. The other recipients were established organizations, like the museum downtown that sustained some structural damage at the hands of the storm, or the theater in Coral Gables that lost its roof. In addition to the King Society grant, Jimena rigorously maneuvered her way through FEMA's complicated website and applications and managed to secure Alex a $40,000 rebate under the FEMA Public Assistance program. Because they removed the debris and rubble of Mecke's so fast, they were entitled to the assistance. FEMA issues rebates to business owners who clear their own debris in a timely and safe manner.

With basically all the money he needed to open, manage and sustain a business, he turned his attention to finding a bigger location for a decent price. Speculators in the neighborhood were open to lowering their leasing prices after the storm, but Wynwood was still overvalued. He only paid ten dollars a square-foot for his old venue and prices like that just didn't exist anymore. However, because he belonged to the neighborhood's Association, he was able to convince one of the bigger real estate visionaries of the area to rent him a prime property one block in from the main strip of Wynwood. The property belonged to a failed restaurant the real estate mogul owned, but closed down due to poor business and logistical stresses for the owner. Alex negotiated a deal for the same price per square-foot he paid at Mecke's. In addition, the property would come with a liquor license from the restaurant, meaning he didn't have to pay the $115,000 origination fee. It was absolutely a game changer. Furthermore, the land was three times the size of Mecke's and designed in a manner so that Alex could create different rooms on and inside the venue. As soon as the ink dried on the lease, Alex began remodeling the new space. Jimena helped him onsite every day. There was a lot of planning to execute. Inside, would be a fully stocked bar with cold air conditioning, two high-definition televisions, a bunch of booths to sit in, dark lighting, a popcorn machine, a jukebox, photo booth, and an elevated deejay area. A typical modern hipster bar, not unlike The Timber or The Spot, but bigger and better and more cultural, with bartenders dressed to the hilt, and a mixture of creative and specialty cocktails with funny or ironic names. Behind the front bar they would build a room for musical, dramatic, artistic or literary performances. It would be simple in design, contain a small mini-bar, and serve as both a theater of sorts, with no seats, as well as a dance hall, for late at night. They could bring in fold-up chairs if necessary. The room would have a variety of lighting options and excellent sound. Both of these rooms would have access to a large outdoor well-lit courtyard, where they would throw a bunch of wooden benches and create a barbecue to feed people. There would also be an area to project films. And he wanted Jacuzzis—two of them with hot water, two of them with cold water. Building The Phoenix in Wynwood was fun and engaging for Alex and more-so for Jimena, who was seeing a different side of her city and meeting tons of new people. Alex insisted that he would only use local artists and small business craftsmen to build the new venue, and Jimena was in charge of hiring and coordinating the designers, carpenters, painters and plumbers, all of whom she would research and then seek Alex's final approval. Jimena also studied mixology online and created the recipes, basically stealing concoctions from the hundreds of online bars she perused. It was pretty easy. She Googled: "Best bars in America," found an article that listed 100 of them, and studied their menus. They hired two local poets to create the names of their specialty drinks. Alex made sure to hire people he knew, or friends of family of people he knew. So, in addition to Jimena's suggestions and research, he constantly posted on Twitter or Facebook, updates like: Anyone know of a good plumber? Anyone know of a good carpenter? Anyone recommend a local sound engineer? Anyone know someone who sells Jacuzzis? He felt very lucky and wanted to pay it forward by rewarding friends and family and the community. He also knew it made him look noble, kind and caring—and that would be good for business. They commissioned a local sculptor to build the main bar, which he wanted constructed from coral. Furthermore, they found local filmmakers and documentarians and asked them to design the booths in the front bar room with advertisements and swag from their films. It gave the room a local feel and promoted the work of the filmmakers and it created more buzz. Of course, they commissioned the best local street artists to paint murals inside and outside the venue. The place looked like Wynwood.

Jimena learned about her city's politics. For example, she learned Miami has two levels of government, with two different sets of commissioners. There's Miami-Dade County, with thirteen districts, and a mayor, and then there's the City of Miami, which is just one municipality, but the biggest one by far within Dade County. The County is the more powerful of the two, and is a larger form of government, dealing with huge monstrosities like the airport and the Port of Miami, not to mention the clusterfuck of Miami-Dade Transit and managing emergencies like hurricanes or terrorist attacks. She learned the difference between County and City. The City of Miami only has five districts and commissioners. And they're only concerned with the incorporated city of Miami. The City of Miami manages its own police and fire departments, and they also have a hand in sanitation and emergency services, but the emphasis is more about community engagement and development. They create and enforce city codes and ordinances, like how late a bar can stay open. They also preserve buildings, designating them historical or not. They fix pot holes and infrastructure. The Film Office is run by the City which determines what movies, tv or commercials are produced in the area. Plus they manage the Parks and Recreation department. She learned a lot building the bar.

And the Phoenix in Wynwood was built by Miami, for Miami, in Miami, and they felt pride. They knew including the city in the endeavor was a recipe for success. They planned to open by the Second Saturday Art Walk in October, three months after Hurricane Catherine, and plenty of time before the chaos of Art Basel week in December.

Everything was going fine until Jimena tried to kill herself.

Chapter 18—

Alex walked into the bedroom to see Jimena sprawled across the bed. He was extremely tired, not only from the events of the last week, undoubtedly one of the most stressful he experienced, but also from managing the logistics of the pending opening of The Phoenix. He didn't want to leave Jimena alone, but there were big issues with the keg lines and he was needed onsite until late. Alex didn't even take his shoes off before crawling into bed next to her. "How's my baby doing?" he asked.

She didn't say anything.

"It's okay, sleep, my love. I'll be in soon."

Alex leaned up to slowly undress. Maybe he'd grab a beer and watch Sportscenter or a rerun of the Dolphins game out in the living room. And then he noticed the bottle of vodka on the nightstand. It wasn't there earlier, nor was the envelope underneath the bottle, serving as a coaster. Judging by the half-empty remains of the bottle, he assumed Jimena drank herself to sleep, again, and who could blame her, in fact, he'd been joining her all week. In fact, he grabbed the bottle and took a quick swig when the envelope again caught his attention. It had his name on it with Jimena's handwriting. He really had no idea. It didn't dawn on him. Not until a few sentences into the two-page handwritten letter. At first he thought it was just an innocent note.

My Dearest Alex—

You must know that I love you. You must know that you are the greatest thing that has ever happened to me. For the first time in my life, you have delivered me true bliss. You must know that what I've done has nothing to do with you. And I beg of you... if you truly love me, please forgive me for what I've done. There are dark things inside me I cannot explain...

He stopped reading the note and put the pages back on the dresser. Running around to the other side of the California King, he sat down on the edge and slowly nudged Jimena. "Babe, wake up, wake up, hey, what is this," he started to talk a little louder, "baby, babe, wake up, come on, stop fucking around, wake up." She didn't budge an inch. Then he noticed the pill bottle on the nightstand—his prescription klonopins. The bottle was turned over and little blue pills littered the table like candy. "Fuck baby, what did you do? What did you do?" Alex shook her like a cocktail sifter but she didn't stir. He put his hand on Jimena's heart and wasn't sure if he could hear a beat. Alex was not a physician. "Baby," he yelled, "what'd you do?" He put his ear to her mouth to hear her breathing, but he couldn't tell. She smelled like vodka and vomit. "Fuck. Babe, baby, come on, no, no," he shook her hard and nothing, "no, wake up, what did you do? Oh fuck, oh fuck." His mind blazed like a three alarm fire as he scrambled for his cell phone.

He dialed 9-1-1 but didn't call.

"This can't be. She's just sleeping."

Of course I knew that it would happen, mami was sick for a very long time, and I knew that he might not be able to take it, that he might go off the deep end, but, but this is too much loss at once. I'm just like him, after all. One of the hardest truths to learn in life is that you are similar to the people who drive you crazy, who you run from. Fuck this shit! Fuck all of this shit.

"9-1-1, what's the emergency?"

"Yes, please, send someone quick," Alex stuttered. "My girlfriend overdosed."

"Is she breathing?"

"I don't know," he looked at Jimena. "Maybe."

"Are there drugs nearby her?"

"There's a fucking suicide note—"

"Sir, please, calm down."

"I'm sorry. There's vodka and sleeping pills and this note. Please, send someone. I live in a condo and it will take time just to get her out of here. Please, please, for the love of—"

"Okay, sir. Calm down."

"I am fucking calm."

"What is your address?"

I blame my mother for a lot, but I loved her. I may have run, fuck, I couldn't even talk to her for more than ten minutes without wanting to run. You stole my childhood, mami, swiped it like a FUCKING burglar and no one can get it back. She always said: you can't serve two Gods. But there is no god! And, you know what, mami? I never ran too far and I could always be found.

The paramedics were on the way. Miami's responders operated fast, but they still had to travel to the penthouse. If the elevator made no stops, it could still take six or seven minutes to ascend from the moment they arrived on the scene. Alex had about fifteen to twenty minutes before there would be a knock on the door. He called the concierge to inform them. Then, in a pitiful attempt to find out how many pills she may have eaten, he fell on his knees, with his unconscious girlfriend a few feet away, and began to count and collect little blue pills.

A lot were missing. He didn't know the exact number of klonopins that remained in his prescription, but he could only account for twelve one milligram pills, and he definitely possessed more. If forced to give a number, he would guess that she ate fifteen to twenty pills. That's not a lot for a junkie. He knew people who could handle double that amount, but not a hundred pound girl with a very low tolerance for prescription pills. One half of a Xanax would knock Jimena into a coma, plus the vodka. "What did you do baby? What did you do?"

The seconds stretched and bended like yoga poses, without any benefits. At one point he ran into the living room to use the house computer to Google phrases like "overdose procedure" and "what to do drug overdose." Web MD told him to call 911 and begin CPR. He didn't know CPR so before Googling "how to do CPR" he double checked to see if there was another method, like smelling salts or something, not that he had any. The National Library of Health website, the official .gov health site, proved convoluted and ultimately provided the same advice. At least the research allowed seconds to fall into minutes. Studying the illustrated CPR instructions proved moot. They made him nervous. This was a guy who hated needles. He almost passed out at the sight of blood, needed a klonopin to give blood. Alex would wait for the professionals. After a few moments, he felt guilty leaving Jimena alone in the bedroom.

I feel so alone. I don't want to leave but the pain is eating me up. Like invisible baby maggots corroding my heart. I'm crumbling into all these pieces, inside-out, like a 1,000 piece of jigsaw, but nothing fits; all my corners and edges are warped. There's nothing left of me. You can't understand. I'm not alone but it feels so much worse than loneliness. I know things like this happen every day, in wars, natural disasters, tragedies. My friend Lucille lost both of her parents in a car accident and she survived. Maybe that's just it. I'm not a survivor.

It happened fast. Two paramedics arrived at the door, a young girl fresh out of Miami-Dade's school of medicine, and a guy a little older than her. Both were Spanish and acted professionally. They left the gurney in the hallway and approached Jimena in the bedroom. They asked Alex what happened, although the scene was fairly self-explanatory, plus they were informed by dispatch of a possible drug overdose. As with any overdoes, the first step was an assessment of the patients ABCs: Airway status, Breathing, and Circulation. The girl took Jimena's pulse and announced she was alive, but unconscious and unable for resuscitation. They would follow the standard orders and protocols for someone in an altered mental state or coma.

They moved the gurney into Alex's apartment and within three minutes of their arrival they already had Jimena on a bed and out the door, equipped with oxygen from a non-rebreather mask. They wheeled her across the marble floors, passed the curious and nosey whispers of neighbors. Soon they descended in the service elevator, held open by one of the security guards to make sure they wouldn't have to wait for an elevator to arrive. The security guard also had a key to assure their trip would be an express non-stop elevator descent. As the doors closed, the elevator cryptically announced they were "going down." "Will she be all right?" Alex must have asked the question to the paramedics ten times since they arrived. "Tell me she'll be all right."

"Seen worse," said the male paramedic, "but it's not good."

Alex followed suit as the EMS pushed an unconscious Jimena through the front lobby, filled with a handful of locals and tourists. Outside people milled as they lifted her into an ambulance. Alex was left standing outside helplessly. They didn't allow him to ride with her. They explained that only parents of young children were allowed to ride in the ambulance. All he could do was head to the hospital. They were taking her to Jackson Memorial. As the ambulance rolled into the night in a colorful and loud collage, Alex realized his keys were upstairs.

Back in the apartment, he poured two shots of Jamison and prepared to head to the hospital, after filling up a flask with whisky. His heartbeat skipped and he was sweating. In the bedroom he grabbed his cellphone charger and the klonopins. Again he saw Jimena's note.

I have a confession. Deep down I think I wanted them dead. I loved them, sure, yeah, I loved them both, but so what? You know how many times I ran away. She was too much. And he was so vacant. I've told you about my father—what happened to him in Cuba. You don't come back. It was just a matter of time. I never told you, but, he's tried before. This time he wasn't taking any chances. I always knew it'd be a gun, just like he lost those closest to him.

Jimena lay unconscious in the ambulance, a ride she wouldn't remember. She needed ER assistance, if she wanted to overcome her own mortality. She wouldn't recall the paramedics applying the Ringer's solution intravenously, a cocktail of calcium, chlorides and sodium She'd have no memory of the cardiac monitor, tests for glucose, no feeling of the liquid Flumazenil, designed to reverse the effects of benzodiazepines, no realization of the night she zipped through the dark and empty streets of Miami arriving at Jackson in ten minutes.

I'm doing something selfish. But I care about you. You changed my life in so little time. I'm grateful for what you've shown me and look at how I repay this debt. I know you are strong. You will be fine. You don't want a selfish bitch like me anyway. My love is totally fucking crazy.

If Jimena assessed her own chart, according to ICD-9 standards, she'd code herself a 969.4, poisoning by benzodiazepine-based tranquilizers—and then throw in a 977.3 for poisoning by alcohol deterrents, and possibly, depending on the outcome of the night, an E950 suicide and self-inflicted poisoning by solid or liquid substance, with an E950.3 to indicate the tranquilizers (Jimena was very thorough when it came to work). At the hospital, they had to decide what to do with Jimena. One of the main problems was the Flumazenil. Imagine a drug that was designed to take away the feeling of the drug that was designed to make you feel mellow. Flumazenil was the devil's ass mixed with pure Nazi venom. Filled with so much rage, it's most common side effect was stroke. The attending physician at the ER didn't like Flumazenil and wanted to treat her differently. Inducing her to vomit would prove impossible because she was unconscious. She could easily choke on her vomit and asphyxiate. Gastric leverage would be the first step and best option. To pump her stomach they inserted a flexible tube down her throat and sucked up what they could. They washed her out with a solution of saline. There wasn't much in Jimena's stomach, so they had to ride out the storm with a variety of other options, including activating charcoal to absorb what they could; they induced urination and defecation, just whatever it took to get the horrible toxic agents out of little Jimena. She arrived in critical condition but in a few hours they had her more stable. With a steady IV flushing the drugs out of her body, and a Hemodialysis to wash her blood, she'd survive this.

Jimena would avoid a dreaded E950 on her medical chart. Who wants to end their chart with an E950? Jimena, apparently, but that would not be her fate. When finally regaining consciousness the next morning, Jimena was still in Jackson Memorial, but she had been transferred upstairs to the psych ward, where she was "Baker Acted" by a forever elated and grateful Alex Lane. He had a friend whose father was a psychiatrist and with one phone call the admission paperwork was approved. Jimena needed to talk to some professionals, he decided, and she ultimately would agree. The mental care would be free and come equipped with twenty-four hour care. Alex would have to wait at least the mandated three days before he could see her.

I'm broken and selfish. And I can't fix me.
You can't fix me,
But I just ask for one thing: forgive me.

Chapter 19—

It was an early November afternoon, brisk for the season and partly cloudy. The sun had its moments and the high clouds looked like an endless river of cotton balls in the expansive sky.

"We don't have to talk about it, babes," said Jackie, lighting a Camel Light. They were outside The Barnacle in The Grove, sipping Coronas at a table during Happy Hour.

"It's okay, Jacks," said Jimena, smiling. "I want to."

"I can't believe Alex did that to you. If my boyfriend, or anyone for that matter, institutionalized my cray ass they'd have a big ass whooping waiting for them when I got home."

"No, I disagree. He's smart. I needed help."

"How long were you in there?"

"Six days."

"Is that a long time?"

"Kinda. By law, you have to stay seventy-two hours, but a lot of people stay longer."

"So, was it like totally *One Flew over the Cuckoo's Nest*?"

Jimena laughed and sipped her Corona. She'd been released for two weeks and decided that going forward the only drug she would consume would be alcohol. No cocaine. No pills. No molly in the butt. At least for a while, if ever, although, she did believe one should never say never. And she also felt recreational drugs, if they didn't interfere with work or life, served a purpose in culture. However, to continue to boil, Jimena knew she needed to reduce the heat.

"It was more like *Goodfellas*," she explained, glancing around. "I was Baker Acted, okay, sure, yeah, it sucks, like bonkers, but one of Alex's best friends, his father is the head administrator of the unit so they treated me differently. Because, you know, getting 'Baker Acted' is like a jail filled with crazy people. Most people don't voluntarily enter, some maybe, but, most no. Most are admitted by the courts or a medical professional, like a doc or a shrink or even a cop. And it's like a co-ed jail. Place is populated with all these aggro junkies and criminals and self-admitted weirdos. They strip search you upon entrance to make sure you're not hiding drugs or weapons. They take your clothes. You can't smoke, which is difficult, not for me cause I don't smoke, but all these other sickos were detoxing and you can see them crawling in their skin for a fucking smoke. Then there are dormitories and rec rooms with televisions. You're assigned a roommate. The food tastes terrible, like old bologna and peanut butter, horrible runny eggs, rubbery chicken, shit food like that. But, Dr. Feldman, that's the administrator's name, he brought me food from Trader Joe's, like every day. Jackie? We have one Trader Joe's in Miami now, in South Miami, he happens to live by it."

"Dang girl—"

"I gotta say, getting 'Baker Acted" for me was sorta pimp. Dr. Feldman made sure I had the best counselors and nurses in the unit to talk to. You know, I was in a dark place. Still am."

"So, you were like totally isolated from others?"

"No, not totally," said Jimena. "I mingled. Dr. Feldman encouraged it. They wanted me to see two things. One, I'm not crazy, and two, people have it worse than me. And he was right. I met a bunch of people that were broken. Don't get me wrong, I feel broken too, well, I did at first, and it's only been a few weeks since they've been gone, but the damage, the hole, it's already covering itself with scar tissue, like, you know, I'm regenerating, and I know that I will heal. But some people will never heal. I mean, we all hurt. We are the walking wounded. But some people never come back from their pain. Some stay broken and will remain broken until the day they die, like some of these people I met at the ward. You could just see it in their eyes. Something or someone destroyed these people. Love. Drugs. An abusive childhood. A broken dream. An abandoned parent. These weren't kids. There's a separate wing for juvies. These were broken adults, raped, pillaged and betrayed by life, love and those they respect. Some were just straight-up-crazy, bipolar, schizo. Like the mind is a powerful tool but when turned against itself it transforms into a nuclear weapon of mass self-destruction."

"That's scary."

"Some people can't be fixed, Jacks. Like my dad, for example. My dad died a long time ago. Fucking Fidel Castro took my dad's life forty years before he took his own," said Jimena.

"You're strong."

"I accept death."

"It scares the shit out of me."

"Find a religion," said Jimena.

"Ha," said Jackie, appreciating the sarcasm. "Talk about manipulating minds."

"Psychology is my new religion."

"Do they have a temple?"

"Your mind is the temple."

"I'm just happy you're okay," said Jackie.

"I'll be okay."

"If you ever need anything."

"This might be the bottom."

"Can you see the light?"

"People have it worse than me."

"So you and Alex?"

"I've never known a love like this."

"Is he the one?"

"I'm not leaving."

"Good," said Jackie, lighting another cigarette. "He's good."

"I could forgive him for anything."

"Can he do the same?"

"He's the one who taught me how to forgive."

"Do you want to marry him? Have kids?"

Jimena laughed. "Whoa, whoa, whoa," she wagged her index finger at Jackie. "Slow down, homegirl." She finished her beer and prepared to get them two more from the bar. "We're not very traditional. And we both have a lot more life to live before we ruin it with children."

***

Jimena lay in bed, not depressed, far from happy, but just. She'd been watching a lot of television lately, getting caught up on shows like *Dexter*, *Breaking Bad*, and *The Walking Dead*. She tried *Girls* but couldn't last two episodes but she absolutely loved *Masters of Sex*. Wearing only a thong and a bra, she buried herself under a fortress of sheets and blankets, with three pillows for her head, and one tucked neatly in between her legs. The room remained dark, except for the slight glow from the plasma flat screen. The Xanax they prescribed at the outpatient center kept her at bay, like a small boat tied to a board in the marina. She wouldn't drift off into the rough and tumble seas; on the contrary, she could go for a ride if someone started her engine.

In the meantime, she waited for her captain, who was out running logistics for the bar, which would open soon. The curtains were closed so zero light could enter and Jimena lay on her side with her back to the window. She wasn't sure of the time. Jimena left the bed only for water and to pee. Alex was gone when she woke and he had yet to return. She ate nothing and felt hunger. If she had to guess, it was probably night time, but not that late, maybe ten o'clock. Alex entered the bedroom. She didn't hear the front door open, but she felt happy.

"How's my baby doing?"

"Kay."

"Yeah," he said, kicking his shoes off and crawling onto the bed. He hovered over her, like a mountain, steady and ever present. "Just okay?" He leaned in for a kiss and she puckered.

"I'm okay, babe."

"Good."

"Just getting in?"

"I might have to go back out," he said, kissing her forehead, "but I wanted to see you."

"Awwww," Jimena said, rolling onto her back. "You're sweet."

"Can I lay with you?"

"Of course."

"The bar's looking awesome."

"That's good, babe."

"And you're looking pretty good too."

"Shut up."

"What's this," Alex pushed aside her sheets, "just in your underwear, I see?" he moved his hand down her back, massaging her in the process, settling like a miner claiming a stake on her ass. He squeezed her round, full bottom, like a sponge, and allowed his pinkie to rub along her inner thigh. "Your ass could run for office. People would vote for just your ass. Especially considering your body type. The Ass-tec Treasurer." She laughed and even maintained the smile.

"Trying to start something?"

"What gives you that impression?"

Alex continued to squeeze her cushy but firm ass, a mountain of golden essence, so present on his horizon, challenging to conquer, but absolutely beckoning, even daring him to try. They've been having sex daily since she arrived back from Jackson Memorial, sometimes multiple times a day, as a form of therapy for Jimena, it helped more than anything else. Jimena used Alex, who insisted that he didn't mind, his dick was her dick, available whenever she wanted or needed it. He made it clear that if he came or did not cum, it didn't matter, and sometimes he did cum, but other times he didn't, but Jimena, she always came. Sometimes Alex simply lay on his back, with his eyes occasionally closed. He'd place his warm hands on her skinny ribcage and allow her to gyrate like the director to the rhythms of her own wet loins. Jimena's favorite position was on top, she could drive his stick like NASCAR. It never took her more than a few minutes with Alex. The size and hardness and girth of his cock fit her pussy like a snug glove on a winter's day. Other times, Alex wanted to participate, to finish, and he gently threw her around, took her from behind, or embarked as a missionary, conducting his own journey, a rhapsody of thrusts and rhythms, until he climaxed inside of her safely and securely.

**

The more he squeezed her ass the closer his fingers traversed towards her inner thighs, eventually parting her moist lips Old Testament style. The waters were welcoming and with the lubrication he moved beyond the normal terrain and used one finger to *tap, tap, tap,* her back door. Each *tap, tap, tap,* opened the back door more, crack by crack, tap by tap: who-o- i-s-s it? "Babe," said Alex, "I wanna do it in the butt."

"You do," said Jimena, her panting slowing down. "Why?"

"Because."

"Because why?"

"Because you scared the shit out of me when you did what you did. Of course I understand all the dynamics and I can't say I wouldn't have done the same, but I'm kind of hurt—that shit scared me to death and I'm actually a little mad and if we do this, it'll help me."

"Okay."

"Okay?"

"Yeah, we can do that."

"We can?"

"Anything, my love."

Jimena stood up, sliding her underwear off. She prepared the normal routine. T-shirt over the head, pop off the bra, find the remote control and maneuver the television to the jazz channel 845, (a habit Alex loved which she also found romantic). But this time, Jimena added a new element: lubrication. She kept it in the middle draw of the nightstand, next to her little vibrator.

"You need to guide me," said Alex. This did not represent his first venture into *that unknown*; first time with Jimena, yes, but not ever. Same with her. "I don't want to hurt you."

"Do you want me on top?" she asked.

"From the back."

Jimena applied some lubricant to *that unknown crevice*, and also to his rock. She bent over, sticking her hips into the air. He knew well enough to push the rock towards the edge of *that unknown crevice* and brush upon its precipice. He stalled, waiting for guidance. "Just go real slow, babe." The rock tried to gently tap *that unknown crevice,* like a pebble thrown at a teenager's window, *tap, tap, tap,* is there anyone home? "Stay still. Don't move." No need to knock at the backdoor, it opened enough so the rock could try to enter, but not open enough to pass through, so the rock stood still, wedged into the backdoor. The rock tried to roll forward.

"Slow, slow, go slow."

Very gently the rock wedged the backdoor.

"Is this okay?" the rock asked.

"Yeah," said Jimena, "just go slow."

"Can I move in and out?"

"Slow, babe."

And the rock slid in-and-out the backdoor, a slowed down motion, so, slow, like, never, before, has, a, rock, moved, in, and, out, of, a back, door, so, slow, so, freaking, slow, as so.

"Ouch, ouch, ouch," said Jimena, and the rock stopped.

"Are you okay?" asked the rock.

"Yeah, keep going," said Jimena, muffled. "It's opening."

"You sure?"

"It's good now, baby. I trust you. I'm open."

"Yeah, you like it when I fuck you like this?"

"I like it, baby."

"You like when I go fast?"

"It feels good."

"You've been a bad girl, do you know that?"

"I know. I'm sorry."

"This is what you get when you're a bad girl."

"I'm sorry I've been bad."

"No, you're not, you like it."

At this point the rock could not tell the difference between *that unknown crevice*, and its more traditional home, all motions and cylinders mirrored each other. Maybe this cave looked darker, but its crevices were just as dank and moist and even tighter for a rock to call home.

"Oh," said Jimena. "This feels good."

"You like it when I fuck you in the ass?"

"It's good, baby. Keep doing that with your fingers."

"I like it too, babe."

"Keep doing that."

"I think I might cum soon."

"I'm building too."
"Oh, oooo, I'm going to cum."
"I love you, babe."
"I love you too," said Jimena, sweating and panting.

Chapter 20 —

The most precious time in Miami was the Magic Hour, near dusk, when heaven lets you know. A slight breeze tickled the palm trees. The temperature settled into the glamorous early 80s, flirting with the late 70s — the type of winter day that made you want to move to Florida.

This was *season*.

Miami was in *season* as if a burgeoning international metropolis could be compared to a strawberry. But that's how snowbirds saw Miami, as in *season*, locals who worked in the hospitality industry threw the same phrase around, waiters just waiting for *season*, servers going to save up some money so after *season* they could travel like a gypsy, a *season* for everything. "The hood looks visually busier," said Jimena.

"Yup," said Alex. "It's season." He held her hand.

A man, dilapidated and dirty, a creature of the streets, approached Jimena and Alex near NW 2nd Avenue in Wynwood. They both intuitively knew what question would be asked.

"Excuse me, do you have a dollar?"

"Nope," said Jimena.

"Fifty cents?"

"We don't carry cash," said Jimena. "You take Square?"

"What do you need the dollar for?" Alex asked.

"The bus."

"You're not going to buy flakka?"

"I need it for the bus."

"I'll give you a dollar," said Alex. "The buses in this city are crazy. They don't even come half-the-time. We normally don t give spare change, but today's a special day, buddy."

"Thank you."

"Just use it for the bus."

"I am," said the man, walking away. "Going to buy flakka."

"Oh snap," said Alex. "He got me."

They both laughed and continued walking. It was the second Friday in November and the official opening of The Phoenix of Wynwood, ahead of schedule, an impossible accomplishment in Miami. Alex wanted to launch the night before Art Walk, to create a buzz. If things went well, they'd hit the ground running the next night during Second Saturday's Art Walk, the busiest night of the month for the neighborhood, which would set the stage for Art Basel next month.

He organized a pretty diverse event for opening night. For starters, he bought three cases of champagne and three kegs of Miller Lite, offering free libations until they ran out. That expense cost approximately three hundred dollars and was worth every goddamn penny. He knew people would buy other drinks and it would also attract a crowd, plus he'd look generous in the process. Alex understood that a large contingent of people in Miami liked their music and drinks free so The Phoenix would always have a drink special, a ladies night and never a cover charge. The inaugural party would start at 8pm and go until closing. From the beginning, like a horse running fast out of the starting gate, exhibiting class and speed, going wire-to-wire, opening night at The Phoenix was a triumphant success. For the start of the night, Alex organized events that attracted an early crowd. In the back room, there was an open mic for comedy, hosted by a professional, someone who normally featured at Improvs. Only professional comedians could perform, this wasn't the suburbs where anyone could sign a list and get up on the mic, this was the city where plenty of seasoned comedians wanted to practice their craft, get up, as often as they could, for free, to hone their skills before different types of audiences, in-between paying gigs, and before ultimate pilgrimages to New York and Los Angeles. In the front room, Alex persuaded a drag queen to venture off of South Beach to host bingo and trivia, replete with a drunk spelling bee. Some people loved bingo, trivia, and drunk spelling bees. Alex offered up bar tabs as prizes and sacrificed a bottle of Jaegermeister ($20 cost for him) for the spelling bee. One would find it hard to imagine the popularity of bingo among a young, hip crowd, but the room was packed, same could be said for the comedy room in the back. And the courtyard outside bustled with action. Alex set-up two tournaments, bocce ball and beer pong (he decided to buy a beer pong table for the outside, as well as the Jacuzzis). The free beer poured like rivers of suds. Jimena actually manned the free beer station and enjoyed the mindless work, and an overflowing tip jar didn't hurt either. The early part of the evening raged. Hundreds of people turned out. All the lights and sound systems were working fine, his staff was just right. Around ten o'clock when the early events ended, more people began to show up. The free drinks were over but the early crowd hung around to buy more drinks from the four bar stations, the main bar inside, a stacked mini-bar in the backroom and beer stations outside, one of which Jimena operated after the free beer dried up. *Ch-ching.* Alex knew there'd be a bridge between the early and late crowd and during that time he coordinated deejays in every room.

As the early birds slowly stumbled into the streets of Wynwood, the night crowd arrived in hordes. He barely had enough security and a Miami city policeman had to linger outside to make sure everything remained copacetic. At night, Alex had an array of deejays set up for the main room and bands for the back room. As a very special event, he asked one of the most popular bands in the city, the Jacuzzi Boys, to play an acoustic set, literally inside the Jacuzzis. Four pseudo-punk-rock kids standing in four different Jacuzzis — somehow it worked out. With a mix of hip deejays, and awesome local bands, the night played itself out as one of the most successful opening nights in Miami bar history. If it seemed like everyone came out it was because they did. So many contributed to the resurrection of The Phoenix in some form, whether building a booth or painting a mural, so many wanted to come through opening night. The free press didn't hurt. The cultural intelligentsia of the city (its musicians, artists, writers, painters, actors and comedians) converging with the city's redeemable philistines and barflies.

This constituted Alex's vision ever since Mecke's was destroyed. Open a bar that included the city, as well as its cultural pioneers. He didn't want The Phoenix to be seen as a moustache twirling hipster haven; on the contrary, he wanted to bridge the gap between the city's thinkers, and its multi-culturally diverse workers—that was the only way Wynwood could succeed. If it felt inclusive and fun—strictly new Miami—definitely not South Beach. It would take time to bridge the diversity, and there would be bumps along the way, but it was possible, through culture, only wonderful culture could bring Miami together.

Judging by the opening night of The Phoenix, it seemed apparent to all in that Alex created something beautiful. In addition, at the end of the night, long past closing time, with only him and Jimena in the back office, after a steady *click, click,* on a keypad, and a streaming trail of e-paper receipts, the first night's final sales topped $14,000.

Towards the end of the night, as a special treat, Alex even called on Uncle Luke from 2 Live Crew to host a booty dancing contest, the most authentic Miami experiences imaginable, a perfect tribute to the old mixing with the new. Alex didn't even have to bribe Uncle Luke to pick Jimena the winner. She danced with Santeria in her blood and felt fine.

Chapter 21 —

Jimena and Alex had nights constantly filled with activity. They probably ventured out six nights a week, except for Monday. Monday *was* the new Sunday, in terms of having a day to rest. They needed a night-in with their full schedules. Sunday they made it a point to get out of the house, no matter what. The Phoenix of Wynwood performed well enough that Alex didn't have to stay on-site every night of the week, nor did he have to close the joint out. He hired a manager with whom he trusted, not a friend, but someone with a strong resume, besides, the place contained enough cameras to catch any thief. Alex and Jimena liked to "make the rounds" on Saturday and sometimes "the rounds" melted deep into the night, but they tried hard not to allow the shadows of a Saturday night engulf their Sunday day. They slept in of course, but not too late. Sunday's were spiritual but in no way religious. They made sure to leave the apartment, usually starting the day at some brunch with a mimosa or a Bloody Mary, maybe journeying towards a park, or the botanical gardens, or the Farmer's Market, perhaps the expansive farmlands of Homestead, and The Keys were always on the table. Often they found a friend with a boat and they used Sunday to explore the bountiful access Miami had to clean waterways, from Fort Lauderdale to Key Largo, there existed a whole ocean to explore. The consistently consistent Miami weather also helped. A blessing, again, even more-so when the lead story in the national media was how many people in the North and Midwest were without power in blizzard conditions. Assume a position of juxtaposition. Adjust your position. Sunday usually morphed into a nice dinner night. Alex wanted to build relationships and felt Sunday night dinners were a good glue to bind a friendship, so they dabbled in Foodie-ism, always with a side of mixology. Monday's were back-to-work days for both of them. Jimena found a full-time position as a Medical Coder with a small EMR (Electronic Medical Records) business in Coral Gables and Alex needed Monday to meet with accountants, deal with weekly receipts, deposits and general management duties at his bar and club. Monday night they stayed in, usually lying in bed just watching television. And there were some quality programs to watch Monday night, either live, or On Demand, and despite old conventional thinking, contemporary television possessed artistic and cultural integrity. Culture became their keyword. Their mistress and muse. Their slut and sultan. Culture. Culture in Miami. Can you believe it? Tuesdays they would leave the apartment for either comedy or jazz. Tuesday was undoubtedly the best night in Miami. The weekend was amateur hour compared to the throbbing pulse of a Tuesday. There was so much to do, all of the events free, many included complimentary drinks for ladies, or drink specials, and no weekend warriors from the western, northern or southern strip mall Florida suburbs ventured out: locals only, intimate and authentic. Wednesday's always had some trivia or bingo night, (the Drag Queen Trivia and Bingo Night at The Phoenix, on Wednesday, was actually voted by the Editors of *New Times* as Best Mid-week Party; consequently, the Readers and Editors also chose The Phoenix as Best New Venue, as well as Best Place to Meet Someone Smart. Thursday's always kicked off some art opening, either at the new museum, or at a gallery in Wynwood or Downtown or Little Haiti. They also found themselves at the theater a lot of Thursday's. Jimena in particular took a liking to dramas with her favorite venue being The Box, located on the premises of the mansion in Coral Gables. She liked the theater, a lot, and often found catharsis on the edge of her seat. She even began to inquire into membership of the Carbonell committee, which would afford her free access to theater spread across South Florida and give her a vote at the annual Carbonell awards, South Florida's version of the Tony's usually reserved for journalists and big donor's, but with a few whispers in the right ears, it didn't seem like it would be an impossible task. Friday's morphed into the same thing as Thursday, just a little bit more crowded. Something always opened: a theatrical piece, a dance recital, the symphony, an art exhibit, or a film or music festival. Sometimes random events popped up like lectures or book readings and they often ventured out, with open ears. In general, they stayed away from the sporting facilities, like the Marlins or Dolphin's, but Alex had a soft spot in his heart for horse racing and if there was a big race, like the Florida Derby, they made the trip to the race track, Jimena donning a fancy hat and Alex a suit. They both also liked basketball and often went to games, pre-partying beforehand. This was their life in Miami, if they didn't jet off on some weekend journey, maybe to New York to see a favorite actor on Broadway, or to Washington, to bounce around the hallowed halls of the Smithsonian, or New Orleans for Jazz Fest, or Savannah for St. Patrick's Day, or Tampa for the pirate party Gasparilla, or to the Gulf Shores of Alabama for the Hangout Music Festival, or a dash to Key West, or a quick drive to St. Augustine. Bigger travel plans loomed on the horizon: London, Dublin, Paris, Barcelona . . . Beijing, Tokyo, Bangkok . . . if the ellipses could continue to keep them together, and it looked like they could . . . see the world. They were culture whores and happily wore the label. But it started in Miami, for here they could give it shape, whisper in its ears, help bridge divided gaps, in a small beautiful city on the Bay, a place most people think existed only for tourists and philistines.

***

Love. What is love? How do you make it stay? Where does it go when it leaves? How can it turn into hate? How can you love more than one person in a lifetime? These abstract questions poets and philosophers have pondered since the dawn of time. Yet no one really knows what love is until maybe now? Maybe this was it. And it still seemed a little complicated. For love manifested itself in so many forms: the love one could feel for their brother or neighbor or pet; a kind and generous love, friendly and stable and reliable. The love people have for parents or children; a selfless abandonment, an endless and bottomless love. The love you have for your God or your Psychology or your Self; a deeply spiritual and omnipotent love. And the love she felt for Alex; a committed and faithful and forgiving love; a passionate and uncontrollable and lustful love. Love inspired so many things: beauty, compassion, romance, attraction, communication, trust, forgiveness, selflessness, faith, understanding, patience, staying in truth, reliability, comfort, safety, companionship, great sex. Jimena felt this for the first time, but to think love was only that invited sloth and ignorance. Love had its dark side. Love was one-hundred percent irrational. Love warped the mind more than a little. It could be obsession. Love could make you do things that you would never do, like blow up someone's phone in a worried frenzy with 100 text messages and 45 missed phone calls. Jimena's been there with this guy. And as his phone turned back on as he walked out of a long meeting, it had an epileptic seizure, *bzzzz, bzz, ding, bzz-bzz-bzz, ding, ding, b-z-z, bzz-z-z-, ding, ding.* When jealous, love put her in a car and drove her in circles, hopelessly looking for what she thought she lost, when it was never even hers to begin with. Of course she kept this secret. She didn't update her status: "just drove by my boyfriend's job fifty times. Anybody see him?" or "texted my boo 86 times, if you see him, tell him he's dead." If heartbroken, love will destroy the mind. Every song on the radio will speak to you. Clouds will shape-shift into the form of your lover. You can't sleep at night. Can't eat. People drown sorrows in alcohol or other self-destructive patterns. Love is never clean. It is filled with mud and we drag each other through this mud, bringing the past into the present, recycling old issues into the moment. Love is also fear and jealousy and insecurity and revenge. People kill themselves and others in the name of love. Love can destroy. We all walk wounded, but some never heal for the truth is love is a monster. Fortunately, the monster can be tamed.

THE END

ACKNOWLEDGEMENTS

This book is the result of a composite of years of writing, teaching, living and loving in Miami. It is most of all for Miami with the generous support and inspiration of so many starting with Lissette Merdez, Nicole Swift, Mitchell Kaplan and all associated with the Miami Book Fair and Miami Dade College. Thank you to John Dufresne, Lynne Barrett, Campbell McGrath, Les Standiford, Jim Hall and my FIU family. Special thanks to Robert William, Didi Contreras and David Anasgasti aka Ahol Sniffs Glue for all your gratitude and talents. Thank you to my editors over the years Brett O'Bourke, Amanda McCorquodale, Ciara Laville, Jose Duran, Liz Tracy and especially Ashley Lucio. Special thanks to Mary Smith, Marlene Lopez and Kacee Belcher. Thank you to the following people and organizations for inspiring the characters in this book: Miami Heat, Miami Bike Scene, The Corner Bar, Gramps Bar, Lester's, Wood Tavern, Moksha Family, Rhythm Foundation, Borscht Corp, Knight Foundation, Miami Foundation, History Miami, Gab Gallery, Krisp, Afrobeta, Telekinetc Walrus, Wynwood Map, Huffington Post, Miami New Times, Prism Music Group, Scratch Academy, Bonnaroo, Mike Levine, Shane Kinsler, Martin Sinclair, Ray Orraca, Chris MacCleod, Brian Basti, Raul Guerrero, Jason Mavila, Kat Bein, Jason Jeffers, Nick Garnett, MJ Fievre, Carl Juste, Connie Ogle, Jan Becker, Stuart Chase, Bridges Aderhold, Maria Ayala, AJ, MJ, CiC, Jay Cowan, Tony, Daylen, and a huge thanks to Mercedes. Thank you to my 1000s of students at Miami Dade and Barry. Thank you to my friends for your endless, eternal support. And of course, thank you to my family.

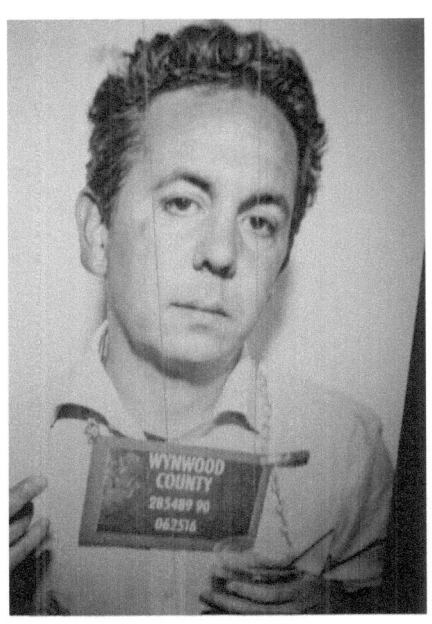

J.J. Colagrande is a Miami based writer and Professor at Miami Dade College. He received his MFA at Florida International and is the author of Headz and Decò.

www.ingramcontent.com/pod-product-compliance
Lightning Source LLC
Chambersburg PA
CBHW021232130626
46554CB00004B/1454